OUTLAW'S HOPE (A VIPER'S BITE MC NOVEL BOOK 1)

LENA BOURNE

Print Edition ISBN: 978-1979174473

CHAPTER ONE

TARA

"You're sure this is the woman you saw?" I ask, shoving another picture of my sister Samantha in front of the former stripper's face.

She snaps a gum bubble in my face. "Yes, for the last time. I saw her brought into the Viper's Nest just after Christmas. I remember her long dark hair. I wish I had hair like that."

She twirls a lock of her thin, light brown hair around her finger.

"Viper's Nest, where's that?" I ask, my hands shaking as I try to make a neat pile of the photos I've been showing her.

She chuckles, revealing two rows of teeth in need of a serious cleaning, and flips a lock of my long, blonde hair off my shoulder. "Not somewhere you want to be, Princess. It's a bikers club HQ, and they're all true outlaws there, killers, not something you can handle."

"Tell me," I snap.

A few other women edge closer to where we're standing just outside the large dining hall of the shelter, leaning in and trying to listen in on our conversation.

"Why's this girl so important to you?" the stripper asks, tapping the stack of photos in my hand with a broken fingernail.

"She's her sister," one of the eavesdropping women explains. "Been missing almost a year now. Right, Tara?"

I'm glad she butted in and answered the question, because there's no way I could've done it without my voice cracking.

"That's right," I manage to mutter.

"It's the HQ of Viper's Bite biker club in Arbor, right on the county line. You must've heard of it," the stripper says, brushing down her tight skirt. "But you don't want to go there by yourself. And you don't want to involve the cops either. They're all connected. And if you do, don't tell them I sent you."

Fear is plain in her eyes, as she stares at me,

waiting for some sort of confirmation. Despite her tough words, she's scared.

"I won't," I assure her.

She nods curtly, then snaps another gum bubble and enters the dining hall.

My hands are shaking even worse now, my heart racing in my throat. But excitement is rising too, hope blossoming around my heart, filling my chest so fast it's hard to breathe. This is the first real lead I've had since my sister disappeared last September. It's the end of May now.

"She's right, Tara," the woman who butted in says. "Don't go there by yourself. Hell, I'd go with you, but you and the other counselors here keep telling me I should stay away from my old life. Though I could use a good time once in awhile."

She laughs after she says it, a grating sound with no mirth to it. The women at the shelter laugh a lot, but it's never a happy sound. Living a hard life will take away your laugh. I hardly remember my own anymore.

"Go into the dining room now, it's almost dinner-time," I say, stuffing the photos of my sister into the back pocket of my jeans. "You just have a nice rest tonight, and don't worry about me."

That's right, no one should worry about me. Just

like no one ever has. No one ever cared for my sister either. I'm all she has. Sure, the cops and the FBI are looking for her, Daddy made sure of that. But it's just for show. He hasn't actually contacted the cops working the case since New Year's. I know because I pester the detective for new information almost daily. I don't speak to my dad much. Most days, I'm sure he'd prefer both Samantha and me to be gone.

The sun has almost set, and a cold wind blowing in from the ocean hits me directly in the face as I exit the women's shelter I've been working at for the past two years. I'd planned to leave early today, go for a swim before I went home, but I ended up staying all day, like I always do. But at least I got a lead on where Samantha might be. Unless the stripper was lying.

Samantha never stopped making fun of me for getting a degree in social services, and for taking a job here in this shelter for former sex workers and abused women. But it's the only place where I ever felt like I matter, like I can do some good. I can help these poor women heal, which helps me in return. And despite her insistence that I should have more fun, worry less, get a job that didn't dredge up old pain daily, I think Samantha understood that, even admired me a little for it. I can almost hear Samantha's harsh laugh as I think that last thought. She lost her laugh too. But if I think really hard, I still remember it from back when we were kids, building sand castles in the playground on my father's huge estate.

"And if I didn't work here, I'd never find you," I mutter to myself, as though talking to her. The stripper who told me isn't the kind of girl who'd give information to the cops. Yet she told me.

A bike engine roars near me, and my heart starts racing again. A group of five bearded bikers are parked near the curb, their eyes fixed on the shelter behind me. They come here almost every evening looking for stragglers from the shelter, trying to lure them away, back to a life of prostitution and drugs. A few of them are checking me out, and their leers feel like grubby, dirty fingers touching my flesh.

I shudder and pick up the pace, get in my car and lock the doors right after. I dial the detective's number to tell him what I found out, while trying to ignore the bikers. But he doesn't pick up.

Through the rearview mirror I see one of the women come out of the shelter behind me, stumbling as she twists her ankle in her crazy high heels. It's Tanya, a former meth addict who's been coming to the shelter on and off since I started working here.

I'm out of the car waving her back inside before I even think about it. Too many women have been pulled back into their old lives by the bikers camping out here, and I have to at least try and stop Tanya from going with them.

"Go back inside, Tanya!" I shout at her.

She eyes the bikers warily, but keeps coming. "I have to talk to you."

I jog over to her and grab her arm, start to pull her back toward the building. "Don't go outside tonight."

She shakes off my arm once we reach the door, rubbing the spot where I grabbed her. "I won't, sheesh. I just wanted to catch you before you left. I'm really glad you finally got some information about your sister."

Her eyes mist as she says it like she's about to start crying, and she's nodding her head fiercely, though I don't think she realizes it.

"Honestly, I have no idea what to do with the information," I admit. I want the cops to go look for her at the club tonight, but I'm sure they won't.

She grabs my hand in both of hers, squeezing hard. "Whatever you do, don't just go there asking for her."

"I..." But I let my voice trail off, because that was

my plan B so far.

"The Vipers are bad, and they don't treat their women well," she says. My heart's racing again, so hard my whole chest is cramping up. What if Samantha is still there, held captive, being forced into prostitution. I'd cry if I could. But as it is, my eyes are just burning painfully.

"But they do have some legit businesses too. Crystal's Lounge is one of them. It's a strip joint, with no extras. You could ask there. Crystal is a nice old lady, maybe she saw your sister there. I stayed with her for a couple of weeks after Tony roughed me up. She wanted me to stay on and strip, but the money's not as good as..." she stops talking, blinking at me like she's afraid I'll reprimand her. "Anyway, maybe you can go there, pretend you're looking for a job, ask around for your sister like you've been doing here."

Me work as a stripper? The mere idea makes me nauseous, but I ignore it, as I smile at Tanya, who's still nodding frantically.

"You gave this some serious thought," I say.

She smiles too, revealing her meth-ruined teeth. "I hope you find your sister. I really do. And my plan would work. Crystal's real protective of her girls from what I hear, wouldn't make you do anything you don't want to do."

I still sometimes get stomach cramps just from a guy looking at me too lewdly when I'm fully clothed. If I had to strip for them, I'd probably pass out. Or just die.

Tanya is looking at me with wide, hopeful eyes, nodding again.

"OK, I'll give it a shot," I mutter, since I don't want to kill the hope in her eyes. I so rarely see it in the women here.

She throws her arms around me and pulls me into a tight bear hug, my nose scrunching painfully against her bony shoulder. "You'll find her, I know you will. Just ask for Crystal when you get there. You can't miss her, she only has one good eye."

I stand there in front of the door for a long time after Tanya goes back inside. The cold wind's beating against me, and it feels like someone's shaking me, screaming at me to make the right choice.

I should call the detective working Samantha's case and tell him all this. But he's given me nothing but promises so far. My dad could maybe intervene, get them to raid the place faster. But from what I learned about biker clubs in the area from the women at the shelter, most of them have law enforcement on the payroll. Besides, my Dad is the last person I want to speak to. I'd actually rather get a job as a stripper.

And Tanya's idea has merit. I've gotten good at trying to get information from women who'd rather not give it. Yet the mere thought of taking my clothes off in front of men is an ice-cold stone in the pit of my stomach. When I think of it, all I see is that group of bikers grabbing me, dragging me to some dingy room and chaining me to the wall.

Stop drama-queening, Tara.

But I've heard too many horror stories about just such treatment at the hands of outlaw bike gangs by the women at the shelter who survived it. Though "survived" is not really the right word here. Even "lived" might be an exaggeration.

A vicious gust of wind sends a strand of my hair right into my eye, the stinging pain finally bringing me back to reality.

Samantha might be chained to a wall right now.

Besides, what's one more nightmare to live through?

No one will miss me, just like no one except me actually misses Samantha. We only ever had each other. And I'll never really live, if I don't know where she is.

CHAPTER TWO

TOMMY

The bar smells like stale cigarette smoke, spilt beer, vomit and fucking cat piss. It's a sickening combination, but I need my morning coffee, and I don't want to share it with whichever one of the girls is taking a shower in my apartment. It must be Lola. I don't think she left last night. Not sure how I managed to allow that oversight, but I've been pretty tired lately. I remember telling her to leave after that amazing blowjob she gave me, but nothing afterwards. Hell, I'd still be sleeping right now if the shower didn't wake me, and my mind didn't go into overdrive worrying about today's meeting the second I realized I was awake.

It's freezing down here like it's not almost June.

I'm glad I at least put on my cut. I hardly go anywhere without wearing it on these days. Must be because of some sick, unconscious wish to hold onto something that gets farther beyond saving each day.

The door to the back swings open with a crash, a loud and jarring reminder to keep my thoughts in check, or else. Crystal walks across the bar, humming some ballad and looking down as se sticks pieces of tape to a cardboard sign. Her dead eye catches the overhead lights for a moment, glowing white.

"Wear the fucking patch over that thing, Crystal," I snap and her humming cuts off abruptly as she turns her whole head to look at me with her good eye.

"It itches," she counters tonelessly and resumes her walk toward the front door.

"And get someone to clean this place up more often," I tell her. "It smells like some cat lady's house."

"Did someone get up on the wrong side of the bed, Tommy?" she asks.

My bed doesn't have a right side anymore. Hasn't for months.

"What's that sign you got there?" I ask.

She holds it up for me to read. It's a generic red and white HELP WANTED sign under which she wrote Enquire Within with a black marker.

"Oh, Hell no, Crystal! The last thing we need is to hire more people." I slam my cup against the counter so hard most of the coffee spills out all over it.

She frowns at me, completely unfazed by my outburst. "I need help around here. I'm too old to stay up until all hours tending bar, and then clean this place all day. I thought you were gonna get the girls to help with the cleaning, but nothing's come of that yet, now has it?"

I wipe off the now empty cup, and place it back on the coffee machine. "Most said they will, I asked Lolita just last night."

She frowns at me again. "You mean Lola?"

"Yeah, her," I say pressing the button to make myself a new espresso. "But Lolita's more fitting. She looks about twelve."

Pubescent looking women aren't really my thing, but I like variety, and Lola sucks cock like she was put on this good earth to do only that.

"She's eighteen," Crystal says, surprisingly catching on to the reference to Nabokov's master-piece I just made.

Yet she said it with a completely straight face, which makes me certain she's lying. But I won't call her on it. If she thinks Lola needs to be here, then

Lola stays. For as long as here lasts. Though I'll try to get her out before it's too late. The list of people I want to get away from this place before my brother turns it into a whorehouse just keeps growing.

"Make me one of those cappuccinos, will you?" Crystal says, and sits down on one of the stools, carefully placing the sign on the counter just beyond my spilt coffee. "I can never get the machine to work right."

She reaches over the bar for a rag to wipe up the coffee I spilt. "So are you ordering me not to hire anyone, or was that just you being cranky?"

I keep my back turned to her as I fill up the little container with a fresh batch of ground coffee. She'd be able to read all I can't tell her about the future of this place off my face, and we must never discuss club business with outsiders, and least of all "property". She's about to lose this place and all she's been trying to do here for the past thirty odd years sure as the summer heat's coming. And sooner too. Even my father let her run this place the way she wanted to. But Shade won't. He'll make all her strippers whores as a matter of principal, and pretty soon I won't be able to stand in his way without risking my own life. I'll do what I can for her and her girls, but I won't die.

"Do what you want, Crystal, you always have," I

say and look back at her over my shoulder for a reaction. Her face is stone, even her white eye grey. She knows what's coming, but she's smart enough not to ask any questions.

"You're VP now," she says nodding slowly. "You have power."

So much for considering her smart. The only way she'll get through this transition my brother Shade, the newly made President of Vipers Bite MC, is planning unscathed will be by keeping remarks like that to herself. Keep her head down and go along. Like she should've done until now, then maybe she'd still have two fucking eyes instead of this scarred, white monstrosity she can't even shut her lid over.

"And if you play your cards right, one day you'll be President and have all the power to do what you want—"

"Shut the fuck up and drink your coffee, Crystal," I interrupt, pushing the cup toward her.

I should be reprimanding her more harshly for talking freely about shit she shouldn't even be mentioning. But I care about her. That's always been my problem. I care. And I lose sleep over shit being done to people who don't deserve it. What's worse, I never actually understood the concept of treating people like property, no matter how hard my father tried to drill that lesson in.

She picks up the cup with both hands and smells it, then takes a sip, smacking her lips afterwards. "This is good."

I nod absentmindedly and check my watch. It's just past three, less than an hour before the Executives meeting starts. Shade'll reveal his full plan for the future of the MC today, I'm sure of it, and then I'll be forced to make my decision. For good or ill.

I dig in the inside pocket of my cut and pull out the patch I picked up for Crystal's owner Bear last night. The word RETIRED is stitched on it in cursive black and silver letters against a pure white background. "Look what I got for Bear."

She visibly recoils from it.

"It could go right here," I tell her, slapping it over my VP patch just above my heart, and in this moment I'm beyond certain I want a patch exactly like this one.

Her face is stone again, but it softens as she reaches over and squeezes my hand. "I know you mean well, Tommy, but you know it's "Ride 'til Death". Bear will never accept this, even if you convince the others to offer it to him."

"He'd take it, if you told him to," I say still holding

the patch over my own, the one that clearly says Life Term even though it spells Vice President. "Would it be so bad to retire out in Arizona somewhere, or maybe Florida? He'd still get to ride his bike and keep his cut this way, and..."

You'd both be safe and out of harm's way, is how I wanted to end that sentence, but I stopped myself just in time.

She shakes her head, and climbs off the stool. "Put that away now, Tommy."

She picks up the sign and goes over to the door. I watch her affix it in silence.

"There, that's done," she says turning back to me. "And while we're talking about things that need doing, get someone to fix the boiler in the upstairs shower. The girls will stop showering if they don't get hot water soon."

She winks at me with her good eye as she says it, and smiles wryly. I can't help but chuckle.

"What? I let them shower at my place. In fact, I insist on it."

That will all end soon too. The other members have been grumbling about me getting all the pussy I want over here at Crystal's, and not letting anyone in on the action. I'll never subject the girls to that, but it won't be easy giving them up either.

"Just make sure whoever you hire understands the rules," I tell Crystal and finish off the rest of my coffee.

Those same rules I wish I could still follow without resentment and without question.

CHAPTER THREE

TARA

I couldn't get to sleep until seven in the morning, and it's past three when I finally get up the next day.

But I have a plan.

I already sent an email to my boss at work, saying I need to take my leave immediately to take care of a family emergency. Then I rummaged through my closet, and dug out my old clothes from high school and college, along with the tight elastic bandage I used to hide my breasts back then. Tears I can't shed are burning my eyes as I wrap it around my chest. I worked so hard these last few years to stop wearing it. Years of therapy is what it took, the three times a week kind, along with a lot of introspection.

I even went on a few dates, but those were all

before Samantha disappeared, and never even got to first base. A peck on the cheek was as close to a good night kiss I could allow. The part of me that might long for a man to touch me, make love to me, is broken, destroyed beyond repair, and I'm starting to accept it. Though I still sometimes miss the children I'll never have. My therapist says I'm too young at twenty-four to make that decision, but she's wrong.

The abuse we endured affected Samantha in exactly the opposite way. She'd go with any guy who so much as smiled at her. From doing teachers in high school, to random bikers she met at the side of the road.

The memory of all the fights we had about her promiscuousness burns a hole in my heart each time I think of it. If only I'd done more to help her, set her on the right path, the path of healing and acceptance like the one I've been trying to follow. But she had a name for that path, she called it *Tara's New Age Bullshit*, so I gave up.

Truth is, I was too busy dealing with my own issues to take care of my little sister. Until it was too late. And that knowledge is so painful I can't even acknowledge it without wanting to curl up in a ball and not move.

The cops think she just took off, and to their

credit there's precious little evidence that anything bad happened to her. But she'd never go this long without calling me. We spoke nearly every day, never less than once a week. She'd call me by now if she could. The day she went missing was no different than any other. It couldn't possibly have been the day she decided to leave me forever.

Samantha needs me to find her. And I won't let her down again.

I grab my hair trimmer and walk to the bathroom. All through high school up until sophomore year of college I kept my hair trimmed to no more than an inch in an effort to look ugly.

But my blonde hair falls in messy waves down my back now, and my eyes are burning again as I look at myself in the mirror. Growing my hair out was a true victory, more so than ditching the boob hiding bandage and manly wardrobe. And I won't lose it now. I kept the undercut until about a year ago. Because with that haircut, if I pin my hair up, it's a rare man that would look at me twice.

With a few practiced strokes, I renew the undercut, then dress in a washed-out pair of baggy jeans and an oversized plaid shirt without thinking any more about it.

Two hours later I'm sitting in a rented pickup.

The bandage hiding my boobs is so tight I'm having trouble drawing a full breath, but I'll get used to that soon.

There's no way I'll be hired as a stripper dressed the way I am. But I could persist, hang around long enough to ask my questions, find Samantha.

And who knows, maybe I'll just walk into this strip joint and Samantha will already be there. Then I can take her home and tell her how sorry I am for not coming sooner over and over again until I lose my voice.

That thought sustains me during the long ride.

The sun is setting by the time I enter the town of Arbor, population 17,121, and dread starts to settle in my stomach. I've been able to keep the worst of it away during the ride by concentrating on the road, but now I've reached my destination. Samantha would call me if she were safe somewhere. So I doubt I'll just find her that easily.

I get lost twice, almost have to ask for directions before I finally pull up into the parking lot of Crystal's Lounge. Muffled music is coming through the black doors, and the sign over the building is already lit, the letters flashing hot pink and green, the silhouette of the woman laying on her side illuminated a bright yellow.

What am I doing?

But I don't slow my steps as I approach the front door. I can't. Samantha could be in there. She could.

A HELP WANTED sign is hanging in the window. No way they're advertising for strippers in this way. They must have a different position they need to fill.

Finally, a stroke of luck.

Maybe the pieces are finally falling into place as they should. No need to ask for a stripper job, if they have other openings available. Even the wind seems to be pushing me inside now, urging me on.

But I stop dead again just inside the front door, caught in the glare of a rugged, bearded bouncer. He's wearing a biker jacket and is weighing me with cold, light eyes.

"I...I saw the sign outside...the Help Wanted one..." I mumble literally shivering. Up on stage a very skinny girl is twirling around a pole to an audience of three. "I need a job," I conclude more firmly.

He eyes me up and down, and I can practically hear his thoughts as his gaze lingers on my haircut. He doesn't like what he sees, which is exactly what I wanted.

He flicks his finger toward the edge of the bar,

where a grey haired woman is bending over a thick notebook, jotting something down. "Talk to her."

My legs are stiff as I make my way to the bar. I have to clear my throat loudly once I reach it to get the woman's attention.

She looks up at me, and I stifle a surprised gasp. She'd be a striking beauty, despite her age, if half her face wasn't covered by jagged scars. One of her eyes is ghostly white, but she's frowning at me with the other one, which is as bright as a clear summer sky.

"Can I help you?"

"I saw the sign outside. That you're looking for help. I need a job," I say in a rush.

It suddenly dawns on me that she might be looking for more bouncers, or maybe some strong guys to carry in the crates of beer and whatever, possibly even a handyman. All the elation I felt reading that sign disappears in a flash of sour disappointment.

"I'm looking for someone to tend bar and help me clean this place," she says sweeping her hand across the vast room. "Think you could handle that?"

I nod fast like I've gone insane. Her face softens as she smiles at me.

"When can you start?" she asks, setting her pen down and closing the notebook.

"Right now?" I didn't mean it as a question, but it came out that way anyway.

She chuckles at that. "And do you have a place to stay nearby? I don't remember seeing you around town."

"I just got here, I'm still looking for a place," I say the first thing that pops into my head.

"What made you choose this town?"

I had a whole story prepared for why I'm here, but I remember none of it right now.

"Got tired of driving," I finally manage with a shrug.

"And you stopped here?" she asks in a mocking tone.

I shrug again. "Seemed as good a place as any."

She looks at me like she thinks I'm full of shit, but then climbs off her stool and stuffs the notebook under her arm.

"Ever work in a bar before?" she asks motioning me to follow her behind the counter.

"I did for awhile," I lie. Samantha worked in a lot of bars, and she told me all about it, down to how to pour the drinks and make some of the cocktails. Samantha always talked a lot, rambled on about anything and everything. My heart cramps up as I realize just how much I miss the sound of her voice.

"It's not a tough crowd here, mostly beer and Jack. Don't stiff anyone and you'll be fine," she says, reaching under the counter and handing me a black apron. "We'll see how you do, and talk in the morning. And there's a room behind the office," she says, pointing to a door at the end of the bar. "You can sleep there if you want. I'll tell everyone to expect it."

"I should just start?" I ask, my voice betraying the panic mounting inside me.

"I'll be back in awhile to check on you," she says and smiles at me. It makes her look ten years younger despite the scars. "But right now, I need to get some dinner and maybe lie down for a bit. I've been on my feet since eight this morning. I'm Crystal, by the way."

I almost blurt out, "I know" as I shake her hand, but stop myself just in time and introduce myself instead.

I suddenly feel bad for lying to her. She seems so open, so motherly, so friendly. She'd understand, maybe even help me find my sister right now, if I told her why I'm really here. But then I notice the jean jacket with cut off sleeves she's wearing, the words "Property of Bear" stitched into the back in black and silver letters. All the horror stories I heard about places like this from the women at the shelter come back in a flash, all jumbled together like a never-ending nightmare inside my mind.

So I just nod, and break eye contact to inspect the bar like I'm getting my bearings though I'm not actually seeing any of it. She's talking to the bouncer when I look up again, pointing at me.

I have no idea what I just agreed to do by taking this job, but my resolve still trumps the fear. If Samantha is here, I will find her. And I will bring her home.

CHAPTER FOUR

TOMMY

Three Prospects I've barely spoken to are digging
large holes in the ground in front of the Nest.
They're for planting a row of trees, which might actually make this place look less like a deserted warehouse, and more like an actual club. It's one of the
only good ideas Shade had since taking over the club.
They all stop working as I get off my bike, mutter
hellos, but I don't stop to chat.

All the execs are already gathered in Shade's
office, sitting around the oval desk my grandfather
hand carved himself when he started the MC back
in the 1960s. One of the legs is shaped like a pin-up
girl, complete with huge breasts. I've been told he
had a tattoo just like it, but I've never seen it since he

died some thirty years before I was born. It's pathetic the shit that makes me nostalgic these days. But there it is.

"You being VP now means you arrive to meetings early," Shade snaps at me as I take my seat at his right. I used to sit at the end of the table when I was still Secretary and my brother Blade was President. He got that nickname by winning a gun fight with a knife when he was about twenty, so it's kinda fitting he died from a stab wound to the heart. In a poetic way, not the practical one. I'm not even fighting the sentimentality this time, just letting it wash over me. It's never gonna be the same again. I might as well miss it, if I can't have it.

"I'm on time, ain't I?" I snap, matching Shade glare for glare.

"I said early."

"Alright, I'll be early from now on, Prez" I say and lean back, folding my arms over my chest. From the corner of my eye, I see Sarge bristle at my disrespectful tone, but I don't think I have to worry about his Enforcers teaching me a lesson in respect out back later. Blade's only been dead for less than two months and we're all still getting our bearings, adjusting to the new leadership.

Shade slams the javelin against the table with unnecessary force, since no one's talking anyway.

"We have lots of shit to discuss, so we better get started," he says loudly, and I do my best to ignore the cramps starting in my stomach.

"Blade had noble ideas of turning this club around, mixing legit shit with other endeavors and slowly phasing the latter out," Shade says, bringing this stuff up plainly for the first time since he took over the presidency. "That's never been my vision, and I don't think it has as much merit as Blade believed. Either way, I'm not the President to carry that out."

You can say that again.

Shade's pale green eyes find mine like he heard me, and I focus hard on not letting a single muscle in my face twitch to betray what I'm really thinking. He has my father's eyes, and I don't enjoy that reminder.

"But it's also true that the ATF is up our asses too far to dislodge anytime soon," Shade continues. "So the time to diversify is now. I propose a two-tiered approach. Whores and drugs. Blade and my father, may they rest in peace, were both against the latter, though whores were my late father's specialty, as some of you remember well."

He shares a knowing grin with Sarge and Treasurer who've both been around since my dad was Prez, but I also feel the cold lick of a look he casts my way. Yeah, dad was into running whores, that's what this MC was founded on. But that ended with my mom's death, and I have no nostalgia for that day, only a cold seething rage I'll never make sense of, or get over.

"I suggest we start with whores, since that's a lot more fun," Shade continues. "Then work our way up to drugs. Blade made no friends keeping this town free of that stuff, so setting up routes and labs could take some time."

"You're talking about manufacture?" I ask, bolting upright. "Fucking shit, Shade, Blade's grave hasn't even settled yet."

Sarge slams his fists against the table, and stands up, glaring at me. He may be pushing sixty, but I still don't want either of his meaty fists anywhere near my face. But he sits back down at a placating wave from Shade.

"Let's all cool down. Brains here is still in mourning," Shade says, which earns him a wave of chuckles.

Brains. I hate that nickname. And it's not sticking, no matter how many times Shade calls me by it. They've begun calling me Viper long before Blade died. It started with the sly way I got the new Sheriff on board with looking the other way, and it's only gotten firmer by me finding ways of keeping the ATF off out backs. But Shade will never let me assume our grandfather's street name, and I don't want it either. Brotherhood and unity mean a lot to me, the importance of it was bred into me. I believed in what Blade was doing, turning this MC from an outlaw one into a legit business. But I can't get on board with Shade's plan.

"We'll need a vote on this shift you're proposing," I hear myself say. "Full attendance."

That should buy me another month to get all my affairs in order. This club has about two hundred members scattered across the country, and I'll insist every one of them is here to cast their vote before I let Shade fuck up everything Blade tried to build. I won't get my way, that much is evident from just the poisonous way Shade's glaring at me right now. And the fact that none of the other execs are backing me up. Shade has them all in his pocket. But he'll have some maneuvering to do before he gets past this stipulation of the Charter. Maybe it'll be long enough to convince Crystal it's over, that she needs to get her girls away before they all becomes whores. Needs to get herself away too.

"Alright, a vote it is," Shade finally says. "As for full attendance, we'll see."

"Tommy's right," the Treasurer says. "It's a big shift, the drugs part even goes against the Charter."

Finally, a voice of reason.

Shade's face is completely frozen, the way it always gets before he blows up.

"Fine, we'll discuss it at Assembly," he says, and I can practically hear his teeth grinding together.

"And while we're on the subject of altering the charter," I say, leaning against the desk and casting my gaze over the others. "I say we let Bear retire."

All I get in response is a bunch of bored mutters.

"Not this again, Tommy," Sarge says. "The rules are the rules."

"Yeah, Ride 'til Death," Shade growls, pointing at the engraving of the club's motto along the wooden tabletop. "No one fucking retires. I don't want to hear any more about it."

His eyes are literally shooting daggers at me right now, but I couldn't give less of a shit. "Fine. But I will put this before the assembly too. Let them vote on it. It's an archaic rule, made when the founders were young. Things change."

Bear is the closest to a founder this MC still has. I'd rather he died in some retirement village and not in the war Shade's new plans will inevitably spark. Bringing in whores will likely do that all on it's own, but drugs on top of it, well, that shit just makes everyone go crazy. But no one in this room is afraid of a fight, so I won't even bring that point up.

Shade is still staring at me like I just destroyed his favorite toy, but the rest are murmuring among each other and it sounds like maybe they're starting to see it my way.

"Fine, you bring your forward-thinking idea to the Assembly, see how they take it," Shade finally says. "But right now we have actual business to take care of. The Vagos are moving a truckload of guns right through our back yard tonight, thinking we're still too rattled by the loss of Blade to notice. But we're gonna teach them to think better next time. And if we get real lucky, that motherfucker Bandido will be among the crew. Then I'll personally skin him alive for killing Blade."

His words are met with a roar of approval and the sound of fists hitting the wooden table. I join in too, since I know when to go along. But I don't think Bandido was just stupid drunk and acting in a flash of rage when he stabbed Blade. I think it was all planned. And as much as I hate to even consider it, I think Shade was in on it.

He's putting on a show of starting a war with the Vagos to get revenge, but it's not a very effective one. And we seem to be in a truce right now.

Shade's no longer looking at me, he's grinning at the men he just spurred into action, and it's not wise to want it, but I fucking yearn for him to know that I know.

We rode to intercept the weapons shipment after the meeting, but it never happened. I'm almost certain Shade just made it all up, so it would appear like the MC's doing something to fuck with the Vagos. And I came dangerously close to calling him on it, but there's really no point adding fuel to his hatred of me. And without anything to back it up, an accusation like that would justify him killing me in the eyes of the other club members. I have no proof, just this nauseating gut feeling that's been giving me night-mares for the past two months. And I want to live.

I already made my decision. I'm leaving the club. What Shade does with it after that is no concern of mine, as long as he leaves me in peace. Blade's dead, nothing will bring him back. It's been weeks since I missed him this acutely, it feels like he just died. All I want right now is a hot shower, a slow blowjob and sleep.

The Lounge is nearly empty when I get there, but the lake of cigarette smoke hanging just below the ceiling suggests thousands are inside.

"Air this place out once in awhile," I bark at Ten, causing him to jerk up from where he'd been dozing off by the door.

Simone is working the pole and judging by the state of her undress she's almost done. Our eyes lock while I scan the room, and she gives me a sultry half smile. But Simone likes it fast and rough, and I couldn't keep up with her tonight. Lola with her skilled little mouth would be perfect.

A girl I've never seen before is working behind the bar. Her eyes are glazed over as she gazes off in the direction of the stage, the light over the bar making her full, plump, perfectly shaped lips glisten. Even under the straw colored bird's nest of a bun on the back of her head and the harsh undercut, hers is a face that belongs on the cover of some magazine, not behind the bar of this sorry joint. And her lips should be wrapped around my dick.

"Who's the new girl?" I ask Ten.

He shrugs. "Crystal hired her tonight, beyond that I have no idea. She said you should talk to her when you get in though, explain the rules and such."

"She ain't a stripper?"

"She look like a stripper to you in that butch dyke get-up?" Ten spits on the floor. "She's here to watch, if you ask me."

"Don't fucking spit on the floor," I bark.

He's probably right about the girl. She's wearing a black and red plaid shirt and a pair of baggy jeans, an outfit that makes her look a lot like the truckers who frequent this place.

I spot Lola nodding off in the shadows at the far side of the bar as I approach, but I ignore her hopeful smile as I rap my fingers on the counter to get the new girl's attention.

"What...what can I get you?" she asks, but she actually recoils from me.

She's either stoned or simple minded, and neither will do her any favors here. But that face. I swear I could just look at her for hours. Especially if her big blue eyes were fixed on me just like they are right now, like I'm the only one in the room. Less fear in them would be preferable though.

"You can get me a beer," I tell her, ignoring the weird trip my mind just took. I'm not looking for a girlfriend. Never did and never will.

She scurries to get a glass, casting glances at me over her shoulder as she pours it. Her clothes are at least five sizes too big for her, but something tells me there's a body to go with those sexy lips under all that cloth. Maybe it's the way what little light there is in this place attaches to her. Might be worth it to keep her around just to find out, if I'm right.

But no.

I don't need any more of Crystal's pet projects to worry about after Shade starts tearing everything down.

I take hold of her wrist as she places the glass of beer in front of me. The mixture of surprise and pure terror in her eyes hits me like a punch to the stomach. I almost apologize, tell her everything is gonna be alright, that I personally won't ever let anyone scare her like this again. *What the fuck am I thinking?*

"I'm Tommy, and I run this place," I tell her instead and only afterwards release her arm, kinda sorry to be letting go of her soft, velvety skin. "Why you wanna work here?"

"I...I...I need a job," she manages, her eyelashes batting something fierce. Only thing missing from this picture is my cock down her throat. She licks her lips like she's thinking the same thing, causing my cock to strain painfully against my zipper. Only one or two of the sweet goodie-two-shoes girls back in college ever had me reacting this way. In as much as I have a type when it comes to women, it's the good girl next door. And without the manly clothes and the manlier haircut, that's exactly what this girl would be.

"What's your name?" I hear myself delivering the question that's always worked better than any ten pickup lines combined for me.

"Tara," she mutters, shaking slightly as she licks her lips again. She's not doing it to entice me. She's still scared of me, but there's really no need. I'd make her feel so good she'd never be frightened of anything ever again.

"You wanna work here, there's some rules. You don't talk to any of the customers, you keep your head down and do as you're told. Don't talk to me or any other member of Viper's Bite MC unless you're asked a question, and generally be as invisible as you can."

I watch Tara's eyes cycle through a million different emotions, from fear to defiance, finally settling on cold resignation.

Lola's smiling at me across the bar, winking each time I glance at her. But she's smart enough not to interrupt, she knows the rules.

"And wear something sexier from now on," I conclude and get off the stool, waving Lola over. She perks up, practically skips over to my side.

Tara's eyes flash at me like lighting illuminating a glacier. "This is all I own."

"Buy some new ones then."

"I'm broke," she shoots right back, the scared creature I saw before completely gone, replaced by this ice queen that knows exactly what she wants.

"Then borrow," I tell her, wondering what other surprise she has in store. "And don't argue with me."

Her eyes settle on defiance as she glares back at me. And all I really know right now is that I want to grab her by the hair and drag her to my bed so I can learn all her secrets the old fashioned way. It's a primal urge, caveman instinct kicking in, and if I don't leave her presence now I'll act on it. The urge to make her mine is *that* strong, stronger than I ever felt for any other woman.

Lola's swaying beside me—if she were a dog, her tail would be wagging. But she won't do tonight. I need to fuck like I haven't needed to in a long while, and I'm sure Simone will oblige.

I leave Lola by the bar, and go pluck Simone off the stage before she disappears behind the curtain, practically drag her through the door that leads to my apartment. She's giggling as she stumbles along, her full breasts bouncing.

But all I really see are Tara's steel eyes piercing me like swords right before the door closed. She's the first woman I ever met that I couldn't figure out at a glance. And I want to peel back all her layers until nothing but the truth remains.

Which is pure fucking insanity.

CHAPTER FIVE

TARA

"I guess you're off the hook," I mutter to Lola, my eyes still fixed on the door through which that guy disappeared with the stripper. And I don't know if I'm actually talking to her or myself. Not sure I'm glad the guy's gone either. Even though he was looking at me like he wanted to rip my clothes off. But a part of me—a very foreign part, one I've never really met before—wanted him to.

"Huh?" Lola asks and takes a sip of the beer he didn't touch.

"You can go to bed by yourself now, I meant," I say.

"Yeah, I guess I should," she says and takes

another sip of the beer. "Tomorrow's another day, right?"

I've been chatting to her on and off all evening and she's nice, but not very forthcoming. Guarded, just like most of the women at the shelter are. So I didn't show her any of the photos of Samantha. She's also not nearly old enough to work in a place like this, I'm sure of it. I'll try to gain her trust, take her away with me when I leave. Which I hope will be soon. Because the heavy ball that's been resting in the pit of my stomach since I decided to come here has turned into full on nausea now.

That guy—Tommy—was something else though. All hard talk, muscles, tallness and testosterone. But his eyes told a different story. Sure I got the familiar jolt of panic and the urge to run and hide when he was staring at my lips and ass, but they changed to something a lot more caring when I stammered on about needing this job. It was enough to make me believe his tough exterior is just a front, a line of protection. Though nothing of what he actually said and how he acted, reinforced that belief.

Lola slides the half empty glass of beer towards me and gets off the stool. "You can borrow some of my clothes, if you want. For tomorrow I mean, though I'm not sure they'll fit. Maybe one of the others can lend you something."

It takes me a few seconds to realize what she's talking about. And all the anger I felt at that guy for telling me how to dress comes back in a rush.

"I like my clothes just fine," I tell her. "Don't worry about it."

He thinks he owns all the women here, that he can take anything and everything from them whenever he wants. It took me a long time to find my anger for men who treat women like that—my father most prominent among them—and no one will ever tell me how to dress again. Or take advantage of me. Not even this dark eyed Adonis who also happens to be the first guy I ever met that I actually want to kiss. But that's just my tiredness talking. I'm dead on my feet from all the excitement of the past two days, so I'm not thinking straight, I can't be.

"Tommy's nice," Lola says and covers a yawn with her forearm. "You should do what he wants."

I'm sure she actually means, "If you do what he wants".

The patch on his jacket read Vice President. So maybe if I do what he wants, let him fuck me like I know he wants to, he'll tell me if Samantha is here. And Hell, if the lingering warmth his gazes left between my legs are anything to go by, I might even enjoy it a little bit.

The idea hits out of nowhere as I watch Lola walk away, and the icy dread that follows it makes me gasp. But it's a good plan, I can't deny that.

TOMMY

Simone faked her orgasm, I'm sure of it, and normally I'd want to fix that problem, but tonight I'm content to play along with her lie. Most of my primal need to fuck disappeared as soon as the door closed on Tara. And I spent most of the time fucking Simone thinking about how I should go back to the bar after, let the new girl know some more about the rules, maybe in that small dark room behind the bar.

"What's wrong with you tonight, Tommy?" Simone asks, trailing her finger over my chest, her long, bleached hair tickling my cheek as she snuggles closer to me.

"You should go now, I need some sleep," I tell her and roll over on my side turning my back to her.

"Sure you don't want me to stay?" Her fingers are cold and clammy like a dead person's.

"Yeah, I'm positive. You know the deal." I never let them sleep over. Though I do usually send them away sated and satisfied.

"Lola stayed last night," she whines.

I wish they didn't all watch me so closely. They're like a bunch of hens, looking to roost with me, since they think it'll benefit them. It's unnerving and very misguided. Even before my dear brother is done restructuring the club, I'll be long gone, with a price on my head, most likely. A true outlaw. The lone wolf kind. It sounds almost romantic, but it fucking won't be. I'm sure of that. "That was a fluke, I told her to leave."

I know what she's angling for, but I won't be claiming any of them as my old lady, I made that decision years ago. And it certainly won't be Simone with her fake orgasms. But I don't tell her that, it'd be too blunt and she needs some hope. So I just turn off the light.

"I thought we had a special thing going, Tommy," she won't let up.

"You're all special to me," I say and make the mistake of looking back at her over my shoulder. Her face looks very sad and empty, bathed as it is in moonlight. It's like she's not even here. Like she's just a ghost holding on with the last of what she's got. But I'm not the guy to make anything better for her. I can make her feel good for a few hours, but that's all she's getting. "Each in your own way," I add.

She frowns at me. But it's the truth. Lola's great for blowjobs, Simone can always be counted on for rough, animal fucking, Ava actually prefers anal, and the list goes on. As for the new girl, she's a mystery. One I'll get started on unraveling first thing tomorrow morning. Because I'm here to have a good time while it lasts. And I don't need any extra baggage to drag away with me once it's over.

She mutters something under her breath as she gets off the bed. It sounds like, "Asshole" but I'm happy to ignore her.

Crystal is alone at the bar when I come down at noon, spraying some caustic smelling cleaner all over the counter and wiping it down.

"I thought you hired that girl to do the cleaning," I say as I squeeze past her to get to the coffee machine.

"Keep your voice down," Crystal says. "She's sleeping in the back room."

"What the fuck? She's not getting paid to sleep," I say even louder, since I kinda want her to get up.

"I went in to wake her about an hour ago, and, Oh my God, it was the saddest thing," she says, flipping a string of hair off her forehead, her good eye very wide. "She was weeping in her sleep with actual tears streaming down her cheeks. Don't be too hard on her, Tommy."

"Me, hard?" I'm hard *for* her. But I ignore that thought, since crying in her sleep does sound like a very sad fucking thing.

"Just leave her be," Crystal says. "I think she's been through a lot."

But Crystal thinks that about every one of the girls here, and as far as I can tell they're all tough as nails.

The door at the back of the bar opens, and then Tara peeks out, so pale her lips are a soft pink. The bun at the back of her head is neater than it was last night, but she's wearing the same clothes, and they're all crumpled up so I'm sure she slept in them. But the soft light in the room still attaches to her, makes her glow a pale white like some fucking religious statue of the Virgin Mary.

I'm not wearing a shirt, just a pair of sweats and her gaze actually tickles as it passes over my stomach and chest, stops dead at my throat. She looks away abruptly, shock plain on her face like she can't believe she was just checking me out.

"What did we say about the outfits?" I blurt out, since I want her to look at me with that same lightening as last night flashing in her eyes.

"Leave her be, Tommy," Crystal mutters behind my back and the look that Tara gives her is one of pure gratitude.

"Fine, wear what you want." I'll back down for now. "Want some coffee?"

She looks at me with wide eyes like she didn't understand the question. I pick up a cup and wave it at her.

"Sure, OK," she mumbles. "With milk."

"Alright, with milk, coming up."

The girl's acting weird, I'll give Crystal that. But I know she likes what she sees when she looks at me, so this shy, scared act of hers makes no fucking sense.

"Thanks," she whispers as I hand her the cup, then actually shakes and stumbles back as I make sure to touch her hand when she takes it. But she smiles at me right after, batting her eyes again, which again makes no fucking sense.

She stands next to me while she drinks it, and I'm just about to break the silence when Crystal hands her the rag and cleaner, directs her to get started wiping down the tables.

The whole thing's super anticlimactic, even though Tara keeps stealing tiny glances at me as I watch her do it.

The back door opens with a crash, and in comes Bear with an armload of tiny cats, Lola and Ava right behind him.

"Get those filthy things outta here!" I yell, more harshly than I intended.

"It's kittens, Tommy," Lola says, pouting at me like the fifteen year old I know she is. So absolutely no more blowjobs from her. "We wanted to play with them inside where it's dry. It's pouring buckets outside. Bear said we could."

"So they can piss and shit all over the place?" I mutter, but it's fitting. Everything else is going to shit anyway. "I told you to keep them outside."

It comes out too harshly, and now even Tara's looking at me like I just killed one of the cats in front of her.

"Whatever, just clean up after them," I say and grab my coffee off the counter. "I'm going out anyway."

To spend the day working on my bike. Hopefully things will make sense again by tonight.

CHAPTER SIX

TARA

I spent the rest of the day helping Crystal clean. It's getting well into the evening now, my back is aching, and all I smell is the lemon-scented disinfectant, but at least I got the chance to meet all the girls working here.

As the day drew on I lost much of my apprehension about this place. Everyone seems so happy, content even, despite how messed up the whole arrangement actually is. But I don't think the girls are forced into prostitution here. At least not by the old biker Bear, who is actually the friendliest of them all. Though I think that might be because he's very clearly very senile. Once it stopped raining, they even showed me the makeshift cat shelter they have out back, where at least twenty cats are housed.

But the more I learnt about this place, the more certain I am that Samantha never came here. Else she would stay put, and she'd certainly call me.

I almost pull out the photos of her more than once, but decide against it each time.

Tommy hasn't been back since this morning, and it's almost opening time now. And with each minute that passes my apprehension grows. Can I even seduce him? I didn't do such a great job of it this morning, judging by the fact that he just left. Do I even want to keep trying? The mere idea wakes a flurry of butterflies in my stomach, which make it even harder to breathe. And even though I'm not sure the answer to that is actually a yes, I do want to try. And that feeling is so foreign it scares me.

"Go on, get some sleep," Crystal says. "I'll tend bar tonight."

"That would be great, thank you," I say. "I could use a shower though."

Apart from bringing in my suitcase, and getting a room to myself on the top floor I haven't even changed since last night. And if I want to give this seduction thing a go, I should make myself look presentable.

"Lola will show you," Crystal says and waves her over.

I follow Lola to the back, but instead of taking me up the narrow, wooden staircase that lead to my room upstairs, she keeps walking down the hallway.

"You can use the shower in Tommy's apartment, since there's no hot water upstairs," Lola says once she notices I'm not following.

"You sure?" I manage to say past the lump in my throat.

"Oh, it's fine, he doesn't mind. Besides, he won't be back for a couple more hours at least," Lola says over her shoulder, already opening the door at the far side of the hallway.

"I don't know...I don't mind a cold shower," I mutter, not moving from my spot. I'm all sorts of scared right now, of him walking in, seeing me naked, and this reaction is one I understand. The voice telling me it's exactly what I want is the weird one, the one I never heard before.

"Come on, don't worry about it," she says and waves me over, flipping the light on in Tommy's apartment.

I'm out of arguments, so I approach the door, even though my heart's beating fast and hard in my throat.

Tommy's apartment is actually just a large room, with a king sized bed at one end, a desk and closet at the other, and a cracked leather sofa in the middle. The bathroom is small, but looks clean enough.

"You can use my shampoo and stuff," Lola says and points to a row of pink bottles at the edge of the bathtub. "Hang on, I'll get you a clean towel."

She scoots past me out of the bathroom and opens the closet, pulls out a greyish white towel and hands it to me.

I grab it automatically. The fabric is rough against my skin and this suddenly feels like the worst idea I've ever had.

Lola smiles at me and then I'm alone in this stark room, which looks and feels unoccupied despite heaps of Tommy's clothes piled on practically every available surface. His smell hangs faintly in the air, and I'm not sure how I even recognize it since I only met him twice. But it's unmistakable.

A couple of skimpy dresses are lying around amid his clothes, along with a couple of bras and thongs. The sight of them jerks me back to reality.

Hoping Tommy's the guy who'll treat me right is a pipe dream, borne of my desperate desire to find my sister as soon as possible, and this weird hormonal reaction I have to him. He's hot. I don't deny that.

But he's also a VP of an outlaw biker club. So he's dangerous by default. He's just someone who will use me and discard me like he does all the other girls in here. And I need that like I need to get raped again.

TOMMY

I enter the Lounge from the back, since I'm in no fucking mood for company tonight. Shade had me riding with him to two meetings. The first was about sorting out what happened to the gun shipment that never came yesterday, and on the second we were checking out whores. If I never have to look at another tweaked-out trafficked whore again it'll be too soon. It's exactly the reaction Shade wanted from me, so I kept my mouth shut. That didn't stop him from telling me over and over that the club's about to earn that 1% patch all over again until I wanted to puke.

I managed to record some of the conversations, and I need to get that shit encrypted and stored somewhere safe. I feel rotten to the core for betraying the MC with these recordings, and the pictures I take of the meetings and the gun shipments, but I need to secure a way out for myself that won't leave me in some shallow grave.

I curse as I enter my apartment and hear the shower running. Whichever of the girls is in there is going right back out tonight.

The tap turns off and the shower curtain flies open just as I enter the bathroom to kick whoever it is out.

But it's Tara staring back at me, her perfect lips forming an O as wide as her eyes. She's frozen in place, making no move to cover herself up. Nor should she. All the blood from my entire body rushes to my cock, making it so hard it hurts. I was right about this body she's hiding under those huge clothes. Her full breasts are so large they'd spill right out of my palms if I held them, and the nipples are tiny flesh colored buds that probably taste sweeter than candy. I'll never understand how she manages to hide that luxurious bosom under that funky plaid shirt.

Her waist is tapered, her hips flaring out, topping the smooth line formed by her shapely thighs and her perfect calves and feet. Her pussy isn't shaved, and the hair there is only a shade darker than her long, wet hair that's falling down the sides of her face, hiding the nasty undercut, and framing her perfect face the way it's meant to.

I knew she was interested, and there's no fucking way I'm kicking *her* out. All other pressing business can wait.

I take a step towards her and she blinks hard, finally waking from her trance.

But she shrieks as I reach out to take her hand, and flies out of the tub so fast, she'd fall if I didn't catch her. She's screaming, clawing at my arm as she drags herself away from me, glaring at me like some wild, caged animal. Her insane reaction shakes loose memories of my mom screaming exactly like this at my father. Painful memories I didn't even realize I still had. But if I release her she'll fall all the way and hurt herself.

So I pick her up, and push her against the tiles. But I have no urge to release my cock and fuck her up against this wall until she screams in pleasure. I just want to hold her, comfort her, wipe that terror from her eyes with a soft kiss.

"Relax, I won't ever hurt you," I say through gritted teeth, and I mean every word.

She stops thrashing, but she's breathing hard, her eyes fixed so firmly on mine, I'm sure she sees right past all my bullshit the way no one ever has. So I know she sees the truth of what I just told her.

And my cock is trying to convince me that I only startled her, and that she wants me to fuck her now that she's calmed down, but my brain knows better. Sure her eyes are softer now, inviting even, but terror and hatred is still mixing in them. And I realize beyond a shadow of a doubt that those are the only things holding her together, that she'd break apart into a million little pieces if she didn't have that.

So I release her, take a few steps back. She's still staring at me, motionless, only the lightening shooting from her eyes telling me she's alive. I still want to pick her up, toss her on my bed, kiss and lick every inch of her until she's begging me to fuck her. Which I would, until she passes out.

But that magical dream is broken as she snatches her clothes off the sink, and bolts out of the bathroom, a photo falling from the back pocket of her jeans right before she disappears through the door. I almost call her back, tell her she dropped something, but that'd be too fucking weird after what just happened.

The photo's of a dark-haired, blue-eyed girl who looks eerily familiar, though I don't think I actually ever saw her. Her eyes have a haunted look to them, even though she's smiling. And I know that look. My mom had those same wounded eyes. I didn't think I remembered that either, but I do.

I toss the photo on the desk and start undressing for a shower.

The woman in the picture is probably Tara's lesbian girlfriend or something. That would explain her hair and clothes, and the sick fear she had of me touching her. And while that opens up a very enticing set of girl-on-girl fantasies, that shit is never fun when they actually hate guys. Maybe I could get Simone and Ava in here later to act that shit out for me. Maybe that'll wipe these painful memories of my mom from my mind.

CHAPTER SEVEN

TARA

I'm shaking so hard my arms and legs are cramping.

When Tommy barged into the bathroom, all I saw was my father's angry face, sure he was about to punish me because I ran from him, hid, make me never do it again. And I'm trying to shut the door on the memories of nights my father did exactly that, bolt it, but it's not working. They keep pushing back, conjuring vivid, nightmarish visions of nights that didn't end with me escaping, nights when I limped away, each step sending shooting pains through my body as I tried to find a safe place to hide. Memories of the years when there were no hideaways.

Tommy telling me he won't hurt me, broke through my panic. And I wanted to believe him, but he was holding me so hard it hurt. I'll never trust a man. I can't. But I know how they think, I had to learn. Slyness and coyness trump brute strength. Almost every time.

Tommy's still my best bet for finding Samantha quickly, if she's here. And if I play my part well, he might even deliver her to me.

That small voice that actually wants him to touch me, make love to me, deliver on his promise never to hurt me, is calling me all sorts of vile names right now. But I ignore it as I drape a clean shirt over my naked body and undo the first few buttons. This shirt's not as oversized as the others I brought with me, and actually looks a little like a dress. I stuff the pictures of Samantha in the breast pocket, and leave my room before I can change my mind again.

I'll let him fuck me, and then I'll ask him about Samantha. It'd work better if I could conjure up some tears while I did it, but I haven't cried since I was thirteen years old and realized that nothing but death will ever erase the nightmare that's my life.

I'm knocking on Tommy's door, with no recollection of actually having walked there. But that's a good sign. It means I'm already blocking it out, that some other Tara is going through with this plan. The strong one. The one that fears no man, and no nightmare. The one that feels nothing at all.

The door flies open, and he's towering over me, wearing just a pair of pajama bottoms, an intricately carved cross hanging from his neck on a silver chain, over a black and white tattoo of the same thing. Around us, the smell of a man's shower gel is mixing with the bubble gum scented one I used. His left forearm is covered in angry red slashes right over the intricate snake tattoo that covers it. My nails left that, and I feel my cheeks grow hot in embarrassment, a pleasant warmth waking in my belly at the thought that I marked him. And that I want to do it again.

"I'm sorry about before," I say, my voice deep and sultry.

"Can't blame me for getting the wrong impression though, right?" His eyes are begging me to agree. And for the first time I notice that his eyes aren't actually black. They're a very dark blue, like the ocean on a full moon night. And the currents in them are dragging me down, past all barriers. The reason I came here is still clear in my mind, but I also know that beyond all logic, this is exactly where I want to be standing.

He moves aside and opens the door wider. I step into the room, passing so close to him I can feel the heat rising from his body as I close the door behind me.

"You didn't get the wrong idea," I whisper and now it's the strong Tara talking, the one that always does what she must. To survive. And make sure her sister survives too. "And you can take me any way you desire. I want you to."

He frowns at me like he doesn't believe me. But then his lips curl up into a grin. I lick my lips.

He's on me in a flash, his hard, strong chest pressing me against the door, his lips on mine soft yet firm, his tongue looking for mine. His passion is sweeping me under, fireworks exploding in all colors of the rainbow inside my mind. Even the strong Tara loses her balance and topples over, disappears in the flood of desire I never felt before, didn't even know I could.

But it crashes against the barrier inside me with the force of an earthquake. I can't do this. I've been raped too many times, and all those memories are now a hurricane inside my mind, attacking the soft pleasure his lips are waking inside me. I want to surrender to it, I want it to win.

One of his hands is kneading my breast, the other cupping my ass. His kiss grows deeper, fiercer, and his hard cock is throbbing against my stomach. All those sensations combined have me skirting the edge of reason, my pussy growing wet, pulsing in need to be filled. I freeze as his hand brushes against my clit, flashes of past pain radiating through me like I'm feeling them now. I can't do this. I'm too messed up. I can never be with a man again.

He stops kissing me, takes his hand away and cups my cheek.

"No?" he asks, his eyes searching mine for an answer that's beyond words. If I said yes now, he'd know it was a lie. And I don't ever want to lie to him.

I shake my head, and look down, closing my eyes. I messed up. Failed. Like I always do. I should pack up and leave tonight, tell the detective everything I know, and let the cops handle it.

He runs his thumb over my lips then lets me go, steps back because he's done with me.

But at least he's not raping me. At least he's respecting my, "No". Now I can at least forever remember what might have been.

"I guess I'll go now," I mutter blindly feeling along the door for the knob. Because I can't actually physically turn my back on him. Even though that's the only logical thing to do.

He just looks at me for awhile, his face blank, but his eyes are studying me so intensely, my knees are turning to mush. Maybe I didn't mess it all up. Maybe I get a do over.

He breaks the eye contact abruptly, walking to his desk and picking something up from it.

"You'll want to take this photo of your girlfriend before you go." He's holding a photo of Samantha out to me, and I'm having trouble swallowing. Hope dying is the worst feeling in the world. That picture was taken a few weeks before Samantha disappeared, and if he doesn't recognize her she was never here. "Next time you want to get back at your girlfriend by fucking a guy, pick a different man."

That's what he thinks is happening?

"She's my sister," I mutter, just those few little words taking the rest of my energy away. Maybe I should've just said, "*Was* my sister" and let go of all the hope from now until forever. It would hurt less, make it easier to breathe, to get up in the mornings, to survive.

Confusion replaces the harshness in his eyes, until they're softer than midnight clouds as he looks down at the photo. "She's pretty, reminds me of my mom."

I snatch the photo from his hand. "It's not. It's my sister."

I'm angry now, because I'll never give up the hope, and I can't believe I even considered it.

"Trust me, I know it's not my mom," he says in a very faraway voice. And I know that brittle strain in his eyes as he looks at me. It comes from trying not to remember something you can't forget. I see it in my own eyes when I look in the mirror, saw it often in Samantha's.

I have the door open before I realize I've moved.

"You can stay, if you want." I hear him say. His voice sounds like it's echoing across a vast distance, calling me home.

I want to stay, but what's the point? He has his pain, and I have mine. I can't give him what he needs. No matter how much I want to.

My eyes are burning with the tears I can't shed as I close the door again. I'm staying. Because even a dash of hope is better than none.

TOMMY

The last thing I expected was for Tara to come back. I almost didn't open the door when she knocked, thinking it was one of the others. And I certainly didn't expect her to stay when I asked her to. I'm not even entirely sure why I did. But she looked so lost holding that photo, telling me it's of her sister.

She's sleeping on the sofa now and whimpering softly, tears streaming down her face. Crystal was right, it's the saddest fucking thing I've ever seen in my life too. And the need to comfort her, make it better, stop her from crying in her sleep ever again, is burning through my body harder than any adrenaline surge I've ever experienced.

But if I wake her, she'll just fly out of here again, clawing at me, her eyes accusing me of doing her wrong, hurting her. I'd never do that to any woman. And especially not this girl who's so wounded, so broken, only her anger and hatred are keeping her from unraveling into a pool of sadness and pain.

I take the comforter and drape it over her, fighting the urge to nestle next to her on the sofa. I've never wanted to just hold a girl as much as I want to hold Tara right now. It'd be enough. I wouldn't even need anything more. My cock's telling me that's a big fat lie, but it's not completely certain of it either.

It's not like me to get all soft and romantic like this. But today was a trying day emotion-wise. I'm no good at handling emotions. Grief is fine, I'm used to that one. Anger I got under control. But these loving feelings...I don't want any of that. They're probably just the consequence of everything else that went to shit today. I'll wake up tomorrow morning and be back to my old self. Because the last thing I need is to grow feelings for one of the girls Crystal's trying to save.

CHAPTER EIGHT

TOMMY

Tara's gone when I wake up, the blanket neatly folded at the foot of the sofa. It's probably for the best she just left quietly, since I have no idea what happened between us last night. Well, nothing actually happened except that she rejected me. But for some reason, my stomach is clenching in nervousness at the thought of running into her later today like I've never felt before with any woman. Except possibly way in the beginning with the first one I had sex with. Those memories are hazy. But it certainly hasn't happened since.

I feel like a total pussy sneaking out the back, but I need to go see Jerry today, get him to transfer and encrypt all these files I have, and I'm already off to a late start.

I get a coffee-to-go from the gas station near Crystal's, and decide to walk to my brother's house where I keep my car, so I can drink it along the way. It's a decision I regret less than a mile into my walk. The sun is beating down, the air hot like it's not barely 11 AM. California's a great place to live, if only it didn't get so hot in the summer. The coffee's scalding hot too, I've already burned my tongue twice trying to drink it.

But all that discomfort fades as I spot Tara jogging down the sidewalk of the street running perpendicular to the one I'm walking down. She hasn't seen me yet, and the nerves from this morning are back in full force. I'm very aware of the fact that I could just keep walking, and she'd never know I was here, but I don't want to do that. I'm kinda enjoying this reaction I have to her. It's fun, and I haven't had any real fun in ages.

So, I stop in the shade cast by the building on the corner, and take another sip of my coffee. Tara's wearing way too much clothing to be jogging in this heat, and her perfect body is completely hidden by the folds of her thick sweatshirt and sweatpants. But I know it's there, and that's enough. She's totally focused on the run, in the zone as they say, seems to have no idea what's around her.

I notice her cheeks are flushed a bright crimson as she draws nearer, a color that reminds me of candy apples.

"Hey, why don't you rest for a bit?" I yell once she's within earshot. "The idea with exercise is to prevent heart attacks, not cause them."

Her bright eyes fix on me and she stops dead mid-leap, landing so awkwardly she barely manages to keep her balance.

"Sorry," I say and walk closer, afraid she twisted her ankle or something. "You OK?"

She's bent double, holding onto her knees and panting. It's such a sexy sound my cock grows half hard just hearing it. I bet her moans would sound even sexier. But her eyes are wary as she straightens up and looks at me. It brings back the unsettling memory of last night and her wild flight away from me.

"You startled me," she says. "I didn't expect to meet anyone here."

She wipes off the sweat from her forehead, slicking back her hair, which is tied up in a bun, revealing the full glory of her undercut. But I could get used to even that nasty haircut of hers. As long as

I also could see the sweat glistening on her naked skin. I honestly can't remember the last time I wanted a girl on my cock as much as I want Tara there.

"It's too hot for running," I say. "Especially since you're wearing so much clothes."

She gives me an angry look, her bright blue eyes flashing with lightning striking on a clear sunny day.

"I'm fine," she says. "I mean, you go running in this heat too, don't you?"

Her eyes are gliding down my arms, making my cock grow even harder. I'm only wearing a t-shirt and jeans, since I left the cut at home. The less clues I give Jerry to figure out who I really am, the better. He's already got access to all the incriminating evidence against the MC I've managed to collect. But maybe visiting Jerry can wait another day. I'd much rather spend today getting to know Tara a lot better.

"I'm not much for running, or cardio in general," I say. "It's mostly weights for me."

I actually flex my bicep as I say it, feeling like a total idiot the second I realize I'm doing it. Don't know what it is about her, but she makes me want to strut around like a peacock. I haven't felt the need to do that in years.

"And swimming, when I get the chance," I add, since she's not saying anything. Her pouty lips curl up into the faintest little smile.

"I love swimming," she says, her eyes lighting up like the sun just came up. "Back home, I try to go to the beach most days."

"And where is home?" I ask.

"Oh...LA," she says, yet I heard the pause. I think she's lying, but I don't care. She can lie all she wants, as long as she's talking to me.

"You're not that far away from home then," I say.

She doesn't say anything to that. I really should've just asked a question, but my mind's completely blank right now. I think her eyes are causing it. They look like two Earths as seen from space, the blue, green, gold and white blending perfectly in her irises. But I've never been struck speechless by a woman before.

"You wanna grab a drink or something? You look like you could use some refreshment."

She blinks, looks down at her sweaty grey sweat-shirt, then back up at me. "I should go take a shower."

It's not a hard no; she almost sounds like she wants me to wait while she showers. The thought of her soapy, naked body sends another rush of blood to my cock. I'm actually fully hard right now, and she's not even flirting with me. She's sweating, her face is covered in red patches, she's wearing man-sized exercise clothes, and she has a shaved head. Yet I still want to fuck her like I haven't wanted to fuck a woman in years. It's bizarre, but then again, it doesn't have to make sense. It just needs to happen.

"Later then," I say and flash her a smile, quite possibly the first genuine one in weeks.

She nods, glancing down the street towards Crystal's, which is also pretty much the only place we could go for a drink around here right now. All the other ones are seedy bars that don't even open until later. Besides I've put off seeing Jerry for too long already.

"Alright, it's a date." I grin at her, but her startled glance as I say it wipes it right off.

She nods, but she's still looking towards Crystal's.

I let her go after that, but I do look back at her a few times. She's not running, just walking, or more like gliding. The outline of her shapely ass and thighs is more visible from the back, despite the heavy sweats she's wearing. I think I have a chance with her, but I'm not sure. And that just makes me want her more.

TARA

The run was meant to clear my head, but that back-fired spectacularly. I woke up before dawn on Tommy's sofa, and I've been unable to stop fretting over my behavior last night. I made such a fool of myself. And what's worse, I couldn't stop thinking about the feel of his lips against mine, his hard rippling body pressing me against the door, his hands cupping my breasts. It felt good, right, natural, but it also brought such dark memories. Not even clear memories, just feelings of dread, primal fear, sadness, all the stuff I never want to feel again. That I'd do anything to never feel again. Yet, it also felt good, promised better things yet to come. Even just talking to Tommy feels natural and right.

And after our chat on the sidewalk, I'm even more confused about it all than I was this morning. Going back to my little dark room in the attic didn't help, taking a cold shower didn't help, scrubbing all the surfaces in the whole bar area didn't help. The run was my last hope. And even that didn't help.

I've agreed to a date.

But he was joking when he said it. Yet why

would he joke? He meant it. And that makes it even worse.

He wants to sleep with me. I see it clearly each time he looks at me. And I'm petrified of that prospect. Because I've never been able to let a man touch me. I always stopped it when it started to happen.

Yet, somehow, the thought of Tommy touching me is exciting, exhilarating. I think I desire it, but I don't really know what desire feels like, so I'm not sure that's it. The whole thing's driving me insane, positively insane. I should just stop thinking. I used to be able to just stop thinking.

A knock on the door makes me leap off the bed, where I've been sitting since I returned from the run. I haven't showered, haven't even taken off my sweaty clothes. Oh God, he saw me sweating like a pig. He was absolutely right about me wearing too much clothes.

The door opens and Lola's head peers in. "There's still some breakfast left, if you want it. Are you alright?"

Her question takes me off guard, but I suppose all those questions racing through my mind must be showing on my face.

"Yeah, sure, I'd love some breakfast," I mutter.

She comes in and closes the door behind her. "I came looking for you before, but you were gone."

"I went for a run," I say, smoothing down the covers of my bed to make it neat again.

She plops down on top of it though, wasting my effort.

"I thought you were still with Tommy." She giggles and it makes her seem very young. Sixteen maybe. She's too young to be working in a place like this. "You're so lucky he let you spend the night in his apartment. He never does that. You must be special."

She giggles again, and I know I'm blushing. "That was just a...I mean..."

She nods like she understands. "I know. I get scared sleeping alone sometimes, so I stay. He never even notices."

And that's just it. Tommy uses all the women here for sex. Even Lola, who's only a child. I can't believe I just spent the whole morning fretting about having feelings for him, when I already figured out exactly what kind of guy he really is. The worst kind. The kind that treats women like they're his toys. The way I acted last night shocked him, and that's why he invited me to spend the night. But that was just my insanity getting the better of me for a minute. I don't think I've ever made a bigger fool of myself in my life.

But now I finally have the clarity I've been so desperately trying to get all morning. And the calm will follow.

"I'll just take a quick shower and then come downstairs," I tell Lola, grabbing some fresh clothes from my suitcase.

She follows me out into the hall.

"What, here?" she asks as I open the door to the small bathroom on this floor. "But the water's cold."

"I don't mind," I say, flipping on the light. "It'll feel nice after the heat outside."

I smile at her, and she returns it.

"You're weird."

She skips down the stairs, and even though she was only joking she's more right than she knows. I am weird. And the part of me that wants to take this shower in Tommy's apartment, even wishes he'd walk in on me again, is the least weird of all.

TOMMY

"Do you plan on ever telling me what all this is about, Tommy?" Jerry asks when I hand him the USB with the data.

"Just do your thing," I say, and sit on one of the three office chairs he's not occupying, and that's not covered by a pile of his dirty clothes, candy bar wrapper, empty beer cans, and who knows what else. My apartment is clean compared to this hacker lair of his.

He frowns at me, but then gets to work. The only light it the room is the one coming off his four monitors. The windows are covered by thick black cloth, blocking out all the desert sunlight, which would be enjoyable, if it weren't for Jerry's BO and the faint smell of rotting food mixing in the AC-cooled air. I wonder if he even opened the window since summer started.

"Do you ever go outside anymore, Jerry?"

It comes out too harsh, but I swear he's gotten even bigger in the last three weeks since I was here last. He was big when I met him at college three years ago, but he has a triple chin now, and the rolls of fat hanging off his arms and stomach are pretty much covering his entire chair. He's 25 years old, like me, but I don't think he has a lot of years left.

He looks at me over his shoulder, with part anger, part something I can't quite define in his face. Maybe it's a cry for help.

"We can go for a walk or something, after you're

done with this," I suggest. Though I'm not even sure how well he can walk with that huge stomach of his.

He pulls out my USB, and hands it to me. "I'm done, so you can stop being rude."

I take the USB and plug it back into the crucifix hanging around my neck. It holds all the data I've collected. Jerry just encrypts it and sends it to some ultra secure server somewhere, but I keep the backup on me at all times. It's waterproof, so I don't even take it off when I shower.

"I'm not being rude," I say defensively. "I'm just concerned about you. It's not healthy the way you're putting on so much weight."

Back in college I tried to help him lose some of it. And it worked for awhile, but it clearly hasn't taken.

"What also might not be healthy is me having access to all this secret encrypted data you keep bringing over," he snaps.

I hope he hasn't been looking at any of it. Apparently it's password protected, so only I have access, but he is a hacker. The system I asked Jerry to set up for me is very simple. I bring him the evidence, he stores it in a cloud, and if I don't call a certain number every four days, all the data gets sent to every law enforcement agency that is even remotely interested in the MCs criminal operations. It's my insurance for when I leave, and I'll make damn sure Shade understands he's going away for life if he tries to track me down and kill me after I do.

Jerry knows it's important stuff, he just doesn't know what it is. Though sometimes I selfishly hope that maybe he does, that maybe he's sneaked a peek. Jerry knowing all about it would give me another layer of protection when I leave. But it could also get him killed.

"You haven't been snooping around in it, have you?" I ask just to make sure.

He shakes his head. "No, I keep my word."

I know he wants me to tell him, but I can't. He doesn't know who I really am, and it's too late now to change that. But he's a good friend, one of my best friends, and lying to him bothers me a lot. Collecting all this evidence against the MC and threatening to expose it all to the cops bothers me a lot too. Yet I see no other way. Some shit just has to be lived with. I learned that lesson a long time ago.

I get up and push the chair under one of his computer desks. "How about that walk now?"

"Nah, it's too hot," he says, swiveling his chair to face me. It groans under his weight. "How about a beer?"

I almost say no, since a beer is the last thing he

needs, but I shrug and nod instead. Though I'd kinda rather be getting back to Crystal's, and having a beer with Tara instead.

———

TARA

I spent the last few hours just hanging out with Ava, Lola and Simone. Playing with the kittens, talking and generally succeeding at not thinking at all. I'm not part of their little group, so I mostly listen. It's a lot like at the shelter, only I have to rein myself in from asking too many questions, or trying to counsel them. I'm succeeding for the most part, but that counselor role is so ingrained in me after all these years of working at the shelter, that Simone is already casting me glances that suggest she's wondering who I really am. Like she thinks I might not be just some woman down on her luck, passing through town. I've been racking my brain over how to ask them if they ever saw my sister here, show them the photos, but I don't think it's the right time yet, they still don't trust me enough. And that look from Simone just proved it.

"When do we open tonight?" I ask at just past three.

Yesterday the club opened at eight, and Crystal was here before then, setting everything up. I haven't seen her at all today.

"We don't," Lola says and screeches as the kitten she's playing with bites her finger.

"What do you mean?"

"It's Sunday," Simone explains. "We're closed on Sundays and personally, I love having a day off. We have to work so much more now that there's only the three of us here. And I get one night of rest from that creep that comes to all my shows."

"You have a stalker?" I blurt out before thinking better of it. Simone looks at me sharply, but Ava and Lola both start giggling.

"Not a stalker, just some guy who's in love with her," Ava explains. "And Simone likes him too, even though she pretends not to."

"I do not," Simone says, closing her arms over her chest. "He's old."

"He's only like forty-something," Ava says. "And he's fit. You should give him a chance. Don't you want to get away from this place?"

Simone gives her a sharp look. Ava shrugs sadly and starts checking over her nails. I have the strongest urge to give her a hug, and I don't get that a lot. I hear so many sad stories at my job, I've grown resistant to them. Compassion fatigue, they call it. I'm not proud of it, but it's part of the job.

"But it's true that only the weirdoes come to the show on Sundays," Lola says. "The rest stay at home thinking about God. So we stay closed, it's better that way."

She's not giggling anymore, and I know that look on her face. She's met some weirdoes in her life. I have too, and I don't like to be reminded. But I never thought God had a big place in the lives of men who come to places like this.

The back door swings open just as I'm about to make a comment to that effect, and Tommy walks in. I'm struck speechless and breathless, and I don't even fully know why. Probably because his eyes are fixed on me like I'm the only one in the room.

"Where have you been all day, Tommy?" Lola asks.

"That's none of your business," he says and finally looks away, so I can breathe again.

He said it pretty harshly, cementing my knowledge that he's just a brute looking for an easy lay. But the girls don't seem bothered by it, just start chattering again, so why am I?

He goes behind the bar and starts fiddling with the coffee machine like we're not even here. I turn away and try to join the conversation, but they're talking about someone I don't know.

"How about we go for a swim?" Tommy asks, startling me. He's standing right next to me, and I didn't hear him approach. His eyes are fixed on my face, like he's asking just me.

"Oh, yes, let's go!" Lola shrieks, jumping to her feet. "We haven't gone swimming in ages."

She's vibrating that's how excited she is, but Tommy's still looking only at me.

"I don't know," I say over the thick lump in my throat. "I don't have a bathing suit."

"A t-shirt will do," Tommy says. "Or just a bra."

He's grinning at me, letting me know he'd really like to see me naked, but what really gets me is that I want him to.

"Nonsense," Ava says and gets up. "I'll lend you a bathing suit. You look like you're about my size."

Ava has the most womanly body I've ever seen, all soft curves and milky skin.

"She is," Tommy assures her, winking at me, and all this feels like a really bad idea all of a sudden. I can't let him touch me or kiss me, my messed up mind won't allow that. And I made that clear to him last night. Didn't I? So why is he winking at me?

Ava and Lola already left to get ready, only Simone is still here. And I'm glad for it, because otherwise I'd be alone with Tommy.

"You getting ready, Simone?" Tommy asks her.

But she shakes her head, her face very hard. "I have to do my nails today."

Maybe I should say I have to do my nails too and get out of this. But I almost never do my nails, and I kind of want to go.

Ava returns and hands me a bathing suit. Once I see it, I do almost make an excuse. It's a hot pink, skimpy bikini that I'd never even consider trying on in a store, let alone wear in public. But it's too late for excuses. I just won't put it on, and I won't go in the water.

"We can take my car," I suggest, because I always need a way out. I need to know I can leave at any time, that I have a clear exit.

"Sure," Tommy says. "But I'm driving."

He sticks out his hand for the keys, and I swallow the argument I was about to make. Because I doubt I'd get very far against his stern, commanding tone. And I don't even really want to try. A part of my mind is very certain that it's alright to let him drive.

CHAPTER NINE

TARA

I'm sitting in the passenger seat next to Tommy. The radio's on full blast, playing some pop song that Lola and Ava are both singing along to. But I'm tense like an overstretched rubber band. I'm not even sure if it's in fear or anticipation of what's to come. This feels like a date, even though we're not alone. Though despite all the noise in the car, I feel like we kind of are. Tommy's not talking, but he glances at me from time to time like he's expecting me to say something. And I'm racking my brain for an opening, but my stomach is a knot of nerves, and I'm pretty sure I'd just stutter if I tried to form a sentence.

The land opens up as soon as we leave town, rolling hills coming into view in the distance, on the other side of vast fields already turning brown from the summer heat. I have no idea where we're going. I thought maybe a pool, since the ocean is too far away for an afternoon dip.

I get my answer as we crest one of the hills. A lovely blue green lake stretches out below us, bordered by dark grey boulders, and thick, lush foliage.

Lola and Ava dart form the car as soon as it stops, and dash away toward the ravine leading down to the lake.

"The usual place, right?" Ava yells over her shoulder, but doesn't stop to hear a reply.

I'm already starting to sweat in my flannel shirt just standing next to the car, since it really is a scorching day today. Tommy grabs a blanket from the back of the truck, then hands me my car key.

"Here," he says. "I just couldn't be seen driven around by a woman."

I take the key, close my fist around it tightly.

His gesture of returning the car key means so much to me, I'd never be able to put it into words. Nor should I try, because he has no idea what he just did for me. I can relax now, because I know I can get away if I need to.

"Thanks," I say and he frowns at me like he heard the genuine thankfulness in my voice.

"It's a bit of a hike to the lake," he says. "And you're overdressed. Maybe you should just change into your bathing suit here. I promise I won't watch."

It's the first allusion to last night's events he's made all day, and he's grinning at me. Some promise, that is. He's just showing me his true colors again. Sex. That's all he thinks about. Even after my clear rejection last night. For some reason I feel more hopeful than mad though.

"I'll be fine," I say and stuff the car key into my pocket, pushing the hot pink bikini I have in there even deeper. I'm not putting it on. No way. "Where to?"

He points and starts walking and I follow. But he was absolutely right about me being overdressed. Sweat's running down the sides of my face within a few paces, and the elastic bandage hiding my breasts is chaffing my skin, its tightness making it even harder to breathe. This was a bad idea. On so many levels. Samantha's not here. She was never here. Why am I even still sticking around?

I'll show the girls Sam's pictures tonight and then leave before morning. It was crazy to think I could find her here on my own, just as its crazy how I can't wait to see Tommy undress and go swimming. He's walking a few steps in front of me, but not so far that I lose sight of him.

I'm breathing heavily by the time I can finally hear the splashing of water and the girls' excited screeches.

The rugged slope we walked down opens into a small half circle of pebble covered lake shore. Tommy dumps the blanket he's carrying on the ground and pulls off his shirt. I actually stumble.

His back is covered in tattoos over the bulging muscles, but his skin is milky pale, with just a hint of a caramel colored tan.

He looks back at me over his shoulder, and I avert my eyes hastily. He knows I was checking him out, it's loud and clear in his chuckle. "Don't know about you, but I'm going in."

He has his jeans and boots off before I can even draw a full breath. And I'm both hoping and fearing his boxers will be next, but he doesn't take those off. He wades into the water, and leaps in head first, doesn't come back out for a good while.

Some alien part of my mind is directing me to go change into the bathing suit behind those boulders we passed getting here and follow him in. But instead I take the blanket, spread it over the pebbles and sit down.

The breeze coming off the water cools my face, and I soon get my breathing under control again. I hope my face isn't too red from the exertion. Lola and Ava are splashing each other and giggling in the shallow part of the lake. Tommy is swimming further out, his perfectly formed arms cutting through the calm water with the precision of a pro swimmer, his whole body one with the water.

I lean back on my arms and look at the sky instead, because I'm getting really tired of the voice telling me I should go in and join him. It's not possible, and the edges of that happy thought are already shrouded in darkness. The one no light in this world can ever chase away. If I don't acknowledge it, it won't hurt me.

"Well, just FYI, the water's fantastic," Tommy's voice flows down to me, followed by a few cold drops of water dripping from his body onto my face.

"I'm sure," I mumble, straightening up and wrapping my arms around my legs.

He lies down on his stomach next to me, looking off at the water. He's so close I can feel the coolness of his skin through my jeans. I'm keeping my eyes fixed straight ahead too, because otherwise I'd just stare at his arms, and his back, and his...

"I thought you said you liked swimming," he says.

"That's why you wanted to go swimming? Because I said I like to swim?" The words are out of my mouth before I even decided to speak. It's touching that he remembered what I told him.

He twists his head and grins at me, nodding. His eyes are kind of the same color as the lake right now. Only the blue in them is much darker, and the green too.

"I do love swimming, but..." How were you even going to finish that sentence, Tara? But...I don't feel comfortable wearing a bikini. But...I get physically sick when a man even glances at me in a sexual way. That wouldn't even be completely true with Tommy. At least not until he actually touched me. Last night was a great example of what would happen then. But that's my problem. My curse. He certainly doesn't need to know about it.

"Thanks, that was thoughtful of you," I say instead. "Do you come here often?"

He rises on his arms, the cross around his neck glinting in the sun. "Yeah, quite a bit."

"I'm more used to swimming in the ocean," I say. "Or the pool."

I can't believe how easy it is to talk to him, despite all his suggestions that I get undressed, or the fact that he's already seen me naked last night.

"There's sharks in the ocean," he says and grins at me again. Surprisingly he doesn't follow up by suggesting this would be a great way for me to try swimming in a lake.

"But there's snakes here," I counter.

He looks around in alarm. "Did you see a snake?"

I'm not entirely sure he's just joking.

"No, I just meant there could be."

He lifts himself up in one fluid motion, the way his muscles flex and roll actually reminding me of a snake, and sits next to me.

"Can I tell you a secret?" he asks, glancing over at Ava and Lola, but then locking eyes with me. "But you can't tell anyone."

"Umm, yeah, I guess." I say breathlessly, completely unsure whether he's asking in earnest, or I'm about to be the punch line of another lewd joke.

"I'm terrified of snakes. I can't even watch a documentary about them."

I snort. Of course I'm the punch line, what else? At least it wasn't lewd.

"I'm not kidding," he assures me, and his face does look very serious.

"You're not? Come on," I say in my most sarcastic voice. "You have a huge snake tattoo all over your arm, and you belong to a motorcycle club named after a viper."

He rubs his snake tattoo. "That's why it's a secret. And it's the Viper, not a viper. It was my grandfather's road name, he started the MC."

He sounds bitter, despite the slight smile playing on his lips as he glances sideways to see my reaction. And maybe he can puzzle it out, because I'm so conflicted in my emotions right now I have no idea which one is showing on my face.

He's not just the Vice President, he's third generation founder. Even if Sam wasn't trafficked by his MC, he can ask around, find out if she's being held by one of the others in the area. He's trying to be my friend. Maybe I could just ask and he'd help me find her. Help me bring her home. A friend would do that. But then he'd know why I'm really here. And I can't figure out if asking, or just thinking about taking advantage of his friendliness in this way makes me rotten. I could also go the same way Sam went, if he's not as friendly as he seems.

"How can you stand having a picture of a snake on your arm if they scare you so much?" I ask to stifle all these thoughts firing off in my brain.

"I was young and stupid when I got this," he says. "I thought seeing a snake every day might help me get over my fear."

"And did it work?" I no longer think he's joking. He told me a real secret. Maybe I could tell him mine too.

"Yeah, not so much," he says. "But it's a cool tattoo, don't you think?"

He shows it to me, making a fist and flexing his bicep so the snake seems to move. It's kind of mesmerizing, and I reach out and run my fingers along it before I realize what I'm doing. The jolt of electricity as my fingertips brush his skin, snaps me right back to reality, makes me snatch my hand back. But the electricity is still coursing through me, causing sparks. Yet it doesn't touch the darkness, nothing can dispel that darkness.

I thought that mass of bad memories only came out when I attempted to be intimate with guys, but now I see it's always there, watching over me, making sure I never forget what was done to me, and how different I am to everyone else because of it, how I don't really belong in this world of normal people.

He's frowning at me like he's trying to figure out what I'm thinking, but the edge of his lips curls up when our eyes meet, and I know what he's thinking.

He's thinking I've just come on to him, and that's not even remotely true.

I look at the lake. Lola and Ava are still in the water, and it doesn't look like they'll be coming out anytime soon.

The sun glints off the silver cross hanging around his neck again. I very nearly touch that too. I don't know what's happening to me, but I want to feel that jolt of electricity again.

"So are you religious?" I ask. It comes out like an accusation.

He touches the cross, rolls it on his fingers. "Not especially. This is more like insurance."

"I've never heard anyone say that so bluntly," I mutter.

He glances at me. "That offends you? Are you very religious?"

I laugh, and it's an especially jarring sound even for me. "Me and God are not on very good terms. Haven't been for a long time."

I used to pray so hard for the parties to stop, for my dad to stop, to just be my dad, to not touch me that way, not touch Sam that way, not get so very angry when I tried to get him to stop. The nuns at the Catholic School I went to told us God always listened. I fell asleep feverishly reciting the Hail

Mary prayer more times than I can count. I even learned it in Latin, thinking that would help. None of it did.

"That was pretty blunt too," he says, smiling at me, but his eyes are serious.

"It is what it is," I say. It took me so long to come to terms with that. And I'm still not entirely sure I ever did.

"So what came first? The necklace or the tattoo?" I ask, pointing at his crucifix, and the tattoo of the same thing it covers.

"I got the tattoo first," he says. "Then had this thing made to match it."

"Well, I hope God listens to you more than he does to me," I say not even sure why I'm still continuing this conversation. I almost feel like I could just tell him everything, and he'd understand. But that's insane.

"Yeah, I don't know about that. I don't even remember exactly why I got the tattoo, or when. It must've been in my darker, teenage years." He looks like he's my age, so that can't have been very long ago. "In fact, I don't remember getting at least half of these tats," he goes on, looking over his ink covered skin. "But even wasted as I was back then, I made some pretty good choices, don't you think?"

I'm actually afraid to look too closely, because I'll just end up tracing the outlines of the dark ink drawings on his body again.

"Yeah, they're all nice." What a great thing to say, Tara. No wonder he's laughing at you.

"Alright, so I told you all sorts of things about myself, for some reason. Now it's your turn."

He didn't actually ask me, just suggested I do it. But I don't think there's anything about myself I can actually tell him. I'm the daughter of one of the most famous movie producers in Hollywood, I work as a counselor at a women's shelter, I think his MC abducted my sister, and is forcing her into prostitution, I can't get close to a man because I've been raped so many times, that most days I can't even think about sex without wanting to puke. And all that pisses me off, because I really want to keep talking to Tommy.

Lola and Ava are out of the water, but they're sitting right next to it, glancing back at us from time to time, but showing no signs of coming over.

Why do I even want to be friends with this guy? He's a criminal, has quite possibly benefited financially from trafficking my sister. He sleeps with underage girls for sport. We're not the same and we never will be.

"Lola's very young to work as a stripper," I say.

He's looking at the two of them too. "Crystal says she's eighteen, but I don't know either. Maybe sixteen or seventeen, what do you think?"

"Younger," I snap. "And you sleep with her anyway?"

The anger coursing through me right now is making me nauseous. And I know it's a reaction to other things, things done to me when I was her age and younger. Because Lola looks very happy. She even laughs like a teenager still. But she is just a girl.

Tommy is looking at me now, but I refuse to meet his eyes. This is all so messed up. I'm leaving tonight.

"I haven't actually fucked her, just gotten some blowjobs from her, but I won't do that anymore either." He sounds very sincere and apologetic. I hear no fakeness in it. "I haven't been myself lately. She's not even my type. But I can do better. Please don't be so mad at me right now."

He grins at me as he says it, and I know he's referring to the anger that must be flashing from my eyes. I know what it looks like, Samantha describes it as terrifying, calls me Tara the Mad Ice Queen. I'd like to tell him I think he's just full of shit. But I don't. He sounds so sincere. And I know what he's doing. He wants to change the tone of our conversation to something lighter, *fun* not heavy. And I want that too. I want him to tell me more secrets, show off his tattoos, I want the rush and the sparks I got from touching him. I don't want this anger.

But I'm afraid it's all I have left.

"Good intentions count," I mutter. And I do mean it. My whole career is built on good intentions. That's all we really have in the fight against the injustices of this world.

"Yeah? I heard the road to Hell is paved with those," he says, and fiddles with his cross again. "But I have this."

I look at him sharply, but he's smiling at me, looking straight into my eyes, intently like I'm the only thing worth looking at. "You're a very serious girl, aren't you?"

He means angry, but he's being tactful. And it's a rhetorical question, so I treat it as such. But it changes the energy between us, dulls the sharp edge of my anger because yeah, I am a serious girl and an angry one, and he seems to get that, it doesn't actually bother him.

"Everything's gonna work out, don't worry so much about it," he says, smiling at me.

"Yeah, how would you know?" I can't help but ask.

He shrugs. "That's just how it works."

I would love to have the ability to blow off the hard truths and just enjoy life. I crave it right now, and I don't know how I've lived this long without it. Sam found it. She could stop thinking and just be, just enjoy herself. Until she disappeared.

"Come on, let's go for a swim," he says and stands up. "You'll feel better afterwards."

A part of me knows he's right and wants to go. But I can't forget.

"You go, I'm fine," I mutter, even smile at him because I know he means well.

Then I watch him stride into the water, leap in and swim away. And I really want to be the carefree girl who wouldn't even think twice before going with him. But I'm not, and I never will be.

It's still light out when we return to the club, but the sun's already set. I watched it disappear behind the rolling hills as we drove back.

Lola and Ava rush towards the club, muttering something about wanting to take a shower first, giggling and glancing back at me as I wait by the truck to get the key back from Tommy.

"Excuse me," he says and reaches over me into the back of the truck for the blanket, making absolutely no attempt to avoid towering over me as he does it.

I gasp, paralyzed by my sudden inability to flee, by his smell all around me. His body's so close I can sense the strength of his muscles. He's head and shoulders taller than me, and much wider, but it's not actually flight I'm considering, not entirely.

"How about that drink now?" he asks and my head jerks up, my eyes fixing on his. The sudden jolt of butterflies his voice woke in my stomach is overwhelming. My whole body is tingling from the energy coiling between us.

He leans down for a kiss, his lips less than an inch from mine when I finally regain my senses. I put my hand up, move my head to the side.

"Can we just be friends?" I deliver the line I always use when dates get to this point. They all say sure, but none of them ever stick around.

"Sure," he says and backs away. A sensation like something ripping passes through me.

I don't even know what to think as I watch him walk away. Maybe I'm just phrasing it wrong. I meant, I'm not ready, I can't, but I want to try, slowly. But no one sticks around for any of that. Why would they? And Tommy is least likely to of all. He has his pick of other girls. I'm no use to him, if he has to wait around for sex with me.

And I can't even drive away, because he never returned my car key.

CHAPTER TEN

TOMMY

Friend-zoned? By the first girl I really want to fuck in years. It fucking figures. I have no sort of luck lately, and I just can't catch a break.

Ava and Lola are taking a shower together, and normally, that'd be enough to get me at least semi-hard, but tonight I just throw them out.

"Where's Tara?" Lola asks from the doorway, peering around the room like it's not obvious Tara isn't here, and she's just hiding behind the bed or something.

I almost slam the door in her face, because she looks so hopeful and excited about Tara being here. But I don't, because she looks so hopeful and excited.

"Never mind that, I have some work to do," I say

instead and close the door firmly. It's a total lie. I have absolutely nothing to do, and I'm not even remotely in the mood for sex with anyone other than Tara. Which is worrying, but I won't dwell on it now.

My friend Brett called while we were at the lake. I wasn't planning on calling him back, since it's probably over some MC business, and I'm sitting that shit out tonight, but I suddenly have nothing better to do.

"Hey, I'm at Sara's," he says when he picks up. "Wanna come down for a drink. She needs some more bodies in here."

"She needs to sell that place, is what she needs to do," I snap.

"You want me to relay that message?" Brett asks wryly.

"No way," I say. "I'll tell her myself when I get there."

Since why the fuck not? A cozy drink with my old friends might be alright for tonight. Pretty soon I'll never see either of them again.

Sara's new bar on the edge of town is more or less deserted. There's only her and Brett at the bar, and a group of teenagers drinking juice at one of the tables by the open windows. I tried to tell her this whole ocean-side resort look she's going for with the decor won't go over well in the hills, but after she spent all her inheritance on it after her mom died last year, I stopped pressing. And the place does have a kind of Caribbean vibe to it, with the dark wood tables and the large, open sitting area. The breeze coming through the open floor-to-ceiling windows, making the white linen curtains billow in and out, doesn't exactly smell like the ocean, but that's what your imagination is for.

Kind of like the way I imagined Tara wanted me to kiss her earlier. I was completely off on that one. *Friends? Jesus.* Why couldn't she just say, "Get lost"? That'd be easier to process.

"You don't look in the best of moods, Tommy," Sara says as I sit down next to Brett at the bar. "What will it be?"

It's too bad about having almost no customers, but at least she has the bartending gig down pat. Fake sympathy followed immediately by the offer of a drink. Though I've known her since kindergarten, so the sympathy's probably not fake in this case.

"I'll have a scotch, double. And a beer." And keep 'em coming. But I don't add that.

"That bad, huh?" Sara says wryly as she pours.

"I heard some rumors that Shade is..." Brett starts saying, but shuts up as I give him a sharp look, glancing at Sara's back and shaking my head.

Brett shouldn't even be hearing any rumors about the execs meeting a couple of days ago. But it figures he has. Shade admitted a lot of new guys to the MC, guys completely loyal to him, in the last couple of months. They're probably the source of those rumors. And Shade's behind them. Despite agreeing to put the matter up to a vote, he's already making sure everyone's informed about the shifts he's planning for the MC.

"Yeah, Brett, no discussing club business in front of the old ladies. Don't you know the rules?" Sara says, placing my drinks in front of me. "But I'm not that anymore. And I won't ever be again."

Ian, her long time boyfriend and my best friend went to jail in February and she broke up with him because of it. But they must have broken up and gotten back together a thousand times in the last ten years since they started dating.

"Ian'll be out by New Year's, he says," I inform her. *And then you'll just start again right where you left off.* I know that's what Ian wants, he keeps telling me when I visit him, and I also know Sara's not very good at saying no to him.

"That's great, but I'm through," she says. "For good this time."

"Yeah, if I had a dime..."

Sara fixes me with one of her piercing gazes that make her look cross-eyed. "What's with all this interest in my love life, Tommy? Are you having girl trouble and don't know how to ask for advice directly?"

Brett barks a laugh. "Yeah, that'll be the day. He never sticks around long enough to have a conversation after sex, let alone a troubled one."

He punches me in the arm like it's all a funny inside joke. I like Brett, he's been my friend for ages, but the way he looks up to me when it comes to women irks me.

"Maybe I am," I say and take a long swallow of my drink. Mostly to get from under Brett's shocked expression.

I can't believe I even said anything. The conversation can't go anywhere good from here.

"Did you get one of them pregnant?" Brett asks. Sara has a very strangled look on her face as she waits for my answer.

"No, it's not that."

"I can never figure out how you don't have a

whole kindergarten of kids running around by now," Brett muses.

I can't either; maybe I just can't have children. It'd be for the best, if it's true. "I'm careful that way."

"So what is it?" Sara asks. "Did you finally fall in love?"

She's says it like a sarcastic joke. She never made it much of a secret that my never ending series of one night stands and casual-sex-only policy offends her.

"She blew me off, said we should just be friends," I say. "I'm just not used to not getting laid when I want to."

I'm plenty used to it. In college, I had to work pretty hard with some of the girls. But it's fun riling Sara up. Her ears start twitching when she gets mad.

Love? Give me a break. I've only known Tara for a couple of days.

"So be her friend," Sara says. "What's so awful about that?"

"We can be friends after I fuck her," I say and earn an appreciative chuckle from Brett. Which offends me for some reason, though maybe what I said did that all on its own. Tara seems so troubled by something, so sad and lost and alone, and she deserves a friend if she asks for one. She certainly doesn't deserve me talking this kind of shit about her.

Sara's ears are twitching uncontrollably now. "I know you're just saying this to mess with me, Tommy. This girl touched you, else you wouldn't even bring it up. And it's high time one of them did. You can't just go through life without love. That's not how it works. And now excuse me, I have to go take care of my customers."

The teenagers want to pay, and she leaves to bring them the bill. I'm glad for it, because I really don't need her harsh assessments of my life choices on top of all the other shit that went wrong today. Brett seems to still be processing all that just transpired. A lot of people think Brett is dumb, but he's very smart, he's just not sharp. He needs time to figure things out before he speaks.

"I'm just afraid I don't have the time to be her friend," I admit once Sara returns.

"Are you going somewhere?" Brett asks pointedly. "Only you've been alluding to not having much time left a lot lately."

Have I? I really need to start watching what I say from now on, if Brett's picking up on my plans to leave.

"I think she might just be passing through," I say to avoid answering his question. It's the truth too.

"Things work out, if they're meant to," Sara says

reassuringly. I think she's sorry for speaking to me so harshly before. She knows *exactly* why I refuse to date. "I know what you can do. You can bring this girl to the concert on Wednesday night. I have Midnight Kiss booked."

"Who?" Brett and me say at the same time.

"You remember Marshall Jones from high school? It's his band. They're pretty famous these days, and I finally managed to convince them to come play here." Sara's positively beaming.

I remember Marshall only vaguely from school, but I do remember he had a band back then already. I also remember him and Sara had a thing once, while her and Ian were broken up. Ian got very violent about it, and I think I helped.

"It'll draw quite a crowd, I'm sure," Sara adds.

"Not on a Wednesday night, it won't," I say, not even sure why I'm trying to spoil her enthusiasm.

"Even on a Wednesday," she won't be deterred. "Like I said, they're quite famous now."

It's a good idea, I guess. Maybe after Tara's had a few drinks, she'll reconsider. Because those looks she's been giving me, those aren't, "Let's just be friends" looks.

CHAPTER ELEVEN

TARA

I felt a little better when I woke up this morning, and my run helped clear away the rest of the debris left by the excitement of yesterday. Running usually helps, but I also haven't seen Tommy all day, so that might be why I'm so calm.

Though I don't think so.

It was clear to me from the second I saw him that he will never be my friend. He wants sex. From me, from one of the others. I don't think it matters to him. Though I'm pretty sure he slept alone last night.

I watched him ride up at around two in the morning, heard him go into his apartment, which is right below my tiny room. For some reason it was easier to get to sleep after he got back. Though I was also dead tired, so that probably had more to do with it.

Today, Crystal asked me to help her clear out the garage attached to her home that's right behind the strip club. So that's what I've been doing since noon. It's almost opening time.

"I think this is some more of your stuff from the seventies," I say peering into a large cardboard box way in the corner, and spotting a pair of ancient looking bell bottoms.

"Is it?" she asks excitedly. "Let me take a look."

I hoist the box onto the worktable by the door so she can sift through it and decide what to keep. We've already filled at least twenty garbage bags with stuff she's throwing out.

A small cloud of black dust blows in my face as the box hits the tabletop, making me sneeze. I'm sure she hasn't cleared up this place in ages, and my fingernails and hands are so grimy it'll take ages to clean it all off. I'm also afraid some big spider will crawl out of one of the boxes I'm shifting. But whatever, at least the work keeps my mind off Tommy.

"Wow," she says in a broken sort of voice. When I look at her she's holding up the jeans, her good eye a little misty. "I remember when I could still fit into these. I was hot in the seventies."

It sounds so whimsical the way she says it that I get a little homesick. Or Sam-sick, because I never really missed my home.

She folds the jeans up neatly, then pulls out a framed photo from the side of the box. She goes completely quiet as she stares at it. I can't even hear her breathing. "And here's a photo of me when I still had both eyes."

She's trying to make light of it, but her breath hitches as she shows it to me. The photo's of her and a biker, who I don't think is her husband Bear, because he looks about her age, and Bear is much older. I was right about her. She was a stunning beauty when she was younger.

"You're still gorgeous," I say, meaning it completely. "Beauty comes from the inside, it's not just skin deep."

I'm fully aware those are just clichés, but they convey what I want to say perfectly. I hardly even notice her scars anymore. And what Crystal is doing for the girls here makes her so beautiful that no scar and no amount of years will ever mar it.

"You're a very beautiful girl too, Tara," she says, sliding a lock of my hair that's come loose back behind my ear. "You should embrace it now, while it lasts. One day you'll miss it."

She's wrong. I'll never miss it. I can't wait to get so old and wrinkled that no man will ever look at me twice. I just shrug and nod, hand her back the photo.

This is another great opening for me to tell her why I'm really here, show her the photos of Samantha, ask if she passed through here. I've had many such openings with Crystal today, but I lost my nerve each time, because then I'd also have to tell her I'm a liar and I don't want this kind woman to think ill of me. But she'd know, perhaps she even knows more than Tommy does.

I reach into my pocket to pull out a photo, but change my mind again. The other reason why I haven't asked Crystal is because I want to stay, spend more time with Tommy. And as much as I try to ignore that knowledge, I can't deny it. If I tell Crystal the truth, I'll have to leave. And maybe I should. He'll never just be my friend anyway. He made that pretty clear last night. But the thing is, maybe I don't want to be just friends with him either. I never really felt this way about a guy before, so I'd like to try and explore it.

"Look at the time," Crystal exclaims, checking her watch. She removes the bandanna holding her long grey hair out of her face. "We should get to the club."

I let go of the photo of Sam in my pocket, and follow Crystal into the club. And I'm not disappointed at all that I missed another chance to ask about Sam. Though I probably should be.

TOMMY

Shade woke me early, had me meet him at the Nest for an urgent meeting then just left me sitting there for two hours, waiting for him. When he finally showed, he dragged me along to another whore shopping trip, and now this. Whatever *this* is.

For hours now, we've been laying in the dirt on a hill overlooking a decrepit warehouse in the middle of nowhere. Apart from Billy, who's been an MC member since before I was born, Shade only brought his new recruits to this stakeout, the ones he brought in and who are completely loyal to him. So I don't even have anyone to talk to.

"I'm telling you," Shade whispers in my ear. "The Vagos are moving those guns from here tonight."

We've been here since sunset, and it's almost one AM now. No one's coming here, not now, not for the next hundred years. In fact, I'm pretty sure that's how long it's been since the last time anyone was here.

"Let's just go down there and steal their stash while we wait for them to show," I suggest. "We'll see them coming a mile away."

I actually get a few grumbled agreements from the others. Another flash of lightning illuminates the horizon, and this time I actually hear the thunder follow it. The storm that's been threatening to come down all afternoon is almost here.

"We're waiting for them," Shade hisses. "I want them to know it was us."

"No one's fucking coming, Shade." The rocks are digging into my stomach and my whole body is stiff from the hours we spent lying here. Shade's little excursion has also put a dent in my plan to return Tara's keys to her in a friendly way sometime today. At this rate she'll be asleep by the time I get back.

He turns to me sharply. "You anxious to get back to your whores?"

He said it loudly, so a couple of the guys laugh.

"They're strippers, not whores."

"Same difference," Shade says. "Kinda like your mother."

Every time someone brings up my mom it feels like a heavy wall shifts in my mind, and I'm always afraid I won't be able to stop myself from unleashing all the rage I keep behind it. It's worst when Shade does it.

"You know, back when Blade was in charge, we never went on pointless runs." I can only see the faint outline of Shade's face, but I know he's pissed now. The tension between us just quadrupled, if nothing else. He hates it when I compare him to our late brother.

"Blade hardly ever organized any runs. He was always a very slow mover."

"Maybe, but he got shit done." Blade was more of a thinker, I can't deny that. But he was moving in the right direction, even if not very fast. Not fast enough, anyway. Because Shade will have no trouble setting the MC back down the shady path now that Blade's dead. Shade and his shady path. It'd be funny if it wasn't so fucking sad.

"But very slowly, like when it came to your mom for example."

He's trying to rile me up, wants me to make a mistake, go for him, and one of his guys is probably ready to stick a knife in my back the moment I do. It makes sense that Billy is here. Shade brought him so the other MC members, the original ones, will hear from him how I was out of line, how I provoked

Shade, how he had no choice but to put me in my place and things got out of hand. And I'll be dead. Just like Blade. And there'll be nothing blocking the Shady Path any longer. I see this version of events unfolding like he just told me his plan. But I don't even know what he meant by this last jibe.

Blade would never murder our father just to take over the club. He was all about brotherhood and loyalty. None more so, and nothing would prevent him from honoring that. He's not resting easy in his grave, if he knows I'm planning to leave. I know that, so I try not to think about it.

A couple of thick rain drops land on the top of my head, slide down my forehead and cheeks as I glare at Shade. I'm struggling to stay calm, not say or do anything stupid. Then the rain just comes down in a freezing deluge. And it helps a lot.

"Let's get the fuck outta here," I say.

But Shade has us wait in the pouring rain for almost another hour, because he's certain it'll stop just as fast as it started.

It's still raining when I pull into the parking lot behind Crystal's.

Three of Shade's guys followed me here, and I'm not looking forward to the conversation we're about to have. It's almost three AM, but the music is still playing inside. Tara might even still be up. My clothes are soaked through, and all I want is to give her the car key, try and be her friend for a bit and then go to sleep.

Slim, or whatever his name is, gets off his bike first, gazing at the club. "Looks like the Lounge is still open. I wouldn't mind a little party before bed."

The other two laugh at that, as they climb off their bikes too.

"No, Slim," I tell him. "There are no parties at Crystal's, you know that."

The others heard me say it too, are drawing closer. I get the feeling this meeting was staged. Technically I can't stop them from going inside without starting shit. Maybe Shade sent them here after me knowing I'd try. Three against one are no kind of odds. At eighteen, I'd probably try to take them anyway. Hell, I might even have walked away from such a fight back then. But that won't be happening now. These days, I can't even call up a shadow of the vicious rage I once felt all the time, and which helped me win every fight.

If they kill me out here in the rain tonight, it could easily be explained as a needless brawl that got out of hand. Shade was never very imaginative. That's exactly how he's trying to explain away

Blade's death. What worries me is that most of the guys are starting to buy it.

The other members would never dare press like this to get access to the club while Blade was still alive, but now I'm the only one standing between them and Crystal's girls.

"Come on, Tommy. It's not fair you get all the pussy you want over here. How 'bout you start sharing?" Slim snarls at me, his tone mocking and cocky, since he has the advantage of numbers. He's talking to me like we know each other, like we're equals. I'm in no mood for this bullshit.

"You just let me worry about what's fair. The club's closing soon, go find somewhere else to get laid."

I turn my back on them and walk away. It's a move that could go either way, and I'm fully prepared to feel a knife in my back at any second. I can only hope they're not the kind of cowards to stab me in the back.

Nothing happens, and I hear them rev up their bikes and drive off just as I reach the door. One night they'll just come, demand what they want. But at least it won't be tonight.

Crystal, not Tara, is behind the bar. I'm so disappointed it stings, but it's fitting too, the perfect end to this shitty day.

Only the old man who has a crush on Simone is still in here. He's watching her dance like she's a mermaid and he a lost lonely sailor. But she's only got eyes for me as I approach the bar. Simone's looking at me like she wants something, but she won't be sharing my bed tonight. Maybe never again.

"Do you want me to kick him out so you can close?" I ask Crystal pointing at the man mesmerized by Simone.

She stifles a yawn with the back of her hand and shakes her head. "No, leave him be. It's sweet how in love with her he is. He's here every night, and I don't think he even wants her in a sexual way."

He's a man and he's old. Of course he wants Simone in a sexual way. He just knows he'll never have her. Women. I'll never understand how their minds work.

CHAPTER TWELVE

TARA

"Good morning, Tara." Tommy's voice startles me, almost makes me drop the coffee cup I'm holding. I've been trying to make myself a coffee on the fancy espresso machine for at least half an hour, but I can't get it to work right.

"Umm, morning," I mutter, trying to hide my shock with a smile. Which I'm not even sure he deserves with the way he just walked away from me the other night.

"Make me a cup while you're at it?" he says, sitting down on one of the stools and folding his huge, perfect arms one on top of the other on the bar.

"Actually," I say, dangling the cup at him from my finger. "Can you show me how?"

"Oh, sure," he says, getting off the stool and coming around the bar. He spoke like it's the most natural thing, and he just wants to be helpful, but there's a slight grin on his lips. And that's the only thing that betrays he even remembers me rejecting his advances two nights ago.

He stands very close to me as he starts making the coffee, explaining what he's doing. He's not towering over me like he did in the parking lot, and there's nothing overtly sexual in his stance, but I still can't concentrate on what he's saying. Because covertly, there's just something about him that calls to me, makes me wish he'd stand closer. And we're already so close we're almost touching.

By the time the coffees are ready, I still have no idea how to make one myself. Now we're just standing next to the machine, side by side, each holding a cup of steaming coffee, and not looking at each other, but not moving apart either. It might have been awkward, if it didn't feel so pleasant. He glances at the back door I left open to air the place out.

"Looks like the rain stopped," he says. "Good."

"Did it rain last night?" I ask. "It didn't when I went to bed, and I just got up." He's listening to me like I'm telling the most interesting story, and we're not just having a stupid conversation about the weather. "And it's sunny now," I conclude, finishing my monologue in the dumbest way possible.

"Yeah, it is." There's no trace of mocking in his tone. I'm so glad for that.

"Here," he says, digging in his pocket and producing my car key. "I meant to give you this yesterday, but things came up, and you were already in bed when I came back."

"Thanks," I say, pocketing the key.

"Wanna take me to breakfast?" he asks, smiling at me. "As friends, I mean."

The stone that's been resting in my chest since he walked away from me in the parking lot drops into the pit of my stomach. But he's not joking, and I don't think he's just teasing me. I think he's being serious. I want to believe he's serious. That he really wants to be my friend. That he's OK with it.

"Sure," I mutter. "But Crystal—"

"We can agree that Crystal's cooking leaves a lot to be desired. No need to pretend otherwise, she's not here."

I chuckle at that. It's true what he said about her cooking, I've never tasted more tasteless scrambled eggs in my life.

"I meant she might want me to help her finish clearing out the garage," I say.

Tommy smiles. "She has you clearing out her garage? Good."

"Why?" I ask wryly. "Did she ask you to do it a bunch of times, but got tired of waiting?"

His eyes finally fix all the way on mine for the first time this morning. They're clear like a moonlit night sky after a hard rain, and I'm suddenly very aware of just how close we're still standing.

He looks away first, shifts, drinks his espresso in one long gulp.

"Something like that. I even suggested she just burn it all, since it's all ancient history anyway." He places his cup on the counter and turns to me. "Although there might still be some of my old stuff in there. Did you find any of that?"

I try to think, but I didn't really get a good look at the stuff Crystal was sifting through. I mainly just helped her get it off the shelves, and out of the corners.

"You should ask her," I offer.

He shakes his head. "No point. It's all really old stuff, from back when I lived with her and Bear for awhile. How about that breakfast? I'm in the mood for pancakes."

"OK, sure, let's go," I say, placing my untouched cup of coffee on the counter and reaching into my pocket for the car key. "You can drive, if you want. And you'll have to pick a place too, I don't know anything around here."

He glances at the key then grins at me. "I thought we could take my bike."

I literally feel my eyes bulge. And I can't deny a part of me wants to get on the back of his bike with him, wrap my arms around his waist to hang on, but...

He takes the key from my hand, his fingers brushing my palm, but in a friendly, off-hand way like it was just by accident. "Another time then."

And I almost say thank you, that's how messed up my mind is right now.

He makes no more allusions that he wants to be more than friends all through breakfast. Our conversation's just easy, light, right in all the ways my conversations never are.

We don't even talk about anything serious, just random stuff like music, movies and the weather, even books. After we finish the pancakes, we get some more coffee, and then some ice cream on top of that, since I didn't get any with my pancakes, but then spent the whole time I was eating them wishing I had, until he finally convinced me to just order it. We've been here for almost three hours, all the other tables in the place have changed customers at least twice in that time, but I don't think he wants to leave any more than I do.

For the first time in a long time, I'm sitting in a restaurant with a guy and thinking of nothing but the conversation we're having. Not dreading the end of the date, just enjoying time with a friend who knows nothing about my past, and doesn't need to.

His phone's rang a few times already, but he didn't answer it. It's vibrating again now.

"Maybe you should just get that," I say, smiling at him.

"Yeah, I will," he says, and his tone suggests he'd rather do just about anything else. "Speaking of music, do you know the Midnight Kiss?"

"Do I? Of course. I love them," I exclaim. "Their lyrics are so deep and multilayered."

This serene half-smile if playing on his lips as he listens to my excited chatter. It makes me blush, I'm sure of it, because my cheeks are suddenly very hot.

"Well, they're playing at my friend's bar tomorrow night," he says. "Wanna go?"

My mind's exploding with all the ways I could say no, get out of this, all the reasons I should say no, but that's not the Tara I am with Tommy. I don't want to say no.

"Yes, that'd be great. I haven't been to a concert in ages." This will actually only be the third concert I've ever been too, but he doesn't need to know that. And I've wanted to see Midnight Kiss play live for ages.

He smiles and his whole face brightens up. "Great, it starts at ten, I think. I'll let you know."

We stay for another half an hour or so, before he says he should go. And there's nothing awkward in our parting, nothing to make me wish I hadn't said yes to the concert. So I can just look forward to tomorrow night without worrying about anything else.

CHAPTER THIRTEEN

TARA

I was hoping to find Tommy by the bar when I came down on Wednesday morning and invite him to breakfast again, but there's only Simone and Crystal there.

"Tommy said you should be ready at eight," Crystal says, only briefly glancing at me before resuming the task of emptying the dishwasher. "He also said to tell you he'd be busy all day."

"OK," I say. She's making quite a point of relating all this. I wonder if Tommy actually told her to say all that. It feels nice thinking he was so thoughtful. "I can finish doing that, if you want."

"I'm nearly done," Crystal says. "But I could use your help in the garage later."

I really want a cup of coffee, but I don't want to disturb Crystal, or dirty any of the dishes she's putting away. So I just stand there, shifting from one foot to the other, and looking through the back door. The sunshine outside is so bright it's white. I wish Tommy would walk in. I haven't seen him since he brought me back to the club yesterday.

"Alrighty, all done," Crystal says, wiping her hands on her denim shirt. "I'll be in the garage whenever you're ready."

She smiles at me, but it's a hurried thing and then she rushes out the back, the brightness swallowing her up. A black spot from staring out the door is obscuring my vision, as I fumble with the coffee machine.

"Maybe that's what I should have done," Simone says, tapping her foot against the wooden side of the counter. "Played more hard to get."

A few more hollow thuds follow her words. I'm not even entirely sure what she means, let alone how to reply, so I just shrug noncommittally and resume fiddling with the machine.

"With Tommy, I mean," she clarifies. "You seem to have the act down cold. Maybe I could learn something from you."

I finally manage to attach the little holder with

the ground coffee to the machine, but it makes a terrible noise when I turn it on. I hope I didn't break something.

"We're just friends," I mumble, not looking at her.

She barks a harsh laugh. "Sure you are. Just a word of friendly advice, don't get too attached, because you'll end up hurt."

There's nothing friendly in her tone though. I suppose that she got too attached, and he hurt her. But she has no right to speak this harshly to me. I'm posing no threat to her, anyway.

"Don't worry about me," I say, glaring at her over my shoulder. She's glaring right back, then her lips twist into a half smile suggesting she wasn't worried at all.

"Good to know." The stool rattles as she gets off it, her heels tapping against the hardwood floor as she leaves the room.

The whole exchange was rather tense and awkward. She sounded jealous, and it made me angry more than anything else. So maybe I'm the jealous one. But that's just stupid. Tommy and me are just friends. And I'm really looking forward to maybe finding some of his old stuff while I help Crystal clear the garage, so I can tell him about it later. Yesterday, he sounded like that would make him happy.

"Don't you want to start getting ready?" Crystal asks, glancing at her watch and then smiling at me.

It's only a quarter to six. I've been racking my brain as to what to wear tonight all day. The baggy jeans and flannel shirts I brought with me are not exactly going to a concert sort of attire. For awhile, I even considered going shopping, but then I realized the concert will be packed, and I certainly won't feel comfortable wearing anything too revealing. And I want to enjoy the concert. Though I also kinda want to look good for Tommy. In the end I just stopped thinking about it, since I was driving myself insane.

"Yeah, I think I better go now," I say, lifting up a couple of the garbage bags to carry them outside to the trashcans.

"You should ask Ava to do your makeup," Crystal suggests. "She's really good at it."

Makeup, clothes, hair. It all seems like such an overwhelming task all of a sudden. And that place *will* be packed. I'm sure of it. Maybe I should just say I have a headache. But even as I think it, I know I won't. Tommy will be with me. It'll be fine. And I really want to see Midnight Kiss live.

I go through my suitcase twice, before I concede that I packed absolutely nothing that could be even remotely considered going out attire. I didn't even pack a bra, though the bikini top Ava lent me to go swimming in would work. Maybe she has something else I could borrow, a pair of jeans maybe. Then I could wear that one shirt that's not flannel or five sizes too big like a tunic. It's not too flattering, but not hideous either. It would work.

I rush from my room and knock on Ava's door before I change my mind again.

"It's open," her voice floats to me, and I could still just leave, but I enter.

"I was wondering if you have a pair of jeans I could borrow," I mumble before I lose my nerve.

She's ready for her performance tonight, wearing a gold, frilly dress, and putting the finishing touches on her makeup. Her room smells of roses, and everything is so neat and proper I feel like I've just walked into a doll house. She even looks like a doll, if you ignore the overly sexy dress and crazy high platform shoes she's wearing.

"Sure," she says and smiles widely. "I heard

Tommy was taking you out tonight. I can do your hair and makeup if you want."

She puts the mascara down and walks to the small closet. I will never understand how she can walk so gracefully in those shoes, or dance for that matter.

"How about these?" she says, unfolding a pair of glittery blue jeans that look more like a pair of leggings.

"Umm, do you have something..."

"Less tight?" she asks, finishing the sentence for me and giggling. "I think I have just the thing."

She tosses the leggings on her bed and pulls out another pair of jeans. They're straight cut and don't look very stretchy at all. "And I have the perfect top to go with them."

She digs through her closet and pulls out a purple shirt with a low hanging cowl neck.

"I was just going to wear this," I say, and pull on the off white tunic I'm already wearing.

"Oh, OK," she sounds disappointed, but smiles right after. "I think it'll look great with these jeans. I can also lend you some shoes, if they'll fit." She digs in her closet some more, and just as I'm about to refuse, since she's bound to pull out a high-heeled pair of shoes, she turns, handing me a pair of ballet flats. "What do you think?"

"They're awesome," I say, taking them and checking the size. 7.5. They'll be perfect.

"Now for the makeup," she says, smiling at me. "And I could fix your hair too."

She sounds so excited about it that I don't have the heart to tell her I'd rather just do all that myself, or not at all. So I sit down on the edge of the bed like she directs me to. I can wash it all off before I go out, she'll never know.

"You have the nicest hair I've ever seen," she says as she brushes it out. "It's so thick, and the color... wow. It's like liquid gold."

"Thanks," I mutter. I don't like getting compliments. Not even from women.

"I know what I'll do with it," she says, standing in front of me know, so I can't see my reflection. "How about a nice low ponytail?"

"Sure, yeah, whatever you think is best." Honestly I don't even know what one of those looks like.

She laughs, a sweet sound that goes perfectly with her rose scented perfume. Then she gets to work, her hands so deft and skilled, I hardly feel her touching me.

"There," she says once she's done, stepping aside so I can see my reflection in the mirror over the vanity table. She parted my hair at the side, pulled it all back into a thick, pony tail at the nape of my neck. The undercut isn't visible at all.

I nod and smile at her. The hairstyle looks great, but I look too good this way.

"Now the make-up and you'll look just like a Hollywood movie star." Her words feel like someone grabbed my throat and squeezed. Of all the things she could compare me to, she had to go with the one that hits closest to home. But I won't think of any of that tonight. I just won't.

"Nothing too fancy," I manage to mutter.

She grins at me over her shoulder from where she's sorting through her make up. "Trust me, I know what I'm doing."

She busies herself applying powders and blushes, eyeshades and lipstick to my face. I try to catch glimpses of myself in the mirror as she works, but she keeps blocking it. And I'm sure there's no way I won't look like a stripper by the time she's done, but she seems so happy doing all this, that I won't do anything to spoil her fun.

"Voila...or whatever they say," she breathes, and finally steps aside.

"Wow, that's so nice," I say without having to fake it at all. Despite how long it took to apply, the makeup look completely natural. She just accentuated my best features, like my high cheekbones and plump lips, but she overdid none of it. I do look ready for a photo shoot. And I kind of like it.

"Did I tell you to trust me or what?" she says and giggles. "You know, I wanted to be a beautician growing up. Maybe have my own place in town, or something. I think I'd be really good at it."

"You would," I say, still looking at my reflection like it's the first time I'm seeing myself. Sam always tried to get me to wear more make up, but apart from some mascara and foundation, I never did. Then Ava's words finally register. "You can still be a beautician."

She smiles faintly, and shakes her head. "No, that was just a dream I had a long time ago. Before all this."

She doesn't sound chipper anymore, just tired. "I should go now. Just take anything from the closet you like."

As soon as she's gone, I grab the jeans and a gold belt that's hanging on the door and leave to get ready in my room. Ava's room looks so dreamy, but there are no dreams left there at all.

It's almost eight, and I still haven't gone down to the bar. I can hear the music playing, and even though I know there won't be a lot of guys down there this early to gawk at me, I still don't want to go sit at the bar. I also almost washed off my makeup and put my hair into a messy bun more than once. But Ava went to so much trouble.

A loud knock startles me.

"You about ready?" Tommy asks without opening the door.

"Sure, just a sec," I say, jumping out of the chair and grabbing my purse.

His eyes literally swallow me up as I fling the door open, and I know he likes what he sees, can feel it like a warm breeze all over my body. And it's jarring, but not in an unpleasant way.

"Wow," he whispers softly and I don't think I was meant to hear it. "You ready?" he adds quickly.

I nod and close the door behind me. He waits for me to precede him down the stairs, and even after my back is turned I still feel his eyes on me. Maybe Simone was right. Maybe he does still just want sex from me. But maybe that wouldn't be so bad.

"Here," he says, taking a helmet off the rickety table by the back door, and handing it to me.

"We can take my car," I say, not taking the helmet.

He grins and shakes his head, his eyes once again taking in all of me, though he's trying to hide it, I think. "Not tonight."

I'm sure I could argue some more, maybe even get my way, but I don't even want to try.

Yet my hands are shaking as I take the helmet and put it on, and I have some trouble getting on the bike behind him. The Tara that worked at the women's shelter and came home every night by eight can't believe I'm doing this at all. And she's a little scared right now.

"The concert's not 'til ten," he says. "I thought we could have some dinner first. What do you feel like?"

The fear is melting away with the sound of his voice, just falling away in chunks. Though I am very aware of our closeness, his smell, which reminds me of clear flowing waters like maybe a waterfall, for some reason.

"Tacos maybe?" I say, but he groans.

"Mexican's not my favorite food lately."

"Something else is fine, whatever you want," I add hastily.

He smiles at me over his shoulder. "No, let's get tacos. You just hang on."

He revs up the bike, cutting off my protest that I'm fine with whatever. He's not going very fast, and I don't need to actually hold onto him, but I put my hands on the sides of his waist anyway, just in case. There's still space between my wide open legs and his broad back, and I want to slide closer, but my reasons for doing that wouldn't be very friend-like at all. And I shouldn't lead him on, not even a little bit, because I mustn't start anything I can't finish.

***

The parking lot of the bar the concert's at is packed, people milling around everywhere. My fingers dig into Tommy's sides involuntarily as we drive across it, and I'm sure he feels it even through the thick leather of his jacket. I'm trying so hard to keep my anxiety at bay. I knew it would be like this. I expected this. It'll be fine.

"I didn't think there'd be this many people here tonight," he says, after he finally manages to park the bike at the side of the low wooden building and away from the main entrance.

I have trouble unclasping my helmet, because even my fingers are stiff from the fear.

"There's always a crowd for Midnight Kiss. They played near where I live a couple of months ago, and I couldn't get in," I say like I'm just gonna tell him all of that story. I shut up before that happens. The truth is I could've gone in, because I bought a ticket weeks in advance online, but I just couldn't handle the crowd. Tonight's quickly going down the same path as I eye the crowd in front of the door, cramps starting in my stomach and the world suddenly feeling very small and oxygen-less.

Tommy's looking at me, but his face is too blurry for me to read his expression. How can I tell him I want to leave without seeming like a crazy woman? But we could just go to a quiet bar somewhere, just the two of us, that would be great too.

I realize I'm still gripping the helmet as he yanks it from my hand, which I don't think he meant to do. "I'll get Sara to let us in through the back."

He has the phone pressed to his ear before I can say anything, and the next thing I know, I'm following him around the side of the building. A short, voluptuous blonde woman is holding the back door open for us.

"Come on, come on, it's chaos in there," she urges,

but the nervous excitement on her face fades as she gives me an appraising head-to-toe look. She grins at Tommy, then offers me her hand. "I'm Sara, welcome to the Breeze."

I mumble my name, which I'm not sure she heard, and then I'm following her inside, Tommy walking very close behind me. I wish he was even closer. I kinda wish I was holding his hand. Especially as we enter the main room through a door at the back of the bar, and it is indeed chaos. The room is just one giant sea of people, and the two waitresses serving the drinks have trouble wading through it.

"What can I get you?" Sara asks, fluffing up her bangs so they're no longer sticking to her forehead.

"Just a coke," I say, and almost add that I can get it myself. At least twenty people are waving money in her direction from across the bar trying to order a drink.

"Come on, have a beer at least," Tommy says, his breath tickling my ear because he's leaning so close. And the jolt of electricity that courses through me freezes the world around us for a second, making even my anxiety fade. It's lessened now that we're inside, and I have little choice but to stay. Maybe that *was* always the key to beating it. To simply accept it, not fight it or try to run from situations that cause it.

My therapist says so, but thus far I haven't been very good at testing it out.

"OK, sure," I say, turning my head slightly to look at him, my cheek almost brushing his.

Sara has a very bemused expression on her face as she hands us the beers, but it's meant more for him than me.

"Go listen to the concert now," she says, shooing us from behind the bar.

The band is already setting up on stage, and we find a spot by one of the windows. The cool glass feels good against my back, and even though it's closed, I still feel like I don't have far to go to escape the crowd. Tommy's side is pressed against mine, because there's not enough room for him to stand next to me otherwise, and it's nice, dulls the edge of my thoughts of escape, makes me kind of wish he'd put his arm around my shoulders, so I'd be even safer.

"This place is nice," I say, standing on my tiptoes and craning my neck up so he'll hear me.

He glances around the room, before his eyes fix on mine. "You think? I find it a little pretentious. Maybe it'd look better in LA."

Something in his voice makes it clear he's refer-ring to me telling him I lived in LA. I'm sorry now that I lied to him about that. Though it wasn't even a total lie. LA was my home for eighteen years, but I moved away as soon as I could.

The singer strums his guitar on stage and the whole room just erupts in applause, hoots, yells, and general cheering. I shake as the fear it causes passes through me, but it all fades to the background once the first song starts. Music was always my escape, could always transport me away from whatever was happening around me to calmer, happier places, even if they were just inside my mind. And this band has the perfect blend of deep lyrics and flowing melodies. I played it down when Tommy asked me to come, but I love them, I know all their songs by heart. They may not be up there with the greats yet, but I'm certain that one day they will be. And I'm so glad right now that I pushed through my fears and came here.

Tommy spends more time watching me than the band, but that's probably just because of the way we're standing. He has to look past me to see on stage. Besides it doesn't bother me at all. His close-ness, this music, it's all just perfect. Back when I bought that ticket to their concert, the one I never went to, I imagined it would be just like this. Well, minus having a guy with me, but this is even more perfect.

I'm actually sad when they announce the last song, and stop playing once it's finished. The crowd agrees with me, starts getting very boisterous, reigniting my anxiety. But it starts to thin out once it becomes clear there won't be an encore.

Sara is sitting on the edge of the raised area of the floor that served as the stage tonight, speaking to the lead singer. Her face is flushed, and she keeps smoothing her bangs off her sweaty forehead. She leans back on her hands, the flowing shirt she's wearing stretching taut across her protruding belly.

"Running this bar must be very tiring for Sara in her condition," I say to Tommy. "Though I suppose it's not this crowded every night."

Tommy looks at her sharply, then back at me. "What condition?"

"Well, she's pregnant," I say, taken aback by the twisted frown on his face. "I thought you knew."

He told me Sara was one of his oldest friends while we were having dinner. How could he not know? She's at least three or four months along.

"She just gained some weight lately," he says. "She can't be pregnant."

He sounds like he hopes she isn't, which is super weird. Unless...what if it's his? Of all things, the thought fills me with dread. As in, I don't like the fact that I'd have to share him with the mother of his child, if things ever go anywhere between us. Which they won't, but still.

Sara notices the way Tommy's glaring at her now, and frowns at him, mimics a "What?" with her eyes.

He shakes his head and looks at me, his face softening as he focuses his attention back to me from whatever that silent exchange between them meant.

"Want another drink?" he asks. "Or would you prefer to just get out of here?"

He sounds like he's more for the latter, but I don't want this night to end yet. The crowd's thinning and they've opened some of the windows. I can feel the cool evening breeze across my face again.

"I could have another beer," I say, and he smiles at me, takes the half empty beer bottle from my hand.

"You hardly touched this one," he observes. "But it's all warm anyway. Let's go get you another one."

His attention is completely focused on me again, and despite the crowd I feel as though we're alone. But that changes again, as Sara passes.

"When were you going to tell me?" he asks her, but she ignores him.

"Is it Ian's?" he says louder, and relief washes over me. The baby isn't his.

She turns sharply, and fixes him with a very angry look. But there's strain underneath it too. And sadness. "Yes, it's Ian's. But don't you dare tell him."

"Of course I'm gonna tell him. Why haven't you?"

She shakes her head and takes a step towards him, like she's about to slap him. They both sound so angry, but it's clear they care about each other too, that this is not good news. I should've just stayed quiet. Why did I have to say anything?

"No you won't, Tommy. And don't you think this baby is any responsibility of yours either," she hisses at him. "I'm raising this kid away from the MC and on my own terms, is that clear? You of all people should understand that."

She struts away and I'm sure Tommy will follow at any second, leaving me here alone, but he doesn't.

"Let's just get out of here," he says. "We can get a drink somewhere else."

He's trying to sound casual, but I can literally feel the effort it's costing him to stay calm. I gladly follow him out of the bar, because the place has grown oppressive yet again.

The parking lot is still pretty full of people, but

it's not as bad as when we arrived. We're halfway to his bike when he suddenly stops and turns.

"I have to go tell Sara something else," he says. "Come with me."

"That's OK, I'll just wait here," I mutter.

I'm not thrilled about being out here alone, but I caused this argument between him and Sara and the least I can do is let them talk in private. A group of bikers standing at the edge of the parking lot have already noticed me, and I feel their looks like so many grubby fingers, but Tommy'll be right back. I'll be fine.

"Hurry back," I can't stop myself from adding though, and he tells me he will.

The wind turns very cold once I'm alone, feels almost wintery. And I know that's just my imagination, but it still licks my skin like I'm not wearing a shirt at all. I left a few of the top buttons of my tunic undone, but I close them now, the collar choking me uncomfortably.

It seems to grow even colder as I spot one of the bikers break away from his group and start walking in my direction. I turn away, hoping he won't stop to talk to me.

"I'd never leave a pretty girl like you on her own,"

his gruff voice reaches me, and I glance after Tommy, but he's nowhere.

I'm frozen. What I should be doing is walking away, or telling him to get lost, but I don't even know how my voice works anymore. And what's worse, I can't even peel my eyes from his face, even though the leer he's giving me feels like a knife ripping through my skin.

"Come, this party is over, but I'll take you to a better one."

All the fear I have of men, every last iota of it, is exploding inside me right now, paralyzing me. My hand goes to my pony tail, and I hate to ruin my hairstyle, but I have to do something, I have to make myself less attractive. Then he'll go away and leave me alone.

"What's going on here, Slim?" Tommy asks, the anger in his voice so raw it frightens me a little.

The guy shrugs, his eyes still fixed on me. Or my breasts, more precisely. "You left, so I thought she was up for grabs."

"She's with me," Tommy says, and his words finally break the paralyzing spell I was under. I manage to take a step back, then another one, until I'm pressed against the wall of the bar. The three other bikers are watching the exchange very closely, bristling, ready to come over. The aggression in the air is palpable.

"She doesn't seem to like that idea," the biker says, still leering at me. "I think she'd rather come with me. Besides, you should learn how to share, Tommy."

He reaches out as though he's about to grab my arm and pull me along. Tommy punches him in the face, which makes his eyes roll into the back of his head. The man's too dazed to put up a fight, but Tommy doesn't stop hitting him until he's on the ground, moaning something incoherently. Tommy kicks him in the stomach for good measure.

It was such a primal, animal act of aggression, but instead of horrified I feel elated, protected, cared for, safe. I wanted that guy gone, and Tommy chased him away from me. He saved me. So many times I wished someone would do that for me, but it never happened. Never ever. Not until tonight.

"What? You gonna start something too?" Tommy yells at the other bikers who are still watching his every move. But they just put their hands up, shake their heads.

"You alright?" Tommy asks, peering into my face. He seems so calm, despite having just beat a man to the ground.

I smile at him, nod for awhile, wanting him to know how grateful I am because I can't actually speak right now.

"We should go," he says and takes my hand. It's such a gentle gesture, so at odds with the aggression he showed mere moments ago. But it's perfect, exactly how I always pictured it would be.

I'm shaking by the time we reach his bike, shock finally catching up to me. But it just melts away as I lean against Tommy's back, wrapping my arms all the way around his waist. I don't even think about it, I just do it. Because it feels right, the way it always should've been. The way it always should be from now on.

***

He takes the long way there, but it's in the parking lot behind Crystal's that he stops. All that's left of this evening's excitement, fear, and shock is this warm mellow feeling filling my entire body. I don't want this night to end.

He offers me his hand and helps me off the bike. I take it gladly, because I don't think I'd be able to get off it without his help. My legs are all mushy, and the whole world is soft like we're in a dream.

"I'm sorry you had to see that," he says, not letting go of my hand.

I'm not. He's the first person who ever stood up for me, who ever chased my nightmares away. And tonight wasn't even the first time. That first night he stopped kissing and touching me when I asked, he stayed my friend when I refused to kiss him after our trip to the lake, and now he saved me from that frightening man. I don't know how to put just how much I appreciate all that into words. But I do know something else. Even if it's completely alien to me, I know it.

I stand on my toes, crane my neck back, and pull him closer by his hand. A jolt of pure raging fire suffuses me as our lips meet. He's not even a little surprised, kisses me back like we've done it a million times before. The fire inside me burns brighter, hotter, uncontrollable. It should be bright enough to cut through the darkness, chase it away forever. It should be enough!

But it isn't.

The familiar dark shapes of my nightmares take over, quench it all. They're here to stay. They're the ones that will be with me forever. Them and the darkness.

I try to pull away from the kiss, but he doesn't let

me go so easily this time. I have to yank my hand from his grasp, yell, "I can't!" before he releases me. But he does, and I run to the back door, fling it open so hard it crashes into the wall. Tears I wish I could shed are burning my throat and my eyes. But I won't get any relief because I can't cry, and I'll never escape the darkness.

CHAPTER FOURTEEN

TOMMY

It took an unnatural amount of effort to let her run away. It's still taking it now as I pace my apartment, trying not to go up to her room and...and what...rape her? I've done a lot of bad things in my life, but I've never raped a woman. And I never will. She's driving me insane.

I risked my life beating up Slim today. Him coming on to her had nothing to do with Tara, and everything to do with Shade's sick plan to get rid of me the same way he got rid of Blade. And Sara had no business bringing my mom into whatever twisted game she's playing with Ian by keeping her pregnancy a secret from him.

But all those are just empty rationalizations.

OUTLAW'S HOPE (A VIPER'S BITE MC NOVEL BOO...   155

I'd have hit Slim for bothering Tara a thousand times over. I'd have killed him if he had put up a fight. Just seeing how scared of him she was woke this fierce protectiveness in me that nothing but blood could resolve. I never felt that for any woman. It wasn't even so much about possessing her. I just needed to protect her. I'd have died for her tonight. Or any night.

Her rejection now, after all that, hurts so deep, and on such a different level, I might never get over it. Hell, I might never sleep again unless she takes it back, recants, lets me kiss her, fuck her, show her just how much I'll never, ever let anyone harm her. Because she's mine.

There's a soft knock on the door and then she's standing in front of me. But she shouldn't be. I haven't felt this out of control in years, not since high school when I started fights like the one tonight daily, just for the hell of it. I can't be trusted right now. Not if she won't give me what I want freely.

TARA

This conversation would go OK, I told myself before I came down here. It wouldn't be easy, but it would be OK. He deserves to know why I can't be more than friends. He told me one of his secrets, and mine's bigger, but still.

Only now he's just standing there, holding the door open and glaring at me, and I no longer think I made the right choice coming down here. His eyes are so angry, but so sad too and it's a dizzying combination, one I can't look away from. Just like I can never look away from my own pain.

"What is it, Tara?" he asks. "Come to mess with my head some more?"

He means it. It's not just a throwaway line meant to mock me.

"I came to explain," I say in a barely audible voice. "And then I'll go."

"Alright, let's hear it," he says and finally lets go of the door handle.

I close the door behind me, turn to find him sitting on the sofa. In the dead center of the sofa, so there's no room for me. Which is fine. I'll just say this and go. I practiced some of it in my head already, but didn't get very far. It just needs a few sentences. No more. Just the basics, so he'll understand. Years of therapy have prepared me for this moment. I can talk about it. I just can't crawl from underneath it.

"I'm waiting," he says, but not as harshly as before. His eyes aren't so angry anymore either.

I walk over to the bed, sit on the edge of it and face him. I'd meant to stand for this, but my legs are suddenly very weak and might not support my weight for much longer.

"I'm sorry," I say, because that's the most important thing I want to convey in this conversation. "I like you a lot." On second thought, that might actually be the most important thing. "But I was sexually abused by my father and his friends for years, and now even the idea of intimacy with a man makes me physically sick, makes me feel like I'm dying, and I know it's just in my mind, but I can't escape it. And I have tried. With you, I thought I could get past it, and that's why I kissed you before. The way you make me feel, made me think I could finally go past it, but I can't because that part of me is broken and nothing can fix it. I'm sorry I led you on."

Some other Tara delivered that speech, the strong one, the one that can take any blow. But she's not here anymore now that there's only silence. I don't know if he's even looking at me, because I'm afraid to look. Afraid to see the disgust in his eyes. That's what most people feel when I tell them. Disgust. Because I am broken. I'm not normal. I'm someone that shouldn't be. What happened to me was unnatural. It's not my fault, I know that, but I am what I am regardless.

I get up, not sure if my legs will even take my weight, but they do. I'm still afraid to look at him. Though his absolute silence really says it all. I don't want to hear that either.

"Where are you going?" he asks hoarsely.

I'm halfway to the door, where does he think I'm going? Of all the dumb responses to all I just told him, he found the winner. It's not fair of me to be this harsh. What did I expect anyway? But it is what it is.

Yet my anger vanishes as I turn to look at him, so I can deliver my answer, and sadness is all that's left.

"I'm going now," I say and my voice actually cracks like I'm about to start crying.

"Why?"

He's gonna make me say it? Again?

"Because you're not saying anything." *Because you're not asking me to stay.*

He comes up to me, but doesn't touch me, though I can sense he wants to. Or maybe I just want him to touch me.

"What I want to say is that I'll make you feel so good you'll forget all those horrible things other men did to you, if you'll give me a chance," he says, his words firm, certain, not a trace of doubt in his tone. "But I don't think you'll believe me."

He sounds so sure of himself. Like what he's saying is possible. His eyes are swallowing me up, all of me, not a trace of disgust anywhere in them. In this moment, there's just us in the whole wide world. Only us. And he's here to protect me. I know he is. He's the one I prayed for. It makes no sense to think that, it sounds insane even in my brain. But I know.

"I *would* believe you if you said that."

He takes my hand, a caring gesture that makes me feel lighter than air. So I just float after him to the sofa. We're sitting very close, facing each other, almost touching.

He runs his hand down my cheek and I lean into his hand.

"Tell me to stop and I will," he says, then leans down to kiss me.

The darkness at the edges of my mind flutters to life, begins seething, as I kiss him back and feelings of warmth, of desire, of pleasure course through me. But I ignore it, just let it rage and roil on the edges. Because he promised he can make it better, and I want to believe him. I should take this leap past my fears.

But the dark fears consume my whole mind without warning, as his kiss gets fiercer, more demanding, hungrier. He leans against me, his weight pressing me into the soft cushions.

I don't push him away, or ask him to stop. Because there's peace in the kiss too, a serenity, a rightness I've never felt before. It's just a flicker amid all the darkness, yet it keeps it at bay, keeps it from swallowing up my mind. He leans back, releasing me, pulls me down on top of him like he heard my silent cry to be unrestrained, like he understands me without speaking. The elation that realization brings turns the flicker into a flame that can cut through the darkness, can make it recede. Slowly, inch by labored inch, but it's working.

He stops kissing me, looks deep into my eyes, so deep I know he sees all. His eyes are the color of a moonlit ocean, promising peace, safe passage to worlds I've only dreamt of until now, worlds where everything is as it should be, no one forces me to do what I don't want to do, and no one hurts me. I stopped believing those worlds existed, but they're waiting for me just beyond the horizon, not far at all.

"We should stop before this gets out of hand," he says, grinning at me.

I know what he means, his desire for me passes like a spear through my pussy, the pain shooting up into my belly. But it's not all bad. It doesn't hurt like it used to, and it doesn't seem impossible anymore. All I've forgotten I wanted is possible again with him.

"OK," I say and he kisses me again, softer this time, with less urgency.

Then I follow him to bed. We're both still fully clothed, still have our shoes on, but he's not suggesting I undress, and he's not doing it either. And it's perfect, exactly how I need it. I think he knows that. He wraps his arm around me and I lay my head against his chest. I used to picture falling asleep with someone like this, long ago. So long ago the memory is faded and fuzzy like an old photograph, but it's growing clearer now even as I drift off to sleep.

CHAPTER FIFTEEN

TARA

The grey light of dawn, filtering in through the grimy window of Tommy's bedroom wakes me. We've moved apart during the night, and he's sleeping beside me now, laying on his back. I'm still wearing all my clothes, but my shoes came off while I slept. One of them is poking me in the thigh, the other is who knows where.

Tommy undressed at some point during the night, since he's lying next to me in just his boxers, the covers tangled up in his legs, his torso bare, the muscles all hard despite his relaxed position. His stomach is ripped, more of an eight pack really, rippling like calm ocean waves with his even breaths.

His chest is covered with tattoos, some of which I

can make out right away, but others would require a closer examination. There's the cross tattoo, hanging on a drawing of a silver chain. The real cross slid off his chest while he slept and is lying on the pillow by his neck. A pair of hands drawn together in prayer adorn his left side.

The sight of his naked body is making my stomach clench, but not in a bad way, not at all. A seething warmth resides in my belly, anticipation and desire prominent among the many different emotions and sensations coursing through me. I've never touched a man because I wanted to. But I want to touch Tommy. I want to touch his warm skin, feel his strength beneath my fingers.

I reach out and stroke his abs, my fingertips barely touching his skin, yet the jolt of electricity that courses through me is almost strong enough to make me yank my hand back. Almost. Because the initial burn subsides, turns into a pleasant warmth that slowly filters through my entire body. It makes me bolder, so I touch him again, caress his chest, his bulging arms, trace the outline of his snake tattoo. Snakes don't frighten me. In fact, I think they're beautiful.

A sprinkling of dark hair forms a line from his bellybutton down into his boxers. The happy trail, and it's the only soft part on his entire body. He's so strong. Nothing and no one could stand in his way. He sighs, shifts a little, and I jerk my hand back from touching his stomach.

"No, don't stop," he mutters, his voice muffled with sleep, his eyes barely open. But he's grinning at me, and my cheeks burn. Air is catching in my throat, and I suddenly don't know if I'm breathing right or I forgot how to. It's just a panic attack, I know them well, and I don't want it now. I want to keep touching him, feel this warmth spreading through my body, maybe even follow the happy trail down to where it ends. But the more I fight it, the harder my heart beats, the worse the whooshing in my ears becomes, and less and less air gets into my lungs.

He sits up and takes hold of my arms gently. I can see him looking at me, but his face is blurry like I'm looking at him through a rain soaked window. He kisses me, slowly, gently, and the desire to flee is suddenly the farthest thing from my thoughts. The darkness in my mind is receding, my heart no longer banging in my ears, my blood no longer whooshing like it wants to all flow out of me at once.

I open my lips a little more, so he can kiss me deeper. His hand is caressing my side, the other still holding onto my arm. His lips leave mine, travel down my cheek, making me gasp, forget to breathe all over again as they find my neck, barely touching my skin there, yet igniting such sparks I'm sure I'll burst into flames. I don't feel used as he kisses me, don't want to run and hide, don't want to pretend it's happening to someone else. For the first time in my life, I want a man to keep kissing me.

His hand gets bolder, passes over my breasts, right before he begins undoing the buttons of my shirt. They cause him no problem, and before I realize it, cool air is hitting my naked chest. His hands move behind me, the clasp holding my bra popping open with a barely perceptible sound.

His lips trace a path down my neck until he's kissing the soft flesh of my breast as his fingers play with my nipple. Desire is warring with fear in my mind now, curdled memories rising to the surface, twisted like dry rosebush branches covered in thorns coiling around this sweet kernel of pleasure in its purest form, which is exactly what it always should've been all there was. But it wasn't. It never was. And the darkness is winning.

My fingers dig into his arms, my hands aching from the effort of squeezing so tight. I feel so naked, so afraid of the terror, of the darkness those memories are conjuring up.

He stops kissing me and looks at me, runs his hands up and down my arms. "Had enough?"

Everything in his face is telling me he wants more, that he's not ready to stop. His eyes are calm and inviting, assuring me no bad thing will happen here, not while I'm with him. But the memories are stronger, they're too dark.

I just shrug, my mouth refusing to form the word yes. Because I'd love more. My broken mind just can't handle it.

He lays back down and pulls me along. I squeeze into his side, lay my arm across his strong body, press as close to him as I can. Because that's the only thing that'll chase away those memories. I know it will. I just have to breathe and hold onto him, and it'll all be alright.

TOMMY

It's such a huge thing I promised her. It sounded like a naïve line in my head, but became such a serious thing, so possible when I spoke the words. And the way she latched onto it... She grabbed it about as hard as she's holding onto me now, her whole body pressed so close to me it's not just hot, it burns.

I'm sure at least half of the women I've slept with until now had abusive upbringings. Maybe even more than that. But I've never met anyone this messed up by it. The way she told me about it, her voice so cold and collected, like a stone statue speaking, like it's a done deal that she'll never be loved by anyone, like she's not the most beautiful woman I've ever seen and deserves love. It just tore right through me, left me speechless.

What I promised her wasn't just some line. All I want to do is erase those bad memories from her mind, give her so many good ones, she'll forget all of the old. It'd help if she didn't keep pushing me away. Maybe I should Google this stuff. But no, I've never needed a manual for how to be with a woman and I don't now. Not with her.

It seems like all my past experience with women has led me to this moment, prepared me for helping Tara. Because underneath her cold assessment of her problem, was this sad little cry for help. So, I'll just have to step up.

I have a shit load of things to do today, like going to see Jerry and making sure everything is up and running. Now that Shade is gunning for me, I need that insurance more than ever. Then I should go see Ian and tell him what I know. Sara will bitch and moan about it, probably won't speak to me for awhile, but I made promises to Ian, and I intend to keep them. Then I have to go see Shade and make sure the fight last night doesn't escalate any further. But I'll leave that for last.

That is, if I'll even get out of bed today. Because all I really want to do is lie here with Tara in my arms. All else will keep. This is my most important errand.

CHAPTER SIXTEEN

TARA

Tommy left just before noon, rather reluctantly, but he promised he'd be back by eight to take me to dinner. Crystal had me start doing inventory after lunch, so I've been cooped up in the room behind the bar, the one I slept in the first night I came here, for hours now, checking all the boxes and crates of liquor against Crystal's ledgers. Her handwriting is hard to read, and her inventory system is so complicated I'm still not sure I understand it fully.

It's nearly eight and there's still no sign of Tommy. The music's already playing, and I'm sure one of the girls is already dancing, but I don't know which one, since I can't see the stage from here.

But I can see the mean looking older biker who

came in about in hour ago very clearly. Ava and Lola avoided even looking at him, but Simone spoke to him for awhile, acting all coy and womanly, like she was trying too seduce him. He sent her away curtly. He's in his forties, his dark hair beginning to recede, and he keeps glancing at me like he wants to say something. I don't like him. He makes the whole room tense.

Crystal is behind the bar and she talks to him from time to time, but their exchanges are always brief, followed by long minutes of silence. I wish Tommy would come already. I want to get away from the club tonight, kiss him some more, maybe let him undress me again. Sure I panicked before, but his lips on my skin, his hands caressing my breasts and my nipples is pretty much all I've been thinking about since this morning. The fear's still there, sure, but it's not all there is. Not by a long shot.

Tommy walks into the club just as I'm yet again revisiting all that happened this morning, and I very nearly drop the bottle of Jack I'm holding. The older biker gets off his stool and meets Tommy halfway. I hear none of what they're saying, but it doesn't look like a happy meeting. Tommy's face is a stone mask, only his eyes alive with anger akin to the one I saw there last night, right before he beat that other biker to the ground for me.

He says something and points to the room I'm in, and then they're both coming towards me. The strange man enters first and flashes me a mean look. "Get."

And I trip over my own feet as I scurry to obey.

"I'll be right out," Tommy assures me, calming me a little.

The door closes behind me, but I can still hear their raised voices through it, especially when there's a lull in the music. I shouldn't eavesdrop, but that man sounds so angry. I have to stay here and make sure Tommy's alright.

TOMMY

"What the fuck happened with Slim last night, Tommy?" Shade is practically yelling. "And why do I have to wait for you? That's not how it works. You come when I call."

I've avoided all his calls today, and there were plenty. In hindsight, that was probably a bad idea.

"I had shit to do."

"Over a fucking woman too," Shade says. "You'll answer for this."

"No, I won't," I snap. "He came after what's mine, didn't back off even after I told him to. It's not the first time he's done that. It's beginning to look like he's deliberately trying to start something with me."

My thinly veiled accusation hangs in the sudden silence. I think Shade knows what I mean. I think he knows that I know about his plan to get rid of me.

"I need you on my side, Tommy," he says, changing the subject completely. "What happened to you? You used to be the first to charge into any new endeavor. Especially one as lucrative as the one I'm planning. Sure, Blade had noble ideas about going legit and all that, but he'd never have pulled it off. I think he was even ready to abandon the idea before he died."

Blade was as serious about going legit on the day he died, as on the one when he first told me about his plans. I'd either be dead or in jail right now, if he hadn't pulled me aside and said he needed me to help him with it, needed me to get an education so I could. But Shade's more right than not. Before Blade made his plans, I was dead set on causing as much damage as I could, anywhere I could. I was angry and the whole world needed to pay. And I was charging down a very dark path, before Blade gave me the hope that being in the MC doesn't have to be all bloodshed, violence and crime. Shade is leading us all right back down that path now.

"I was always against running whores," I snap.

"Come on, it'll be fun." Shade play punches me in the arm like we're the best of friends. "Think of all the free pussy. We're brothers, remember? And Slim's as good as now. You wouldn't harm a brother over a piece of ass, would you? Though I admit she's a looker."

It sounds like a threat, the way he says it. How long has he been sitting at the bar checking Tara out? I'm suddenly almost as livid as I was last night when I beat up Slim. All Shade has to do now is mention my mother, and I'll kill him.

"Stay away from her," I say. "She's mine."

He takes a step back, holding his arms up in mock fright and surrender. "Easy there, little brother. You're scaring me a little. But then again, you always did."

Good. He should be scared. Though I know he's just talking shit. Shade's not scared of anyone or anything. Least of all me. He's exactly like my father that way. I didn't do myself any favors coming on this strong, but I really don't care. If he or someone acting on his orders goes after Tara again, he's dead. And I don't care what happens to me after that.

"I need you tonight, so go make yourself look pretty," he says and opens the door. "I'll be waiting at the bar."

There goes my quiet evening alone with Tara. But I'm not going anywhere before I show her just how much I missed her all day.

"Come in here, Tara!" I yell through the open door after Shade leaves the room, making her shake. Shit, that just came out too harsh.

She's not even looking at me as she enters and shuts the door behind her.

TARA

He knows why I'm really here, he knows about Sam. He knows I lied to him. Those things flashed through my mind when he called me, won't stop playing on a loop as I close the door behind me. I couldn't make out all they were saying, but I heard them speaking about whores. They meant Sam. That's why that guy was giving me such mean looks. Why didn't I just tell

Tommy everything last night? I should've told him everything.

But his grip on my arm as he pulls me closer is gentle, his eyes soft as I finally dare to look into them. The last few traces of anger in his features are fading fast, disappear as he rests his arms around my shoulders.

"Did I scare you?" he asks, smiling at me.

"Yes," I say in my best chiding voice.

He draws me closer and hugs me tighter, his hard body pressing against me, just like I've wished for all day. Flight's not my first reaction, it's a distant second, draws even further behind as his lips touch mine, erasing the last traces of my fright, causing cascading rivulets of warmth to gently pool in my stomach.

We kiss for a long time, his arms gripping me tight, mine resting on his waist. It's easier then before to just focus on the sweet warmth rising inside me, the slow building of desire, of fantasies coming true. Much easier than it was last night. The darkness is there too, but I see it clearer now, see what it's made of. Memories of things I went through, things I want to forget but can't. Events I ignore because they're too painful to face, yet I hold onto them anyway.

Why? I don't know. Maybe because of the injustice of it all.

I didn't deserve what happened to me. It's messed me up so bad, and no one paid for it, no one got punished for it. And that's not right. Sam just wanted to forget, told me I should too, but someone has to remember. Otherwise it's like it never happened, and it did. It happened to me. So the memories are always there, gnawing at me, demanding I remember.

But maybe I don't really have to.

Maybe all I have to do is surrender to this kiss, this gentle, soothing softness, that's so simple to enjoy, so right, so —

He starts to pull away, but I follow, kiss him harder, wrap my arms all the way around his waist so he can't escape. And he doesn't even try to anymore, kisses me deeper, his tongue searching for mine in my mouth. And my sudden desire to have him inside me isn't immediately followed by a painful jolt of imaginary, remembered pain. And even when it comes, it's not so strong, not so debilitating as it always used to be.

"I really should go now," he whispers after awhile, growing tense in my arms.

He releases me and reaches into his pocket, pulls

out a key. "I'll try to be back before you go to bed, but if I can't, just let yourself into my place."

I stare blankly at the key. It seems like such an important gesture. The girls said he never even let any of them sleep over.

"Or, I'll just see you tomorrow?" he asks, starting to put the key back into his pocket. I grab his hand with both of mine.

"No. I mean, yes, I'd love to," I say, prying the key from his fingers.

He chuckles at that, gives me a peck on my forehead, and leaves. Now all I really want to do is go curl up in his bed and wait for him to return.

CHAPTER SEVENTEEN

TARA

I was asleep when Tommy returned last night. But he did wake me up before he left this morning, with gentle kisses that went further than yesterday. But still not far enough. Though I wanted them too, I just couldn't.

He promised we'd have tonight all to ourselves. So I need to go shopping. I can't wear my old high school clothes anymore, and I can't keep borrowing stuff from Ava. I also need a real bra. Ava's bikini top works, but it just isn't enough, and I'm not wearing that elastic bandage ever again. My skin's still all chaffed from it from that trek down to the lake.

I knock on Ava's door, find her and Lola curled up on her bed, giggling over something.

"So," I say, smiling at them. "I was thinking I need to do some shopping. Want to join me?"

Lola jumps off the bed, clapping her hands. "Ooo, a shopping trip. I'm in."

Ava gets off the bed too. "We could go to the mall. Or maybe that fancy new Galleria." She draws out the word in a mocking way. "Though that place is super expensive, I hear."

"Let's go there," I say without thinking. I'm supposed to be a broke, down on her luck woman, not someone who goes shopping at the most expensive store in town. But I want some nice clothes. I want to look good for Tommy tonight.

Sam always made fun of me for hiding myself behind oversized clothes, saying what a waste it was. She'd be proud of me now. The second I think of her, all the elation I felt seconds ago just disappears, washed away by the river of icy water the thought brings. I came here looking for her, and I've done none of that. Instead I've just selfishly followed my desire to be with Tommy, forgot all about Sam.

"Are we going or what?" Lola asks.

No, I didn't forget about her. I'll tell him tonight. He'll help me find her, I'm sure. I try not to think about how he might be the one keeping her locked up as I follow the girls out to my car. He's not like that. I know he isn't.

By the time we're driving I almost manage to convince myself of it completely. But underneath all the soft kisses, the loving touches, he's still a criminal. Someone dangerous. Someone to fear.

We've been shopping for hours, but I still only have a few pairs of jeans and a couple of tees picked out. It's all exactly the same as the clothes I already have back home. Not too tight, not to revealing, just normal.

"How about this one?" Ava asks, holding up a lilac wraparound summer dress. "It would look amazing on you."

The fabric is too thin and way too stretchy. This dress would hide none of my curves. "I don't know."

"Come on, just try it on," she says, shoving it into my arms.

"And maybe these jeans too," she says, picking up a pair with large holes at the knees.

"OK, sure," I mutter.

Maybe this is exactly what I need. Someone else picking out clothes for me. Then maybe I wouldn't dress like a grandma all the time. Sam's words, not mine.

"Any other suggestions?" I hear myself say. If she's not here, I can at least honor her this way. By living, being carefree, like she tried to convince me to be for so long. I always avoided going shopping with her, because she'd always want me to get sexy things. And I'm so sorry about that now. So sorry I brushed her off, never listened to her suggestions, because I was always right and she was always wrong.

I leave the store with five large shopping bags full of clothes I'd never buy for myself. Clothes Sam would want me to buy. But all that euphoria is fading fast as we make our way to my car across the scorching parking lot. I should be looking for her, not doing things in her memory like she's already gone forever.

"That cost a fortune," Lola says as we get in the car. "I wish I had that much money to spend."

Lola says it with all the innocence of a teenager, but Ava's not that naïve, and she's looking at me from the corner of her eye, awaiting my explanation for it. I didn't think before I whipped out my gold card to pay for it all. Not having money was never a problem for me, there's millions in my trust fund. And that's on top of the more than generous allowance my dad wires me every month. I'd like to think of it as guilt money, but that man is incapable of feeling guilty. I've tried to get him to stop giving me money more than once, but that ten thousand is there in my account on the first of every month like clockwork.

"I sold everything I owned before coming here," I lie. "And the money just came through yesterday."

Ava glances at me like she doesn't believe a word I just said, but doesn't challenge me.

"But you're staying with us, right?" Lola asks, bouncing in the back seat. "For awhile longer, at least. I really like you. I don't want to lose another friend so soon."

I look back at her, almost swerve onto the sidewalk. "Who was your friend that left?"

Please let it be Samantha. Please.

"Tabitha. But she left after just a couple of weeks," Lola says looking up as though trying to remember. "And then there was Rhonda, and Gwen was nice too."

"Gwen was such a bitch," Ava snorts.

"She was alright, her and Simone were really close," Lola says. "But she did steal all that money. And then last year there were Betty and Melanie, I wonder what happened to them."

She keeps talking, but I'm no longer listening. I

already knew Sam was never at Crystal's, so why am I so sad right now, why do I feel so hopeless? That stripper might not have seen her at all. Maybe Sam really just met some guy and ran away with him, like the cops keep suggesting. I hope she did.

I changed five times before I finally decided to wear a flowery wraparound dress. Ava picked it out, but it's not as tight as the other ones I bought, or as revealing. And I paired it with a jean jacket, which hides what the dress doesn't, though I still wish I just wore jeans and a tee-shirt. Even despite the look I got from Tommy when he picked me up. It was all desire, no dirtiness, and exactly how I want to be looked at from now until eternity.

He took me to a quaint little rustic restaurant on a hilltop outside town. We finished dinner awhile ago and now we're just watching the sunset and finishing our drinks. The sky's lilac and white, the sun long gone behind another set of rolling hills in the distance. I can't stop thinking about Sam, haven't been able to since I left the mall. I'm so selfish for not telling Tommy right away. But I just don't want our closeness, this healing bond between us to ever end.

And end it will, as soon as I tell him. There can be no other way. He makes money off prostitutes. And Sam is probably just one in a long line of many.

"What's on your mind, Tara?" he asks.

He's been looking at me questioningly, wondering this same thing for awhile now. I saw it clearly, but I ignored it. It's time though.

He's fiddling with his napkin as he looks at me, waiting for an answer. I take his hand, going for one last touch, would prefer it to be a kiss, but I'll take what I can get. It's time.

"I didn't come to Crystal's because I needed a job," I say, watch his eyes narrow. "And I'm not running from anything either."

I pause, unsure how to continue, hoping he'll say something. But why would he?

"So you're telling me you came here under false pretenses?" he says, not sounding angry at all. In fact he grins, of all things. "Who hasn't?"

"You're not mad that I lied?" I ask, completely taken aback.

He brings his hands from under mine, and grips it in both of his. "You didn't tell me anything about your life, Tara, so you didn't exactly lie. But you can tell me something now. I'd love to know everything about you."

I gasp, his words filling me with such hope, such happiness it's almost like I just found Sam. Almost.

"I work as a counselor at a women's shelter in San Sebastian, and I'm here looking for my sister who went missing about nine months ago." I say it fast, don't want to stop now that the words are finally flowing. "A woman at the shelter told me she saw her at your club at Christmas. So I came here looking for her."

He frowns at me, his grip on my hands relaxing. "She's the girl in that photo you dropped? I haven't seen her at Crystal's."

"The woman said she saw her at some place called the Viper's Nest," I admit.

He lets go of my hand, leaning back in his chair and exhaling loudly.

This is it. Now he'll tell me to get lost. Or maybe...but no, Tommy would never hurt me.

"Saw her like how?" he asks. "Partying?"

His eyes are very serious as he waits for my answer.

"She said she saw her brought in. It didn't sound like that was a good thing." It sounded like she was there against her will. But what if she wasn't? What if Sam *was* just there to party? I suddenly don't know anything anymore. Except that I want Tommy to stop looking at me with those serious eyes. I want him to smile at me, tell me everything is alright, that no one from his MC harmed Sam, because he'd know and he wouldn't allow it.

"So you think she was trafficked?" he asks instead, his words hitting me like boulders flung directly at my chest.

I shrug. "Yes, that's what I fear happened."

He nods, but doesn't say anything more, just waves the waitress over to pay. His silence is scaring me, fear so strong, so black rising inside me I can hardly see anymore. But he wouldn't hurt me. I know he wouldn't, and he sounded sad when he asked me if I think Sam was trafficked. Not mad at me, just sad. But what if he's sad because now he can't be with me anymore, because I know too much?

"Let's get out of here," he says, pocketing the change and getting up, offering me his hand.

I take it, let him lead me out of the restaurant. The parking lot is dark and deserted, the cricket song and gravel crunching under our feet the only sound around us.

I should be afraid, because he could be taking me anywhere right now. We came here on his bike, and there are only hills, woods and fields between here and town for miles and miles. It's almost dark. I should be afraid, because even if I run away, I might not make it. But I'm not afraid. Because whatever happens, at least I had these last few days with Tommy. At least I now know I'm not as broken and damaged as I thought, and at least I get to hold his hand a little while longer.

He stops once we reach his bike, lets go of my hand and cups my cheeks gently. "I'll find her for you, if she's here. But the MC hasn't dealt in prostitutes for over ten years, I doubt that woman saw your sister. Especially not at Christmas."

The cold fear forcing it's way into my mind is completely blown away by the warmth of hope his words bring. I throw my arms around his waist, hugging him tighter than I ever hugged anyone, even my sister. Tommy wouldn't harm me, and he'll never let me down willingly. I felt it before, and I know it now.

CHAPTER EIGHTEEN

TARA

I feel so clean, so light, so new as I precede him into Crystal's through the back door. The wind picked up as we rode back, caressing my body, blowing away all that I no longer need. The walls are thudding from the loud music playing in the main room, but despite all the noise, I feel like we're alone. Just me and Tommy, together against the world. I no longer have to carry all my burdens on my own. And I'm so happy, I could hoot with joy.

I wrap my arms around his neck as soon as he closes his apartment door behind us, kiss him hard, because no darkness can come between us tonight, I won't let it. He responds in kind, kissing me deeply, taking my air with his urgency, his tongue demanding entrance. He's kissing me the way he kissed me that first night I came to his apartment, not holding back at all, his whole body tense, hard like a snake ready to pounce.

And I'm trying to match his urgency, give him all he wants, the way he's given me all I want, given me things I never even dared ask for. But all the wishing in the world can't keep the dark memories away. I knew that, am realizing it all over again. Because this is too rough, too raw, too fast, and I can't keep up.

His kiss lessens in intensity like he knows, his hands leaving my ass, travelling up and down my back gently.

"OK, slow," he says, and I don't know if he's telling me or himself that. But it doesn't matter, because it's exactly what I need and I didn't even have to ask.

He releases me, leads me to the bed by my hand.

"You do want this don't you?" he asks, staring deep into my eyes.

I just nod. I want this more than I can ever put into words, every cell in my body wants this. I just don't know if I can have it.

He removes his jacket, lets it fall to the ground,

and does the same with mine. Then he pulls on the string holding my dressed together. It flaps apart and he makes a sound somewhere between a groan and a moan, as he sees me in my underwear. I got the really expensive kind, white laced with gold. He slides the dress off my shoulders, kissing my neck as it slithers off, rivers of warmth flowing through me from all the spots his lips touch, forming a sea in my belly.

Before I realize it, he's sliding my bra off too, the air-conditioned coolness making my nipples stand out. He takes one between his lips, nipping it softly, causing a spasm of need to rip through my pussy, making me wobble. He steadies me, guides me onto the bed, and it passes, melts in the warm rivers still filling my belly.

His kisses travel down the center of my stomach, each a little harder than the last, his hand caressing my breast, pinching my nipple, making me moan. I jerk, try to snap my legs together as his kiss lands on my clit over my panties, but he's holding my legs open, prevents it.

His hand leaves my nipple, moves down my stomach on a clear path to exactly where I want it. His eyes are fixed on mine so intently it feels like we're one. There's need in his, a predatory hunger, but softness too, tenderness. But I still gasp as his hand reaches my pussy, still try to jerk away. Because my desire is congealing now, becoming one with the dark memories of pain, and I'm afraid. Afraid that this one will become one of those too, one of the dark ones. I survived those, but I don't think I'll be able to survive that.

He kisses me, and the fear fades. His hand is resting against my pussy, not moving, but I know he wants to rip my panties off, have his way with me.

"Come on, just let me?" he asks, his eyes fixed on mine again. And I know he's asking me to let him make me feel good, so good I'll forget all else.

"OK," I mutter, and he smiles, kissing my neck again.

This time his kisses don't stop when he reaches the edge of my panties. Instead he pulls them down in one swift, practiced motion and kisses my clit before I even have a chance to react.

His kisses and licks get harder, faster, fiercer, bringing pleasure in such strong waves I can't even focus on my fear anymore. It's like I'm floating, can't even feel the mattress beneath me, and I'm aching for more, for him to take me even higher, for these waves of pleasure to become tsunamis. For them to never end. He pushes a finger into my pussy. My mind conjures up pain at the intrusion, but that's not what I'm feeling as he works his finger in and out of me, adding another, his lips and tongue playing with my clit. All the fear, all the protests of my dark memories are silenced by an orgasm which racks through me like a thousand needles piercing me at once, the pain instantly transforming into rivers of pleasure.

"I want you inside me," I mumble before the pangs of my orgasm even begin to fade. Because this second, it's all I want, all I ever wanted, but I don't know what will happen a second from now.

He doesn't need telling twice as he kicks off his pants and boxers, reaches into the nightstand for a condom. His hard cock is pulsing, seems to expand even further before my eyes. It's thick and long, but not curved. And my fear of big ones rushes to the surface, makes me choke on my own breaths.

He's looking at me, questions he'd rather not ask clear in his eyes. Or as clear as they can be behind that haze of desire. It's fine, he won't hurt me. He won't ever hurt me.

So I just smile at him, wave him over before I change my mind, before the fear wins again.

He enters me slowly, stretching me open, the pain only mental, but I feel it regardless. Yet it won't win, I won't let it win. I want him, I need him, and that knowledge becomes clearer, more pronounced with each thrust of his hips, each inch of his cock he gives me. The sea of pleasure still filling my belly starts roiling, waves forming, his cock the cause of it all. And if I think of nothing else, then this pleasure he's giving me will be all there is. As it should be.

His thrusts get faster, deeper, more out of control, his hands pressing my arms into the bed, my whole body rocking from his need, my need, my fear of it all. He's not holding me down to restrain me, I know it's a possessive thing, but right now I don't really see the difference.

He stops suddenly, pulls out his cock and smiles at me. "Maybe you better get on top."

He plops down on the bed beside me, pulling me to him by my hand. And I don't need a second invitation.

My hips know what to do even if I've never done it this way before. I always had to be held down or else I'd kick and hit, run if I could. I never stopped fighting unless they made me.

But I don't have to fight now, as Tommy's cock slides in and out of my pussy, and I'm in control, of my own body, of my own pleasure, which builds and builds, no longer hindered by the dark memories. We climax together, his cock buried deep inside me, pulsing, filling me like he was made just for me.

I see stars in his glorious, deep, dark blue eyes, and soon they're filling the whole room, twinkling, shimmering, guiding me to a world where only pleasure exists, where there is no pain. Guiding me home.

I'm woken by Tommy kissing my neck softly. He's spooning me, his arms wrapped tightly around my torso. I know what he wants, his cock is rock hard, pressing against my ass. And I want to let him take it. I really do. But I didn't sleep well. Nightmares kept waking me, and I don't remember any of them now, yet they left a sour feeling in the pit of my stomach.

I grab his wrist as his hand covers my breast. I don't yank it away, just hold it, so hard my hand is shaking. I so want to want this.

"Not in the mood?" he asks, kissing my neck again without waiting for a reply.

"I just...I don't know..." He takes it as an invitation, kisses me harder, grinding his pulsing cock into my body.

"Later," I whisper, because my heart is racing, my vision blurring. I hope there will be a later.

He releases me, rolls over onto his back. I can tell he's disappointed, but he's trying to hide it. And I want to lay down next to him, press my body against his, wrap my arms around him, and let him hold me. But I don't know if I should, if he even wants me to. So I just lie down on my back too, pulling the sheet over my nakedness and stare up at the ceiling, willing the darkness to fade, my heart to stop beating so very fast.

"Why are you even doing all this for me?" I woke up in a dark mood and it's only getting worse. Even my voice sounds like it belongs to some bitter old woman. But right now I don't know if I can ever give him what he wants. Maybe last night was all I had in me to give.

He doesn't answer right away, but when I glance at him there's no trace of disappointment left in his face. But there's this pensive look in his eyes like he's trying to figure that out too.

He rolls over again, rising up on his elbow and looks down at me, all of me. I don't want him to see the darkness, but I fear he probably does. "Because I would do anything for you."

"That's just..." But I stop myself from adding

"insane" because this could well be the nicest thing anyone's ever said to me. No one sticks around ice queen Tara for long. No one offers to help her. Because she's beyond help.

"Crazy?" he asks, grinning at me. "Maybe, but it's how I feel. Isn't that how it's supposed to work?"

He doesn't add "in love" but I hear it loud and clear, see it plain in his midnight eyes.

But I can't stop the darkness of my mind from covering everything, mixing with even the happy memories, the ones we created together. The ones I hoped would be safe from it. This is too perfect. It can't be real.

"But you're used to treating women like property," I mutter.

He chuckles. "That's not necessarily a bad thing. It also means you'd never have to worry about anyone harming you ever again. And I wouldn't want you to be my slave or anything like that."

He's saying exactly what I want to hear, so why am I resisting? Why is my twisted mind trying to hold onto the pain so hard?

"Besides, my mom taught me to treat all women like princesses, especially the one I chose to be mine forever. And that I should do anything for her." He's smiling as he says it, but his eyes aren't clear anymore as though thick grey rainclouds just covered the starry midnight sky.

"That sounds a little childish," I mumble, but there's no mistaking the sarcasm in my voice. He certainly hasn't treated the other women here as princesses. Maybe he didn't treat them badly, but none of them was his princess.

"Yeah, I was very young when she told me that, she just wanted me to get it." His tone is no longer playful, carries an edge now, and I never want to hear that. Never want to be the cause of that. He's given me so much. If he never gives me another thing he's already given me enough.

"I'm sorry," I say, running my hand along his cheek, as though that will erase the pain that's now plain on his face. "I didn't sleep very well."

It's no excuse. But it's the truth.

He lays his hand over my palm, brings it to his lips and kisses it. "Don't worry about it, I just..."

But he doesn't finish the sentence and I have no idea what he was going to say. I can no longer see what he's thinking just by looking into his eyes, and it's like an invisible wall is blocking him from me, separating us. I want it gone, I want us closer, as close as we were last night, for those few glorious minutes when I managed to climb from underneath all the pain and crushing darkness, and give myself to him.

"Your mom sounds like a fun lady," I say. "I'd like to meet her sometime."

I don't even know what possessed me to say it. I guess I just wanted him to know I want to be a part of his life, a big part, for a long time, forever. But the clouds covering his eyes only grow darker, more threatening, the wall between us thickening, growing opaque. He's still holding onto my hand, but he's no longer kissing it.

"Yeah, that's a story for another day," he finally says, sounding as though he speaking to himself as much as to me. But at least he's speaking, at least I haven't chased him away yet. I never wanted to do that.

So I do the only thing that seems right, natural, what I should've done from the start. I pull his head down and kiss him. He responds immediately, kisses me back. I don't know how much time passes as we just lie there in each other's arms, our tongues entwined, dancing a dance that's ours and ours alone.

"I'll need those photos of your sister," he says later, as I'm watching him get dressed. My mind's still filled only with the sweet memories of our kiss, all that happened before not even registering.

The mention of Sam cuts through them like a wrecking ball.

"I'll get them," I say climbing off the bed.

I wrap my dress around me and rush from the room.

It's fine. He'll find her now. It'll all be fine.

CHAPTER NINETEEN

TOMMY

Promising Tara I'd find her sister was the easy part, actually delivering might not be. But I'll do the best I can, save at least one girl from the fate Shade has in store for hundreds more like her before I leave him to it. Just thinking it leaves a bitter taste in my mouth, but what else can I do? He's the President of the MC.

I know of only one way to make this search go smoothly, and I'm getting nauseous just considering it. But it will kill more than one bird with one stone, provided I'm believable. Which I will be. Deception comes naturally to me.

Apart from one of the prospects scrubbing the floor, the Nest is deserted. I asked Shade to meet me here, but he's now more than an hour late. He probably wants to pay me back for keeping *him* waiting and not answering his calls. It's fine. It gives me the chance to have more than one beer before I have to face him. I'd go for something stronger, but then I might not stop.

The bright sunlight as he opens the front door blinds me, since I've been sitting in this dark room for so long.

"You wanted to speak to me, Tommy?" he says pulling up a chair. But I get up.

"Let's go in the back."

His acquiescent shrug still somehow lets me know he's the one giving the orders around here, but he follows me into the conference room without saying anything.

I don't like being in this room. Everything in it reminds me of being the snake that I am, because I'm planning to leave all this behind and betray my brother our leader, spitting on the loyalty that is the backbone of this MC. But I've made my choice. I can't be a part of Shade's plans. I'll find Tara's sister and then the three of us will leave together.

I turn to face him, wiping all that from my face. "I don't want to fight you anymore, Shade. I'm sorry for being so difficult lately—"

"Difficult? That's one way of putting it," he interrupts.

"You're the President now, and I will fall in step behind you, like I should've done from the start," I continue as though he didn't interrupt. "If you think running whores is the future, I'm behind you. I've kind of been itching to get my hands dirty again. It's been too long. Like you said, Blade had noble ideas, but all that was actually very boring. I miss the excitement."

I grin at him, and he's grinning back, but I don't know if he's buying any of this. I used to be wild and vicious, there was no job too dirty for me. And that wasn't so long ago. I'm counting on him still remembering that.

"As for the drugs," I say, chuckling. "Hell, I'm not even against that. I even tried to convince Blade it was the way to go for awhile."

"I remember that," Shade muses. "I remember you made him very angry suggesting it."

It's true. But that was a long time ago, back when I spent my days and nights completely wasted.

"So we're cool?" I ask.

He extends his hand for a handshake, pulls me into a hug when I take it, slapping my back hard.

"But no more talk of full attendance, Tommy. I call the shots and the execs vote, like it's always been."

"Yeah, I don't know what got into me," I say. He's still gripping my hand, and I'm not entirely sure he believes any of what I just said. But I'll find out in due time. For now, I'll assume he does.

"As for the whores," I say, releasing his hand and sitting down in one of the chairs, right by the carving of the naked woman. "I think the first step should be reclaiming the local whorehouses. We can start with the ones we get rent from and then move on to taking over some of the other ones. What do you think?"

The MC hasn't been running whores for years, but we still collect money from the establishments that do on what was once our turf. I always thought it came to the same thing, tried to get Blade to give that up too, but he was a slow mover, Shade is right about that.

Shade is looking at me like he's impressed.

"I like your way of thinking," he says, taking his seat at the head of the table. "But let's do it on the DL for now, just scope them out to start with, go around checking that they're all up to date on their payments, and that they're not misrepresenting their earnings. That way we can get a feel for what we're dealing with before we start running them out."

I lift myself out of the chair by pressing against the table. "Sounds like a plan. I'll get started today."

He frowns at me, his eyes narrowing. It's the first real sign that he thinks I'm full of shit.

"I've been dying for some productive action," I say, grinning at him. "It's what's been making me so antsy. But if you want to send someone else, that's fine."

"No, no, you go, but don't go alone," he says, and I have to fight down my sigh of relief. As it is, I'm not sure it's not showing plain on my face.

"I'll take Brett," I say and head for the door.

Hopefully, I'll find Tara's sister today. If I get started right now, I should have most of the nearby whorehouses checked out by the time Crystal's closes.

I had no luck in the first ten whorehouses we visited. Calling those places houses is actually generous. Mostly they're just containers, or old converted warehouses, places that no one should be forced to live in. Just the idea makes me nauseous, and that on top of seeing all those poor girls makes me wish I'd had that stronger drink before I went on this errand. Or ten, with maybe a line or two of Coke to chase them down. But I'm done with all that. Forever.

The sun is setting, and Brett and me just pulled up to yet another whorehouse. This one's even worse than the others. It's made up of a series of dilapidated warehouses surrounded by a thin wooden wall. There are four more places I still planned to check out tonight, but I don't think I can. I just want to return to Tara now, hold her, and kiss her for awhile. We don't even have to do anything else. I wanted to return to her with good news tonight, but the truth is, if her sister has been held in one of these places since Christmas, even finding her won't be entirely good news.

"Why are we doing all this again?" Brett asks as I get off my bike, looking at me like he's trying to find that out without me having to speak.

"Shade's orders," I say and walk towards the biggest and foremost building, which I'm sure is the reception area, or the office, or whatever the fuck they call it.

What's left of the paint job on the once red metal door is peeling off, revealing gashes of rust. I'd hate to be locked up behind that door, it looks like something out of a horror movie.

"It's good that you're starting to follow his orders

more willingly now," Brett says, jogging to catch up to me. "But you're VP now, you can make some of the choices yourself. Visiting these places can't be what you want to be doing."

He's not quick, but he always gets to the right answer eventually.

"Brett," I say, stopping suddenly and blocking his path. He almost runs right into me. "Let's just get this done. We'll talk about our feelings some other time."

I try to sound mocking, but it comes out very serious. I was barely able to stop myself from yelling at him to shut the fuck up. I'm so angry I need to lash out, at anything or anyone. But it won't be at Brett. He's quite possibly the last true friend I still have in the MC.

"Alright," he mutters at my back as I walk on towards the door. I know he has more things to say, but he's wisely choosing to keep quiet.

I swing open the door so hard it crashes against the wall, the metallic thump echoing through the courtyard.

"What can I do you for?" a sweaty, bulky man asks. He shot up from behind a rickety desk as I opened the door, and assumed a not very welcoming stance. But his face slackens and pales as he recognizes me.

"Tommy, is that you? To what do I owe the pleasure of this visit?"

He looks vaguely familiar, but I can't quite place
him. Maybe I met him back when I still did most of
the dirty work for the MC. Those years are more or
less a blur.

"I'm here to check that you haven't been falling
behind on your rent money," I say just as Brett closes
the door behind us.

"Of course we're up to date. I got the ledger right
here," the man says, digging through a drawer, thick
drops of sweat falling off his forehead.

"I also want to inspect your offerings, make sure
you're not keeping anything from us."

The man straightens up, fidgeting under
my glare.

"Sure, sure, let me just get the keys," he finally
says. "But I assure you, everything is as it's always
been. We don't keep secrets."

It's a little irregular that I want to see the women,
but none of the proprietors of the whorehouses we've
visited so far objected much. I was almost hoping this
guy would refuse to show me, so I could punch him a
few times. It's scary how much I'm craving to beat
someone up. I haven't felt like that in years.

If word gets back to Shade about me asking to see

the whores, I'll just tell him I was checking out the wares.

It's Tara I see every time I peer into one of the rooms. And I don't know if it's because I want to be with her right now, or because the fear, the cold, useless anger, the resignation I see in the girls' faces reminds me of how she looked when she told me about the abuse she endured. It's the first, it has to be. Tara isn't as beaten down as these poor women. Most of them don't even dare meet my eyes as I look into their rooms, some don't acknowledge my presence at all.

The sadness and hurt is palpable, grows worse, more tangible by the minute until it's filling the whole building, crushing the life right out of me. None of the girls in the first or second building look anything like Tara's sister.

But the girl in the last room of the last building I'm inspecting has long dark hair. She doesn't even flinch as the door opens, just stares out of the black painted window. Her room smells of dirty sheets, piss and semen and the paint on the window is cracked and peeling off in places, so I guess that's what she's looking through.

"Hey! Turn!" the proprietor yells at her, and I

come very close to punching him in the face, just for his mean tone alone.

She does it, slowly like she's just sleepwalking, like none of this is really happening to her, my heart thumping in my ears.

But my hopeful anticipation crashes like a full bottle hitting concrete, once I finally see her face. She has the same hair as Tara's sister, even has blue eyes, but it's not her. Not even close. This girl is ugly. And I hate myself for thinking it, almost as much as I hate myself for failing to find Tara's sister tonight.

"Shade called while you were inside," Brett informs me when I return to our bikes. He didn't follow me on the rounds. "Says your phone's off and you should charge it."

Shit. I hadn't even checked my phone once all day. Now it looks like I'm dodging Shade's calls again. Not the best start to getting him to trust me.

"Is that the entire message, or was there more?" I snap.

Brett pockets his phone and straddles his bike. He doesn't like my tone, but he's the last person in the world to just call me on it, especially since he understands how repulsive I find this work. I really appreciate that right now. "He wants you to meet him at the Nest for a drink. Told me to go home."

Great. All I want to do is be with Tara. Take her out somewhere, far away from all this. Or we could just spend the night locked in my apartment. That would work too.

It's getting light out by the time Shade finally lets me go home. We spent the whole night reminiscing about the good old days, while he drank a whole bottle of Jack by himself. Talking about the past is possibly my least favorite thing to do in the whole world, but I couldn't just leave. At least he seems to believe me that I'm back on his side. In as much as I ever was in the first place. Shade and me were never very close. He's too much like my father, and I could never see past that.

Tara's curled up on her side of the bed—the left side, the one closest to the door. But she's facing the center, the side where I would be sleeping. I want to wake her up so bad my whole body aches for it. Literally aches.

She's not crying now, but she was, the traces of tears still visible on her cheeks. I want to be the one to stop her crying in her sleep. I fucking yearn to be that guy. So I can't wake her up now, because I'll just be giving her bad news, more reasons to cry. She didn't believe me when I told her I'd do anything for her. But I meant it. And if she won't take me at my word, I'll just have to show her.

The sun rises before I finally start to doze off, and I only managed that because I caved and took hold of her hand.

CHAPTER TWENTY

TARA

Crystal left me alone to finish cleaning the garage now that she's gone through all the boxes, while she had an errand to run. Tommy's still sleeping. I didn't have the heart to wake him when I got up this morning, since he must've returned very late last night. I know since I stayed up until after five waiting for him. I was curious if he found out anything about Sam, but I also just wanted to kiss him, hold him, maybe do even more than that to show him how sorry I am for being so argumentative with him yesterday morning. It means so much that he wants to help me find Sam, and that he wants to be with me despite all my problems. I don't think I can ever quite tell him just how very much it means. But I plan on showing him.

I'm almost done sweeping up the floor now, and then I'll go to him. He's slept long enough. I can wake him now, maybe the same way I did that first morning. The thought makes me smile and start sweeping faster.

A shadow crosses the entry to the garage, and I look up hopefully, the smile still playing on my lips. But it's Bear, Crystal's husband. Despite being over eighty years old, he's still an imposing man. He's nice to the girls, and they all seem to like him, but all that about women being the property of MC members has me weary of him. And Crystal wears that jacket with the words "Property of Bear" embroidered on it a lot. Though I think Bear is suffering from dementia, maybe even has Alzheimer's, because sometimes he has no idea where he is.

Today doesn't seem to be one of those days. His eyes are clear and sharp as he greets me. He walks over to the table where Crystal left a couple of boxes she still hasn't finished going through.

He pokes around in one of them, pulls out the framed photo Crystal showed me a couple of days ago.

"She's throwing all this out?" he growls more than says. "Good."

And he punctuates that by spitting at the photo. I'm so shocked I nearly drop the broom. But he's smiling at me now.

"Did I ever tell you the story of Crystal and me?"

I've hardly spoken to him, so I just shake my head, still shocked that he would spit on a picture of her like that.

He shows me the photo. "She was with this piece of shit when we met. Giant Red he was called, on account of his flaming hair, I suppose. Because he wasn't very tough at all as it turned out."

The mischievous way in which he's grinning makes him appear much younger than he is.

"Now see, Crystal was his old lady," he continues. "I knew that, but the moment I saw her, I knew she had to be mine. He didn't treat her right, see, and it didn't take long to convince her she should be with me. But he took the bottle to her face in revenge. My poor, beautiful Crystal." He picks up the photo again, wipes away the spit with his thumb and gazes wistfully at her face. His story is touching me in ways I never imagined I could feel. It's almost enough to bring tears to my eyes.

"And what happened then?" I breathe.

He looks up and smiles at me, his eyes cloudy, but I think that's just from remembering. "I made sure he paid for it, and that he never hurt anyone again. Then I stayed at her bedside night and day while she recovered."

"And you never left her side since," Tommy says. He's leaning against the doorframe of the garage, but moves towards me as our eyes lock. His are letting me know he feels the same way about me, that he'll always be there for me no matter what, no matter how damaged I am, even if I was disfigured.

He wraps his arms around me, and I lean against him, suddenly finding it very hard to stand on my own.

"Yes," Bear says. "I told you that story before, haven't I Tommy?"

"Only about a million times," Tommy answers, his voice reverberating in my ears.

"Well, I'll leave you to it then," Bear says, a playful tone in his voice.

I look up into Tommy's eyes, want nothing more than his lips on mine. And he obliges, kissing me like he read my mind, like it's the only thing he wants to be doing too. The dusty garage disappears, the world melting away, wiped clean by the blinding sunshine we create together, ready for us to remake it.

"That was such a beautiful story," I say later. He's only wearing a pair of sweatpants and no shirt, and I'm a little jealous he walked through the entire club like that for all the others to see. But he's in my arms now, so I shouldn't even be thinking that.

Tommy steals another kiss from me. "Wasn't it? Though to be honest I never really believed it until right now."

His words hit me right in the chest, causing rivulets of bliss to flow all through me. All I want is for this feeling to last and last.

"I didn't find your sister yesterday," he says, his words driving a stake through all that bliss. "But I'll check a few more places today. If she's anywhere around here, I'll find her."

I feel the truth of his words, his desire to do just that somewhere near my heart. But my chest is filling with icy despair regardless.

"I'll go now, so I can be back early tonight, then we can go do something fun. Last night they opened the drive-in cinema for the summer. Ever been to one of those?"

I shake my head. I know what he's doing, he's trying to cheer me up. And I want it to work, I want to let him.

"The movie starts at ten. But I'll be back before

then," he says, wrapping his arms around me even tighter. "Maybe you can even wear that pretty dress of yours again."

He's probably referring to the jeans I'm wearing, but they're not even the baggy ones I brought with me. And I'm not wearing a flannel shirt over them, just a t-shirt.

He sighs, a flash of anger ripping through the velvety soft night of his eyes. "Is your father in jail for what he did to you?"

His question comes from left field, completely surprising me, my chest filling with another jet of icy cold water.

I shake my head. I tried for so long to make him pay for what he did to Sam and me, reported him, even sued him, but his money and his connections kept him safe, and his lawyers made *me* look crazy.

"And your mom? Did she do nothing to stop the abuse?" he asks.

"She died when I was two years old," I tell him. "I don't even remember her."

I wish I could, but I only know what she looked like from photos. His eyes are filled with such compassion, I want to cry. But the softness starts congealing into a very hard edge in front of my eyes as I gaze into them.

"What's your father's name? Where does he live?" he asks harshly.

My eyes widen, my breath hitching in my throat. There's no mistaking the look in his eyes now, it screams murder.

"Why?" I mutter, not even sure why I'm asking since I already know the answer.

"I'll make him pay for it," he says. "I'll kill him for what he did to you."

The words pierce me like a thousand knives flung at me at once. I hold him tighter, burrow my head in his chest. "Oh, Tommy, no. He's not worth it. It's not worth it. He's too well connected, and I...I don't want to lose you."

His hands are stroking my back, my hair. "Don't you want him to pay?"

The real answer's yes. To everything he's suggesting. And it scares me. Shakes me to the core that I'm even considering it, that a part of me is rejoicing at the thought of my father dying a bloody, painful death.

"I'm trying to forgive," I mutter.

"Yeah, how's that working out for you?" His harsh, bitter tone makes me shiver.

"I mean, I personally never got very far with that," he adds, stroking my hair gently.

I look up into his eyes, which are cold like a frosty winter midnight now. "Thank you for offering, Tommy, but no. It means so much to me that you'd even consider it. No one's ever done more for me than you. But I...I just couldn't...just couldn't live with that. Or with something happening to you because of me."

I'm rambling so I shut up. He frowns and shakes his head like my answer didn't please him at all, but then he smiles, kisses me again, gently this time, tenderly and slowly. And I know I should be scared of him, because he just suggested murdering my father like it would be an everyday sort of thing for him, but I'm not. I just feel very safe and protected.

The movie's about to start, and I'm leaning against him, his arm around me, resting against my hip. Today's search for Sam didn't go any better than yesterday's. It upset me, made me fear the worst even more than I already feared it before. Because this was my best lead to find her, and it's very quickly coming to nothing. But he's so certain I shouldn't lose hope yet, that there's still more places to look, that I believed him, managed to chase my doom and gloom thoughts away. Though the weird stony look in his eyes didn't fade all through dinner. It's probably still there, only now it's too dark to see clearly.

"I've never seen this movie," he says. "Did you?"

It's Casablanca. I've seen it a bunch of times. "Sure. It's a classic, you know?"

I'm trying to keep my voice light, match his tone, but I'm not sure how well I'm succeeding.

"Classic movies aren't my favorite," he says, his hand sliding over my ass.

"Oh, come on, I'm sure you've seen your share of classics bringing girls here," I say. "Don't drive-in cinemas only play classics? Though I suppose you probably didn't come here to actually watch the movies."

He squeezes my ass for a moment, before resuming the slow caresses. "Are you suggesting something, Tara?"

That smirk on his lips tells me he was thinking about it long before I sort of suggested it. "People come here to make out, don't they?"

He chuckles. "I actually wouldn't know, this is my first time at a drive-in."

"Oh, come on, you expect me to believe that?"

"No, I'm serious, I was never much for dating before I met you."

"Yeah, me neither," I admit. So much of what he says sounds exactly like what I would have said. Like we think the same. And it's a little weird, but feels so right.

"So, for example, a blow job at a drive-in movie is something I've never gotten," he says, grinning at me. "I imagine it must be tha bomb."

"Easy, there," I breathe and kiss him softly. Because even though a flash of something very close to fear passed through me at his lewd suggestion, I know he's just playing with me. That he'd never want something from me that I can't give.

The movie's almost halfway done by the time we stop kissing. My skin is tingling from his touches, my mind fuzzy, all of the darkness swaddled in soft mists of pleasure, desire, pure bliss.

"How about we go back home now?" I ask, still breathless from all the kisses we shared. "I've seen this movie a hundred times."

It doesn't really have a happy ending. And I want only that tonight.

The music from the club is thumping through the walls of Tommy's apartment, but it's a muffled sound, and it only accentuates how alone we are. How it's just the two of us here, the rest of the world far removed, distant, spinning around without us.

Fear of what's to come is mixing with the tantalizing sparks of arousal inside me, but it's not quenching them, not making me reconsider. Though I am a little apprehensive, because the loving softness in Tommy's eyes has a jagged edge that's all predatory desire.

But I can do this. Because I want to.

We're still standing by the door, kissing, and I take a step back, sliding out of his arms. He lets me go, only gripping my arms tight for a second before releasing me. And it's all the reassurance I need. Even if I say no right now, after being the one to suggest we come here, he won't force me to do anything I don't want to do. I already knew that, and now I'm sure.

I untie the strap holding my dress together, and undress for him, smiling as his eyes take in all of me with such hunger I feel it everywhere, deep in my chest, in my belly, in my pussy. His look is bidding me come closer, and there's no force in this world strong enough to prevent me from ignoring that call.

I return into his arms and kiss him, the soft firmness of his lips between mine so sweet, so tantalizing

I can't help but bite down ever so slightly. He responds instantly, grabbing my ass and grinding his hard cock into my belly as he deepens the kiss, his desire for me ripping through my entire body all at once. But I slow him down, not because I fear it, but because I have different plans for him tonight.

My fingers are fumbling with his belt buckle, not quite succeeding in undoing it, since I've never undressed a man before, never even wanted to. He takes over and does it himself, lets his pants drop, and steps out of them. I trail my hands down his defined chest, let my fingers bump against the hard six pack of his abs, as I kneel in front of him.

He's grinning down at me as I free his cock from his boxers. I'm completely lost in his eyes as I take a tentative lick. The darkness is there, but it's no more than shadows on the edge of my awareness. It's more like a grey mist than anything tangible.

He groans as I take the head of his cock between my lips, his hand stroking the back of my head. I feel him tense as I take even more of his hardness in my mouth, enjoying the velvety firmness, the pulsing heat against my tongue. His cock fills my mouth completely, and I gag as I reach my limit. He exhales harshly, his hand tightening its grip on my head. And I know how much he wants to take over, thrust his cock deep into my throat, yet he's letting me do it at my own pace, surrendering all the control to me.

It emboldens me, makes me flick my tongue out, stroking the shaft, as I work on just the head, rolling my tongue around it, tasting every last, sweet millimeter of him. His fingers are tangled in my hair now, his eyes glassy, half-closed, fixed on my face. His breaths are coming faster, more jagged, his stomach taut. I know he's close to coming, and I want him to, want to be the one to give him pleasure tonight.

"I'm gonna come if you keep that up," he whispers hoarsely, and I just continue to bob up and down on his cock, letting it invade my throat now, my gag reflex finally under control. And still he's just letting me have all the control, letting me set the pace.

He's trying to hold out, I can feel it in the tension radiating from him, but he has no hope of succeeding. I want him to come, give him back just a little of what he's given me. He makes a fist in my hair right before his hot semen floods my throat, and I'm trying to swallow, but I can't do it fast enough.

He lifts me up in one fast motion, displaying energy I was sure I'd drained from him. Before I know it I'm on my back on the bed, braless, my panties hanging off one ankle, my neck and breasts, belly and thighs, tingling from his kisses. I'm giggling, thinking of nothing but where his lips will touch me next. They land on my clit, making me gasp and moan at the same time as his tongue goes to work, stoking the embers of desire smoldering inside me into flames.

He knows exactly what he's doing, and my body's responding in ways I didn't know it could, my breaths coming in jagged little moan-laced exhales, my fingers making fists in the sheets. I'm so close to coming, but he keeps me on the edge, my orgasm so near I can almost feel it consuming me, yet so far beyond my reach it's driving me insane. Just as I'm sure it'll come, and I open to let it flood me, he pulls away kissing me wetly.

I'd protest, but he doesn't give me the chance to as he climbs on the bed and leans against the head-board, pulling me into his lap. His cock enters me in one long stroke, and the orgasm that washes over me is explosive, so all-consuming I forget where I am, who I am, know only this searing pleasure ravaging through my body.

He keeps thrusting into me, his strokes sure and precise, hard yet controlled, and before I even recover from the first, I'm cresting another wave of intense searing pleasure. I'm holding onto the head-board, screaming, no longer aware of anything but his cock deep inside me, his arms holding me firmly in place as he takes what he needs from me, but gives me what I need too.

I may be straddling him, my way to escape easy and clear, but he's in complete control of my body now, of my pleasure, and this is exactly where I want to be. Because I've never experienced a more satisfying escape than the orgasms ripping my body, my soul, my everything to shreds right now, revealing a lightness, a weightlessness, a brightness that no dark memory can ever weigh down or conceal again.

CHAPTER TWENTY-ONE

TARA

It's been over a week since Tommy started looking for Sam, but he's had no luck. He's still trying to convince me he'll find her, but I don't think either of us believes that anymore. Losing hope sucks, it hurts and angers me, but the pain isn't as pronounced as it would have been before I came here.

These last few weeks with Tommy have cleansed me. I feel as though I'm finally recovering after a long illness, kind of like I'm getting over a flu, only the sense of healing is so much stronger, so much better than that. I'm still not quite there yet, still get overwhelmed by my dark memories sometimes, but those times are fewer and farther between now, and the darkness is growing less threatening, less consuming all the time. It's hard to feel despair amid all that joy and healing.

Tommy's been coming to see me during the day too lately, just to steel a few kisses before he sets out again. He told me not to expect him today, but I can't help it. I am expecting him, keep glancing at the back door hoping to see him walk through as I wipe down the tables with the lemon scented disinfectant.

The door opens, and I look up again, butterflies fluttering in my stomach. But Crystal walks in, a very hard expression on her face. She's followed by Simone and— My breath hitches in my throat as I see the woman who told me to look for my sister here walk into the bar. She closes the door behind them, hasn't noticed me yet. But she does as she turns, her eyes fixing squarely on me.

"You can have your old room back, Gwen," Crystal is telling her, sounding very stern. "But this is your last chance here. And the money you stole is coming out of your paychecks until it's all paid off. Is that clear?"

Gwen finally looks away from me, and nods sheepishly, looking down at the floor. "I'm so sorry for that, Crystal. I had it so good here. I don't know what possessed me to steal money from you and run away."

Crystal grumbles something incoherent, but her expression visibly softens.

"You're working tonight, so you might as well get some rest now," she says, and Gwen nods so enthusiastically you'd think she just got the staring role in some blockbuster movie.

Crystal gives her another stern look, then walks over to me and hands me an unsealed white envelope.

"What's this?" I ask, wiping my hands on my jeans before taking it.

"Your pay for the last couple of weeks."

I don't want to take it, but I see no way to refuse that won't look suspicious, so I just pocket it without checking how much is inside. I'll give it back to her before I leave, once I finally come clean about my real reason for being here. And maybe I should do that right now, because Gwen and Simone are huddled together by the bar, Simone's mouth and eyes very wide each time she glances at me. I'm sure she's telling Simone all about who I really am, so I should just tell Crystal right now before they do.

I can't believe it never occurred to me some woman from the shelter where I work could come here and expose my lies. Thank God I at least told Tommy, because I certainly missed my chance with

Crystal. She's already heading out the door and I can't very well go running after her without looking like an idiot.

Gwen and Simone are both glaring at me now, Simone especially. She hasn't been very friendly these last few weeks, and I assume it's because of Tommy and me. I've been trying to smooth things over with her, but haven't gotten very far.

"You know Gwen, don't you, Tara?" Simone asks, approaching me slowly with Gwen in tow. I could just lie, deny it all. But I've never been any good at lying. Yet I can't quite bring myself to admit it either.

"She's been telling me an interesting story," Simone continues. "All about how you're some do-good social worker looking for your sister."

"Please don't tell anyone else," I hear myself saying.

"Yeah, Simone," Gwen says, looking from me to her, her face kinda pinched like she's regretting saying anything. "I don't want any trouble with Crystal."

"Relax," Simone says. "Crystal hates liars and cheats almost as much as I do."

I could point out that Crystal just took Gwen back after she stole money from her, because she's a kind and caring woman who understands that sometimes people just do what they gotta do. But I don't want to piss off Simone even more.

"I just want to find my sister," I say. "She's been missing for more than nine months. And Gwen said she saw her here, so that's why I came looking for her."

"After I expressly warned you not to," Gwen puts in, then turns to Simone. "Come on, leave her be. It's her life, she's not doing you any harm."

But Simone is still glaring at me, anger the only emotion in her light blue eyes.

"Does Tommy know?" she barks.

I almost say yes right away, because I want to put her in her place, make her back off. I'm not hurting her in any way. Except that I took Tommy away from her. But he was never hers. Yet that's what this is all about. He hasn't even spoken to any of the others much since I moved into his apartment, and I know that because I've jealously watched him interact with them so closely I'm ashamed of it.

"Yeah, didn't think so," she says, chuckling. But it's a hollow, mirthless sound. "I wonder how he'll take it. Not too well, I'm guessing."

"Don't tell him, OK?" I hear myself say, but it's more of a command than a plea.

He's out looking for Sam every day, and I'm sure

he's doing it in secret, and that no one from the MC knows about it. He hasn't said as much, just told me not to worry about it when I asked, but I can't imagine any of the other members would be too happy about his plan to find and free one of their prostitutes. I can't reveal that secret. Especially not to Simone. She's too vindictive.

"He deserves to know, don't you think?" Simone says smugly, like she'd already won.

"I'll tell him myself," I snap. "Just butt out of this, Simone. It's none of your business."

"You think you're special just because he's fucking you every night?" she says grinning widely in disbelief. "Wake up, woman. You're just a new toy for him. But he'll tire of you soon enough. I've known him on and off for years, and I can guarantee that's how this affair of yours will end."

I'm so angry right now, I can't see straight. It's not true what she's saying, I know that. She's just trying to rile me up. I know Tommy really cares about me, it's clear in every kiss, every hug, every look we share.

"He'll discard you soon enough," she says. "Probably right after he learns you've lied to him."

I can barely stop myself from hitting her. I'm shaking from the effort.

Gwen has been standing perfectly still during

this whole exchange, but she moves now, wraps her arm under Simone's. "Let's go get a drink, Simone. This will all work itself out on its own," she says. "And I have so much more to tell you."

"You just mark my words, Tara," Simone says warningly. "Your little fairytale will be over very soon."

But thankfully she lets Gwen lead her out of the room. She's wrong about Tommy and me, but the dread of returning to my old life, the one before Tommy in it, that she conjured up with her jealous words is very real. And those memories are swarming my mind, vivid like I'm living them right now.

TOMMY

I start sweating the moment I enter Jerry's air-conditioned lair, since it's so fucking hot outside it's hard to breathe. I don't know what's happening with the weather, but two weeks ago I was freezing my ass off in the rain, and now I'm dying from the heat.

"Back again already?" Jerry asks in mock surprise, swiveling his chair to face me. His mom let me in, like she always does. I don't think he leaves this room much. On a day like today, I don't blame him. He'd probably have a heart attack before he took two steps outside.

"Yeah." I remove a keyboard and a dirty plate off the chair next to him and sit. "I need your help again."

"Do you now?" he asks, his voice full of meanings. But I can't answer his questions.

Besides, today's visit has nothing to do with the MC stuff, and I don't even know how to ask for his help on this one. I ran out of whorehouses to check two days ago. Tara's sister isn't anywhere for me to find, but I can't bring myself to tell her that. Not yet. Not after she's been so happy, so carefree these last few days. I can't bring myself to dash her hopes. I just can't.

But I can do something else for her. I can make sure her father never hurts her, or anyone else ever again. She'd never be able to live with herself knowing I killed him, which is still my number one wish. I might even hate him more than I hate my own father, and that's saying a lot.

But there's ways to fuck up a man's life without killing him. And if this fails, I can just break his neck or something, make him a fucking tetraplegic.

"I need you to do some more of that dark internet magic for me and find some dirt on someone," I say.

The main reason I befriended Jerry in college was because he's an awesome hacker. I'm not proud of that, but we grew close since, so maybe that makes up for it.

"You know, like you did with the new sheriff a year ago," I add since he's just staring at me, not saying anything.

I really hit the jackpot with the sheriff. The man has a big secret, one he can't afford getting out, and he's left the MC in peace ever since I told him I knew. I'm hoping getting dirt on Tara's father will be even easier.

"It's not another law enforcement official you want me to spy on, is it?" Jerry asks. "Because that kinda stuff carries a hefty prison sentence."

The surge of guilt for involving him in all of this makes me nauseas. But I pay him very well for his service. I think he can probably spend the rest of his life in this room playing video games on just the money I paid him so far.

"This is different," I say. "I want you to find something on Vincent Di Marco."

"Whoa, you don't mean the Hollywood producer? That Di Marco?" Jerry says.

"That's him." I'm not proud of myself for checking Tara's ID while she slept to get her last name. Feel very icky over Googling her until I was certain her father was in fact one of the biggest producers currently working in Hollywood.

"I've seen like all of his movies," Jerry says. I have too. He produces action movies, all blockbusters. But I'm never watching another one of his movies ever again. "What's he done to you?"

"It's not exactly what he's done to me." Though it kinda feels like he has. "But he's hurt a woman I care a lot about, and I want him to pay."

Jerry squints at me, probably because I said I cared about a woman, and he thinks I'm lying. But I've never been more truthful in my life.

"He's a child molester," I say, balling my hands into fists until they start shaking. "Likes raping little girls."

"No way," Jerry says. "You're shitting me."

I shake my head. "I want you to find what you can on him. Get me enough dirt so I can bury him."

Jerry is still staring at me, but the disbelief in his face is shifting to something resembling anger. "You're sure about this?"

I nod. "Positive."

He runs his hand through his hair, then bumps the mouse so the computer screen flickers to life.

"These pedophiles cover their tracks very well," he says, powering up some program on the screen. "But if there's something to find, I'll find it. I'll get back to you in a couple of days."

"Could you just check now?" I ask.

"Nah," Jerry says. "It's gonna take awhile, and I like to work in peace. But I'll work on only this now. Nothing else, I promise you. I fucking hate child molesters."

I'd hoped to get all the dirt on Tara's father today, so I could drive down to LA and confront him with it. I make a few more attempts to convince Jerry to let me wait while he searches, but he won't be swayed.

So I have the whole day in front of me now, and nothing to do. I could go visit Ian in prison. Maybe he even knows about some whorehouse I don't. But I still haven't decided if I'm gonna tell him about the baby or not. My policy when it came to Sara and Ian's on and off relationship was to stay the fuck out of it, and maybe this baby secret falls into that category too. And besides, I'd so much rather spend the day with Tara.

The parking lot behind Crystal's is baking in the heat when I pull out, the sunlight so bright it's blinding. I just want to get Tara and take her to the lake, spend the rest of the day enjoying her presence and her closeness. I hope Jerry finds something good on her father. Then she can finally close that chapter of her life for good. She needs that kind of closure, else she'll never be truly happy. Even if she doesn't realize that yet. But she's holding on to those memories to fuel her anger and that's just not healthy. I know, I did the same thing for years.

"Got a second, Tommy?" Simone asks from the stairwell leading up to the second floor.

She's been casting me very angry glances, since Tara and me began dating, but she's all smiles and fluttering eyelashes now.

"Sure, what is it?" I ask.

"Not here," she says. "Follow me."

She leads me back outside into the heat. But this won't take long. I won't let it. She tried to come on to me a few times in the beginning, but I put a stop to that firmly.

"I don't even know how to tell you this," she says,

but I can tell she's lying. She can't wait to tell me. Simone is the worst liar.

"Just say it," I snap.

"Tara hasn't been completely honest with you," she says. "With any of us, really."

No one's been more honest with me than Tara. Not ever in my life.

"She came here looking for her missing sister. She's probably setting us all up to bring the cops down on us soon," Simone says, all the coyness gone from her eyes.

She's looking at me with a triumphant expression on her face. I suddenly realize she's expecting me to thank her, tell her what a good job she's done. And maybe I should. The less people that know about Tara's true reason for being here, the better. But I can't stand anyone talking shit about Tara. Especially not conniving little Simone.

"You should stay out of things that don't concern you. I'll handle this and you keep your mouth shut about it." I bark, even succeed in making her blink in fear. "Do I make myself clear?"

I've never spoken to her like this in all the years that we've known each other. She's already recovered from the initial shock of it though, is glaring at me with pure defiance. "You already knew, didn't you? Oh my God, are you helping her find her sister?"

"None of this is your business, Simone."

"What's Shade gonna say about this?" she asks bitingly. "I'm betting he doesn't know."

"I'm warning you, Simone. Stay out of it, for your own good."

But she won't be doing that. I can see it clearly in her eyes. She's mad, and she'll do anything to drive Tara away. But going to Shade with this...I hope that's just an empty threat. I hope she's smart enough not to even consider it. For her sake and mine too. And especially for Tara's.

"This is MC business and I'm dealing with it," I say as menacingly as I can. "Shade already knows."

She seems taken aback by my tone, and I can literally see her brain working as she tries to reason it out and decide whether I'm lying or not. She's smart, she'll come to the right decision. I'm done talking to her.

If she goes to Shade with this, the fragile web of trust I've managed to weave between us in these last few days will be gone, and he'll probably be right back to trying to kill me. It's time to leave. And Tara's coming with me.

I find Tara sitting on the sofa, hugging her knees and staring out the window, seemingly mesmerized by what she's observing. Though seeing as there's only a row of dumpsters there, I can't see how that can be.

"So, it seems Simone knows why you're really here," I say, all the anger I felt just a moment ago dissolving now that I'm finally with Tara. She has this effect on me, where she makes me think everything will work out, and that nothing is as bad as it seems.

She turns her head slowly. Her face is as white as the walls, her expression just as blank. "Yes, she does. Gwen told her. She was the one who said Samantha was here in the first place."

Her voice is toneless, matches the expression on her face. Though her eyes are filled with lighting.

I take a step toward her, but stop again before I reach her. She hasn't moved at all to welcome me. Actually, she wrapped her arms around her knees tighter.

"I'll take care of it, don't worry." But I say it harshly, not reassuringly as I meant to. Rejection pisses me off more than most things do. Shade says it's because I was spoiled as a child. But right now, it's because I want to hold Tara so bad my stomach actually hurts.

"Yeah, like you'll take care of finding my sister for me. And fix everything else that's wrong with me, right?" she snaps, finally releasing her legs and sitting normally.

"I will find your sister." Though the words just sound hollow now, even as I say them. I might never be able to deliver on that promise, but I'm sure as fuck not gonna admit that to her now that she's angry at me. "What brought all this on?"

"You haven't yet," she says, glaring at me and ignoring my question. "And come to think of it, finding her isn't exactly in your best interest if she was trafficked by your MC. I mean, you'd be risking jail time if she's freed and talks to the cops, wouldn't you?"

She's absolutely right. And I have no answer to give her right now, not where anyone could easily overhear it. Simone might be listening at the door. The fact that Tara's not in my arms, letting me kiss her, that she's sitting on the edge of the couch, stiff as a board and glaring at me, accusing me of all these things, is pissing me off in ways I didn't even know I could get mad in.

"That's all very true, Tara," I say harshly, letting

way too much of that anger into my voice. "I'm a criminal. Would you prefer it if we just called this whole thing off?"

No way her answer can be yes. But I think she's very close to saying it, and it pisses me off even more.

"Am I stupid and naïve for believing you... believing all the things you promised me?" she says, still perfectly calm and collected, anger flashing in her eyes. "Was all that just so I'd let you fuck me... like a challenge or something."

Yeah, it was a fucking challenge. It still is. But even in my anger addled state I know saying that would be a huge mistake.

"I realize you've been through a lot in your life, and that it's made you very angry," I say, way too coldly. "But maybe you can start to recognize a good thing when you see it now."

"What? You mean letting you fuck me?"

"Fuck you?" I snap. "When have we actually fucked? We wouldn't even be having this conversation if we'd done that."

That came out all wrong, but I don't know how to fix it. What to say so I don't make this worse. My anger at her is fading fast. I don't want to be angry at Tara. Ever.

She shakes slightly at my harsh tone, blinking

hard, her face no longer blank. It's sad and confused now. She's like this fragile little bird trying to fly, but can't because she's locked in this cage made of anger and pain she won't let go of. The last traces of my own anger just vanish, replaced by a painful desire to comfort her, care for her, love her. And it's so foreign, yet so strong I'm actually trying to conjure all that anger back, because at least that's familiar. I know how to deal with that. But this, this could kill me if she says goodbye now.

She's still looking at me, but the lightning flashes in her eyes have subsided to a steady, relentless downpour of grey rain. It looks like it'll never end, not until it just washes everything away and there's nothing left.

"I love you, Tara." I never expected to nor planned to say those words to a woman. I never actually said them to anyone, unless maybe to my mom and I don't remember it. But they just roll off my tongue, or from the bottom of my heart more like, and I mean it completely, it's the most true statement I've ever made, and probably ever will make again.

There's still rain in her eyes as she looks at me, but it's abating, tiny rays of sunshine filtering through.

She stands, takes a tentative step towards me, but

changes her mind. The silence is so absolute it's like everyone else just died in some apocalypse or something, and we're the only people left in the world. A lot depends on what she says next, more than I'm willing to admit. My sanity chief among it.

"I...I..." she stammers, but then squares her shoulders and looks directly at me. "I love you too, Tommy."

I grab her and kiss her, pouring all my relief, all my passion for her, all that I never thought I'd ever feel for a woman into that kiss. And she returns it in kind, letting go completely for the first time. It's as though a wall comes crashing down between us, and we're finally standing victorious in the rubble.

"How about we start this over?" I ask later. "I thought we could go down to the lake, since it's fucking hot out today."

She looks up at me, nothing but bright sunshine in her eyes now. "Yes, that's a fantastic idea."

CHAPTER TWENTY-TWO

TARA

We haven't spoken much since we got in the car, but we're almost at the lake now, and I want to apologize for the way I acted, and for letting the darkness get the better of me. Yet I can't quite find the words. But it was for the last time. Today was it's last and final attempt to drag me back under all that hurt and sadness.

I'm leaning against him as he drives, his arm wrapped around my shoulder. My hand's resting on his taut, muscular thigh, the denim of his jeans coarse against my palm. I don't think I've ever been this at peace in my entire life.

"I didn't just say I love you because you said it first, you know?" I tell him as he's getting the blanket and the bag with our towels and stuff from the back of the truck. "I would've said it anyway."

His eyes lock on my face for a second, and it feels like he actually caressed my cheek. "I know."

He heads down the ravine toward the lake, and I fall in step beside him. "And I didn't mean all those things I said either. You've already given me more than I ever hoped to receive."

He glances at me and smiles, but there's a tightness around his eyes that I don't quite understand. "You weren't completely wrong in your assessment though."

His words land in the pit of my stomach like a bag filled with stones. Of course I was right, he *is* a criminal, but does it really have to change anything? The old Tara would have said yes immediately. But the new me would do anything to keep Tommy. Even break the law. It never did a thing for me, so what do I even still owe? Do I have to sacrifice the only person who's ever made me happy just so I can say I've done the right thing, the proper thing, the legal thing? Just so I'll still be obeying an arbitrary set of rules, which never protected me from years of pain and abuse. Not the way Tommy has.

"I'm leaving the MC," he says. My mind's still

reeling from all those hard questions and bitter real-
izations, so his words don't immediately register.

"You're what?" I ask.

"I'm getting out, starting over," he explains rather
breathlessly.

He's gazing at me very intently, not even looking
where he's stepping. I trip on a stone and almost fall.
But he reaches out, catches me before there's any
chance of that happening.

"But can you just do that? Leave, I mean." It goes
against everything I know about motorcycle clubs.

He frowns, releasing my arm and continuing his
trek down the ravine. "No, they won't just let me go.
I'll have to disappear."

The lake shore finally opens before us, but even
all that beauty can't chase away the darkness filling
my mind. "And if they find you they'll...?"

I can't finish that sentence, can't bring myself to
utter the words.

"They'll probably kill me," he says matter-of-
factly, like we're just discussing the weather.

He dumps the stuff he's carrying on the ground
and grins at me. "But I'll make damn sure that doesn't
happen. Let's go swimming now."

He's doing it again. Calming me with his reas-
suring certainty, going for lightness even in the face

of this terrible prospect he just unveiled for me. But it's madly contagious, this ability to let go of the dark and just stay in the light. It's something I've never been able to do before I met him, nor really wanted to, since I thought clutching onto the pain was the right thing to do. But all I want now is to feel good. And it really is as simple as letting him take my hand and lead me into the water.

We don't do much swimming. We just kiss for a long time, my legs and arms wrapped around his strong body, only a thin film of water separating us. This weightlessness mirrors what I feel inside me perfectly, the world outside and the world within blending seamlessly, everything finally the way it should be.

Once it gets too cold in the water, we move outside, lay side by side on the blanket, kissing some more. I've touched every inch his perfect torso, his glorious arms, his stunning face, his strong neck, since we got here. I've also memorized all of his many tattoos, and I know every bump created by his muscles by heart. He's done the same with my body. We're like two blind people getting to know each other. Though all I really need to know I already do. It's all around us, in this sweet, pleasant yet charged energy passing between us, in his love pouring into me through his kisses, and mine flowing right back.

"Want to take this up a notch?" he asks, smirking at me. His cock is rock hard, and I want to touch it, want to taste it.

But we're not alone at the lake. We might be alone in this little alcove, but others are nearby, I can hear them laughing and talking. Every once in a while a motor boat whizzes past, or someone comes paddling by on a SUP board or in a rowboat. Though those are getting to be few and far between, since the sun has already disappeared behind the hills bordering the lake.

I lift up out of his embrace. "Let's go for another swim so you can cool off. That should keep you from getting any more bright ideas."

I smile at him as I say it, and he's trying to look disappointed, but he can't quite fight down his own smile.

"Fine, you go on," he says.

"You're not coming?" I ask, and there's no hiding the disappointment in my voice.

"I am," he says, smirking. "But first I want to watch that perfect ass of yours as you walk down to the water."

He squeezes my butt cheek to accentuate his

statement, and I feel so desired, so wanted, that I almost reconsider, almost tell him he can take me anyway he wants to, right here on this shore.

But that'll keep. I kiss him again, then walk to the water, glancing back over my shoulder every few steps to see if he's really watching, to see some more of that desire in his eyes. But I didn't really need to check, since I could feel his eyes on me the whole way.

Twilight is making everything look washed out, grey and two-dimensional as we sit by the water later. I'm leaning against him, my head resting against his shoulder, our fingers laced together in his lap. And I'm trying hard to hold onto my happiness, but it's fading as fast as the daylight.

"I'm starting to accept that I might never see my sister again," I say.

He grips my hand tighter but doesn't reply, doesn't even look at me.

"And that scares me, as much as it makes me sad and angry," I continue into the silence.

"I know what you mean," he says, still just looking off into the distance. "But you shouldn't lose hope yet. If she was seen alive six months ago, chances are good she still is."

"Are they?" I ask quietly.

"I understand where you're coming from though," he says, not answering my question. "I know what it's like to be angry over something you can never change or fix. But that shit just eats you up inside."

What does he really know about my pain? Him and his kind might be taking advantage of Sam right now. No, not him. And certainly not his kind. I want to believe him, want his words to just comfort me, not open any more terrible, unthinkable questions.

"And it can destroy you," he goes on. "Trust me. I've been struggling with the first line of the serenity prayer for years. Though I'm getting better at two and three."

God, grant me the serenity to accept the things I cannot change,

Courage to change the things I can,

And wisdom to know the difference.

I used to recite that to myself constantly for awhile, after I first heard it during therapy long after I'd given up on God. It sounds so freeing, so attainable, and I like to think I got it down at least to the point where I understand that forgiveness will bring me peace.

"What's the thing you can't change that trips you up?" I ask. "Aren't you planning to leave the MC behind?"

I still don't know if that means he's planning to leave me behind too. I was afraid to ask, since the wrong answer would crush me, so I just let it go as I surrendered to the bliss that was this afternoon. But that's fading fast with the light now. I'd go with him if he asked. There's no part of me that resists that. But he hasn't asked, and I'm growing very frightened he isn't planning to.

He looks at me like my question shocked him. But his eyes are searching my face, not glimmering in anger.

"I am," he says, looking back at the water. "But that might still not help completely."

He's speaking so cryptically, I don't even know what to ask. It feels like he'd rather not tell me, so I probably shouldn't even try to force it out of him. But he sounds like he wants to talk about it, so maybe I should.

"You seem very put together to me," I say, choosing a middle of the road approach, letting him know I'll listen, but not trying to drag anything out of him.

"For the last four years or so, sure, but before that I was totally out of control, did way too many drugs, spent days and nights high, and I did a lot of bad things. I don't even remember most of it, but the stuff

I do remember is horrible enough. And it was all because I was so fucking angry."

"At what?" I say automatically, without thinking. He needs to talk about this. And I'm here to listen. I'll always be here to listen. I want him to know that.

"I don't even know if I should tell you," he says, looking at me again. I hope he can read in my face how much I'm here for him if he needs me. "It's not a pleasant story. And I haven't talked about it very often."

"My story wasn't very pleasant either," I say. "Yet you listened, and you stuck around. I'm tough, I can handle anything."

I said the last as a joke, to lighten the mood, make it easier for him to talk.

"I know you are," he says, smiling at me. "You're a lot stronger than me."

I open my mouth to argue, because he's wrong, I'm fragile and brittle, at least I was until I met him. But he lays his fingers over my lips to stop me.

"I'm still angry at my father, even though he's been dead for thirteen years. I wish I was the one to kill him, but I never got that chance and it tore me up inside for years. It still bothers me on my darker days."

"We have that in common too, then," I say, smiling. "Minus the killing and dead part. What did your father do?"

I meant it as a way to lighten the mood, but it came out somber as though we're at a funeral. Because that's exactly what it feels like right now.

"He strangled my mom and made me watch to teach me how women are just disposable beings, and how they should be put down the moment they get out of line." He says it all in a rush, not even pausing for breath, the panic, fear, sadness, confusion, dread rising inside me at his words nowhere near the peak yet already unbearable. "I was ten years old, I didn't understand shit, and by the time I did, it was too late. She was dead and I did nothing to stop him from killing her. I'll never be able to live with that comfortably."

He glances at me, but looks away immediately, probably scared off by the shock that must be plain on my face.

"That's so...that's..." but I can't find a word strong enough to describe what he just told me. What he lived through.

"Horrible?" he says. But that doesn't even come close.

"What happened to him? Did he go to jail?"

"No, nothing happened to him," he says. "I don't

even know where my mom is buried. He was old, almost seventy, and died a couple of years later of a heart attack. I didn't speak much to him after it happened."

"I can imagine," I blurt out to fill the silence, to let him know I'm still here, still listening, that I am strong enough to hear all this, that it doesn't kill me inside, make me want to hide and cry. Though it does. But my wish to stay by his side, make it all better for him is stronger.

"My mom was trafficked too, just like your sister," he says. "But my father liked her, took her for his own. She was only seventeen when she had me. It could've turned out alright for her if my father wasn't such a women-hating psycho. Or if she kept her head down, and did what she was told to do. But that wasn't my mom. She was a fighter."

He chuckles a little as he says it, gazing off into the distance, his eyes no longer just sad and angry, but kind of happy and proud too. I understand now what he meant when he told me how she taught him to treat all women like princesses. She wanted to make sure he didn't end up like his father.

"So I have her to thank," I say, squeezing his hand tighter. I wish she was still alive, so I could thank her in person.

"Yeah." He turns to me, his eyes darker, scarier than the blackest night right now. "And I want you to know that finding your sister and saving her if she's being forced into prostitution is personal for me. The MC hasn't been running whores since my mom died, my father abolished all that, thinking that would make it right between us again. And I'll do everything I can to stop it, if it's happening again. I'm not just doing it because I want to keep fucking you."

His words sting, but I know it's just anger talking right now, because he's forced himself to relieve all those terrible memories. And I know I'm the one who needs to create the lightness now, needs to chase away his darkness the way he's done so many times for me.

"What did you even mean, saying we never fucked?" I ask snappishly. "I remember that very differently. In fact, I'll never forget last night, for example. Not even when I'm old and senile."

He grins at me, kissing the top of my head. "I just meant you haven't really let me fuck you the way I want to, which is also the way you really need it."

What is he even talking about?

"Is that your expert opinion then, given your wealth of experience in the field?"

He laughs, releasing my hand and wrapping his

arm tightly around me. "Yes, I am very experienced. So you should just trust me."

His voice still sounds weighed down, but it's getting lighter.

"Alright, doctor," I say. "I trust you."

He releases me, and stands offering me his hand. "Let's go then. It's getting dark anyway, and snakes are gonna start coming out."

I smile wryly at his bad pun and let him pull me to my feet. "There's snakes during the day too. They like to sunbathe on boulders."

He shakes like he's trying to get rid of a bad thought. "Don't even say things like that."

I laugh at him, and it's a free, melodic sound, not the strained, choked one I'm used to hearing. He smiles at me, softly and serenely, like he knows it too, knows that my laugh, my carefree laugh is finally back. I thought I lost it forever.

"Just so we're clear," he says as we're walking back to the car. "You can still be on top sometimes, but it's not gonna be all the time anymore."

Oh, that's what he means. It's true that we've only done it with me on top until now, because I've been too frightened by him holding me down. But I absolutely yearn to feel his weight on top of me right now.

"Whatever you say, Doc," I say, but he's too focused on checking the underbrush for snakes to look back at me and smile. But I still know he's looking forward to being alone with me in his bed almost as much as I am.

CHAPTER TWENTY-THREE

TARA

The sky is still tinged a soft purple as we exit the car at Crystal's, a few tiny stars shimmering here and there.

"What? You wanna watch the sky some more?" Tommy asks gruffly, but I know he's just joking.

"Nope," I say and smile at him coyly, loving the tense energy borne of anticipation coiling between us.

He grabs my hand and practically drags me to the back door.

Before I know it, I'm pinned against the door of his apartment, the loud music from the bar thumping through my body, accentuating the volleys of desire racking through me from his kisses, his touches, caresses and squeezes. We're breathless and naked before long, skin to skin, our tongues entwined, battling a friendly battle, but fierce nonetheless.

He's all passion right now, kissing me, touching me as though it's the only thing he wants to be doing, the only thing he ever wanted to do and ever will. And it's contagious, makes me yearn the be swallowed by all that passion, taken under, consumed. My whole body's awash with desire, yet it's still mounting, reaching peaks, traversing them, climbing new ones, higher ones. I can't even spot the darkness from up here.

His lips leave mine, and he grabs my arm, pulls me to the bed and tosses me down onto it, my giggles quickly stifled by his urgent kiss, and the weight of his strong body pushing me down into the mattress. My hands are tangled in his hair, pulling him closer, because I don't want any space between us, not even a breath's worth, none at all.

He shifts his weight partly off me, and I'm about to protest, pull him back. But then his fingers find my pussy, and I forget all else. He kisses me deeper, as he plays with my clit, pinching it, stroking it, leaving me yearning to be filled. His tongue invades my mouth as he pushes two fingers into my pussy, making me shudder, moan and gasp for air.

He pays no heed, hooks his fingers inside my pussy, starts pumping them in and out fast, then faster, hitting some until now unknown pleasure spot inside me. I'm shrieking, moaning, screaming, twisting my nails as I grab the sheets, my body taut and tense, and still my orgasm just lasts and lasts, doesn't abate, until all I am is one giant ball of nerve endings stimulated at once, the pleasure he's giving me so intense it burns through me like electric shocks, the pain and pleasure unbearable yet all I ever want to feel. He's no longer kissing me, just watching my face as I come, harder and harder, until my voice is coarse, and I nearly forget to breathe.

He finally gives me a moment of respite, kissing my neck, my heaving chest, as I struggle to regain control of my breathing. He's still stroking my clit, but the pleasure is soft now, pervasive yet mellow, easy.

I gasp as his cock starts entering me, sliding in slowly, deliberately, meeting no resistance, and opening me up so completely, I'm afraid I'll just break open. No, not afraid, I'm not afraid.

"You OK?" he asks, and I nod, biting down on my lip to keep from coming again.

I want to savor this moment for as long as I can, be present. But it's no use, not once he starts thrusting into me, the entire length of his cock sliding in and out of my pussy. I feel every bump, every vein, see stars, constellations, comets whizzing by. The sound of his jagged breaths and groans, the feel of his hips pumping his cock into me, his hands gripping my wrists, pushing them into the mattress are the only things keeping me grounded, keeping me from just floating away into the stars.

There's no fighting this orgasm, so I stop trying to, just let it consume me. It explodes with such power, I burst into a million specks of brilliant light, become one with the shimmering stars. But it will all come together again, better than before, forming a new Tara.

I'm lying in his arms later, nestled so close I'm not even sure where I end and he begins. He's kissing me softly, playing with my hair, stroking my back, and I'm trying not to doze off, because I don't want this day to ever end.

His hand comes to rest on my butt, squeezing slightly.

"You know how that first night you said I could do anything with you," he asks. "Did you mean that?"

I was a completely different person then, can't even fully remember the way I thought. But I do know my offer wasn't sincere, and that shames me now.

"What would you like to do?"

"I don't know, anal?" he asks, chuckling.

I glide my hand across his stomach, making his breath hitch.

"You don't ask for much, do you?" I ask, trying to sound terse, but I feel so soft, so light that I'm not succeeding at all.

He chuckles again, kissing the top of my head. "I just thought I'd put that out there. You know, something for you to think about."

"Alright, I'll think about it," I whisper.

I don't think I can ever refuse him anything, and it's as scary as it is freeing. Because I know he would never ask me for anything I can't give.

TOMMY

I dream of someone drilling through the walls of my apartment, before I finally wake up enough to realize it's my phone vibrating. It's still completely dark outside.

Tara is sleeping on my left arm, which has no

feeling in it as a result, and I have to use my right one to pull it from under her. But damn, I'd even let that happen all over again, that's how much I love her. The feeling just came out of nowhere, but now it's all I know, and all I ever want to feel from now until forever.

She murmurs something, but then just rolls over and goes on sleeping. Whoever's calling right now is gonna get a talking to. Though it couldn't be that many people. It's probably Shade, and that's the only reason I'm even getting up to answer it.

The phone has stopped vibrating, and it was Shade, I realize as I pull it from my jeans' pocket. He's called twenty-four times already.

I don't bother getting dressed as I slip out into the hall, closing the door behind me slowly, so I don't wake Tara.

"Finally," Shade snaps as he picks up. "Didn't we have the talk about you answering my phone calls promptly?"

"We did talk about that, and we decided I get to do what I want." I should be more apologetic, but he just makes it so fucking hard.

"Speaking of decisions...come to the Nest, I got one for you to make."

His cold, weird tone is finally starting to fully

register. He didn't call twenty-four times in the middle of the night because he needs me for a job, or to have a brotherly chat. It's something else.

"Why are you calling?" I ask.

"You'll see," he says. "But I think you better hurry."

I hear a dull noise in the background that sounds a lot like he's kicked something.

"What's going on, Shade?"

"Less questions, more coming over here, Tommy," he snaps and hangs up.

I dress quickly, only stopping long enough to check that Tara is still asleep and grab my keys.

I won't worry about this until there's something to worry about. But I have this nagging feeling that something's so wrong it might never get fixed again.

The parking lot in front of the Nest is dark, the newly planted trees swaying in the powerful gusts of wind. Only Shade's bike and a couple of the club trucks are parked outside, so he must be in there alone.

I find him opening a new bottle of Jack behind the bar as I enter, his face in shadow, since he's illuminated from behind by the bright light in the hallway that leads to the back rooms.

"Finally," he says, grabbing the bottle and

retreating down the hall that leads to his office. "Follow me."

I smell blood, but that could just be my overactive imagination. Because right now I'm only seeing all the ways this visit could go wrong.

"You know Simone, right?" he asks just as I reach the door into the conference room, and it takes every ounce of self-control I ever had not to recoil and back out of the room.

Simone is lying in a puddle of her own blood, her dress ripped and pulled up high over her hips. Her face is a mass of blood and bruises. But she's still alive, I can tell by the tiny bubbles forming over what used to be her nose.

"What the fuck did you do?" The rage starting to boil inside me is making my voice cold and cutting. I could always control my voice, but never my fists. And right now, I want to beat up Shade as badly as he beat up Simone, or worse. I have no doubt he was the one that did it. The knuckles on his right hand are bruised black and blue, caked over with blood.

"I knew you wouldn't approve," he says, pouring himself a glass of Jack as though a woman isn't dying on the floor at his feet. "But she came here with some tall tales about how you're betraying me behind my back for that new piece of ass working at Crystal's. I couldn't have her spreading that shit about you, but I need the truth from you now. Are you looking for some whore of mine with the intent of stealing her from me?"

"What you need is to call an ambulance," I bark, glaring at him, so I don't have to look at Simone.

"You always were too soft with women. I blame Dad for that, he let you spend too much time with that whore of your mother." I'm barely able to keep it together, one more word and I'll fucking strangle him. "He should've gotten rid of her sooner."

"You're even sicker than he was," I spit. "I'm taking Simone to the hospital. You wanna stop me, now's your chance. See how well you do against a man, not some 100 pound woman in heels."

He's glaring, but he's not really considering taking me up on my offer. I'm younger than him, taller than him and a lot more vicious. He knows all that.

"Didn't think so," I say, bending over to pick up Simone. She used to be so light in my arms, once upon a time, but she's as heavy as a log right now. And I don't even know if she's still breathing. But I need to get her away from Shade, need to get myself away from him too. And Tara, and Crystal and all her girls. And all the girls he's got locked up God knows where.

I'm half-expecting him to shoot me in the back as I walk down the hall, but he doesn't even try to stop me. Nor does he follow me outside. I knew he wouldn't do any of those things, he's too much of a coward, prefers to get others to do his dirty work.

I take one of the trucks, drive like a maniac to the hospital, calling Crystal on the way, telling her to meet me there.

But she's not there yet when I reach the ER, and even though nothing good will come from me carrying Simone inside, I don't even think twice about it. I just carry her right in through the front door, her blood soaking into the patches on my cut.

They take her from me, rush her somewhere. No one stops me as I walk out. And I do want to stay, find out if she'll make it, but there's no time. Shade will have had time to think now and plan his next move. He might have already sent some of his guys to grab Tara from the club, though I'm counting on him not wanting to start an open war with me in that way. No, he'll go after me first.

Crystal is running towards the hospital entrance just as I exit.

"What happened, Tommy?" she asks, her hand flying to her mouth as she sees the blood.

"Simone told Shade about Tara looking for her sister, and me helping her. The worst fucking mistake she ever made," I say. "I should've stopped her."

"She said something about that to me too, but she never mentioned going to Shade," Crystal says, shaking now. "Is she alright?"

"No she's not fucking alright. She has no face left," I bark, but reconsider my tone when I see the stark pain covering Crystal's face, or what's left of it. "Go in now and see if she's alright. Take care of her, I'll pay for it."

She grabs my arm as I pass her to leave, gripping tight. "Shade runs a high-end escort service out of Vegas. Maybe Tara's sister is there."

Her good eye is very wide as she tells me, probably expecting me to yell at her for knowing this secret and for speaking out of line. But I really just want to hug her. So that's what I do, because I love her and there's no reason to try and hide that anymore. After my mom died, and with the way she died, for the reasons she did, I was afraid to get too close to any woman, even Crystal, who practically raised me after it happened. Not only so *I* wouldn't get hurt, but so no one would hurt them because of me.

The guilt I felt over my mom's death was too much to bear, I couldn't handle it, so I put it all squarely on my father's shoulders, where most of it belonged anyway. But I remember it now. And I am guilty if I just stand by and do nothing as Shade treats all these poor women worse than my father did. It took Simone getting almost beaten to death to make me see that, but I see it now. And I need to get Tara away from here before all my worst fears come true all over again. Then I'll deal with Shade. And I need to make sure Crystal leaves too.

"Once you take care of Simone, get out of town. Take the others with you too," I say. "Make them, if they won't go willingly."

I don't know what I'm gonna do to fix all this, but it might get worse before it gets better.

"I'm staying, Tommy," she says, giving me a firm squeeze and then releasing me.

I shake my head. "No, Crystal. You have to leave. Shade is too dangerous, and we're not the best of friends right now. He might come after you because he thinks I betrayed him."

She taps my cheek. "Don't worry about that. I have Bear. Shade wouldn't dare go against him, or me and my club. The other members won't let him, and they certainly won't help him do it."

"I hope you're right, "I mutter. And she could be, Bear did ride with my grandfather, the Viper. But Shade is insane and bloodthirsty as hell, and he has a whole section of the MC that's loyal only to him.

"I am right, Tommy."

I try to warn her again, tell her to be careful at least, but she gives me no chance to, as she rushes through the sliding doors into the ER.

Tara's still sleeping peacefully when I return, the club completely quiet and dark. But it's getting light out, and Shade won't wait much longer before he comes here looking for us.

I change quickly, stuff my bloody clothes and my ruined cut into a garbage bag and toss it into the back of my closet. I hope Shade finds it, knows that I'll never fucking follow his psycho leadership after tonight. I'll tell him all that in person eventually, but right now I need to get Tara out of his reach.

"Come on, wake up," I whisper, shaking Tara awake gently. There's no trace of tears on her cheeks, and I hope that's how it stays forever from now on.

She finally opens her eyes and blinks at me. "What is it?"

"I thought we could go to Vegas," I say, plastering the widest smile on my face.

"What? Where?" she asks, sitting up and rubbing her eyes before looking out the window. "It's barely light out."

"Yeah, I know," I say, kissing her pouty lips because I can't help myself. Even the horror of what just happened is fading fast now that she's awake. "But this way we'll get there nice and early, maybe have time to go swimming in the pool before hitting the casinos. Come on, it'll be fun."

She smiles at me, her eyes sparkling, the sun rising fast and bright in them. "OK, yeah. It might be fun."

She gets out of bed. "I'll go pack."

"Don't take too much," I say, grinning at her.

My plans for what I'll do next are very vague. But they might involve getting her drunk enough to marry me tonight. Then she'll be mine for real. There's such a small chance of ever finding her sister in Vegas that I won't even mention she might be there to her, not yet. Not until I decide on a plan.

There's other ways of finding her sister and making sure she's returned home safely. Ways that sour my stomach just thinking about. But if Tara's my wife, I can take her anywhere with me. And that's the most important thing, all else are just empty words, promises I would never have made if given a choice. The only promises that matter to me are the ones I made to Tara.

CHAPTER TWENTY-FOUR

TARA

We've been driving in my rented truck for about two hours, and judging by the signs we still have about three hours to go before we get to Vegas. The only stop we made before leaving town was at a large house in a nicer part of town not far from the club. I watched the sun peek out from behind the distant hills while Tommy was inside the house, feeling nothing but contentment and bliss, peace. It waned just a little when he returned with a large black duffel beg, the muscles in his arm flexed and taut from the weight. He tossed it in the back seat and then we were off.

I think this is it. This is the day he leaves his life behind. But he hasn't said anything about it, hasn't asked me if I'm coming too, so I didn't mention it either. He took me with him, so in a way I already have my answer. I'd like to be asked, but it's not necessary.

We spent the first hour singing along to songs on the radio, and kissing as much as we can without crashing. Now I'm just leaning against him, handing him the cup of coffee I'm cradling in my lap from time to time, and watching the world whizz by. The sun's beating down on the car, but inside it's nice and cool, yet pleasantly warm too.

The fact that I'm so willing to leave without having found Sam is nagging at me though. And I don't know how to bring it up without causing another argument. He's done what he could to find her, I understand that, know it without him having to tell me. She's not anywhere where he can find her.

But I still feel like a traitor. Like I've let Sam down again, this time because of my selfish desire to just enjoy my time with Tommy. She'd want me to be happy, I know she would. But can I ever be truly happy at her expense.

"I can drive for awhile, if you want," I say, spotting a sign for a gas station coming up in a few miles. He seems so tired.

He looks at me, and then kisses my forehead. "Yeah, it might be for the best."

We pull into the gas station, and I climb over him to get behind the wheel. He stops me mid-effort, holds me tight in his lap and gives me an urgent, hungry kiss that makes my head spin. The passion in it belies his tiredness that was so evident just a few minutes ago, makes me want to get naked, feel his bare skin against mine, have his hands, his lips, his cock bring me to another earth-shattering orgasm.

His hands are already snaking up under my t-shirt, his rock hard cock pressing against my pussy, so we're on the same page, and I really wish I'd worn something else, something easier to get out of, one of my new dresses, instead of jeans and a tee.

"Why does there have to be so many people here?" I mutter in between returning his kisses, spotting a family of four goggling at us as they eat their sandwiches by their RV.

He chuckles and gives me another deep kiss, before removing me from his lap and sliding to the passenger side. "Let's just get to Vegas. There won't be any people in our hotel room."

It's hard to focus on the road, since my body is screaming for more of his touches and his kisses. It's still so new to me, this desire, this wish to be with a man, touched by a man, loved and made love to, yet somehow it feels like it was always there too. Like it was just obscured by all the darkness, and not missing at all.

"So, where will you go when you leave?" I ask.

He looks up from fiddling with his phone sharply, but I keep my eyes fixed on the road. I can't believe I just asked him that so pointedly.

"I'll have to disappear. For awhile at least," he says. "I was thinking South America first, and then Europe. I've always wanted to go there."

"Europe is nice," I mutter. It would be a whole lot nicer if my dad and his friends weren't there with me the times I visited Paris, London and Venice. But I won't think of that now. Those memories already feel like they're from another life, yet they're still horrible. I'd love to go to Europe with Tommy, make some better memories. But he's not asking me along.

"I was thinking it'd be great to get one of those mobile homes and just travel around for years, see it all. Go all the way across Europe, and then maybe to Asia." It sounds so perfect, so peaceful. I'd love it.

"You mean like an RV?" I don't know why my tone is so mocking. Maybe it's because he's just scrolling through his phone like he's already checked out of this conversation.

"Yeah, sorta, but I was thinking more along the lines of something cool like this." He shows me a picture on his phone. "It's a bus that these two love-birds converted into a home and now they're just driving around the world in it."

He flips through more photos, showing me the interior of the bus. And it looks so cozy, so modern, there's even a big kitchen, and the bedroom is this small nook, with only a large bed in it, sheltered from the rest of the world.

"You can get homes like this off Craigslist for pretty cheap," he says. "I checked. And then just put it on a ship and off you go."

"Looks great," I say, my voice choked up, my eyes burning like I'm about to start crying.

He's looking at me very intently, I can feel his eyes literally burning holes in my cheek.

"Well?" he finally asks.

"What? I already said it sounds like a great plan."

He puts the phone away, staring out through the passenger window. The silence drags, feels like it's sucking all the air from the car. Why did I even ask? I could've just enjoyed this trip while it lasted. Why did I have to go ruin it before it even got started?

He turns to me, his gaze so searching I have to meet his eyes, I'm powerless to stop myself. I still see all those worlds I never knew existed in his eyes, those glorious, distant lands full of adventure, desire and pleasure, happiness and peace. But it hurts to look at them now, because I already miss them.

"I know you have your whole life here, and that you need to find your sister," he says, his words coming very slowly, like he's measuring them out, trying to postpone saying them. "But would you come with me?"

"Yes!" I exclaim, and almost veer into the other lane.

He seems shocked by my answer, but he's smiling already. "Really?"

"Yes, really. I thought you'd never ask."

He kisses me, holding onto the wheel and keeping it steady, because he understands I'm not able to right now. The tension is gone, the air moving as though a thousand butterflies are fluttering their wings around us.

"I was scared to," he says sheepishly. "I thought you'd say no."

I shake my head vigorously. "I'd go anywhere with you...just as soon as we find Sam."

I add it as an afterthought, but I know it's a deal breaker, because that could take years.

What I need him to do is tell me confidently it

will happen any day now. But he can't promise me that, and that fact is plain in his stony face right now.

"Yeah, as soon as we find your sister," he says, but quietly, lost in thought. Probably already regretting he even asked me.

He doesn't say anything else, just leans back and closes his eyes. So I don't say anything either, just drive, trying to think of nothing. But I'm already imagining all those old world buildings and castles in Europe whizzing past us. I hold on to that happy thought until it's all I know, and everything else is just fading memories of another life, one I never want to return to.

We arrive to Vegas just after two PM, and despite the midday heat the strip is awash with people, all wide-eyed and smiling, rushing to and fro, excitedly admiring the glitter around them. I've never been here, only seen pictures, and I can't wait for it to get dark, so I can see all the lights.

I nudge Tommy awake, since he slept the rest of the way here, as we approach the huge fountain in front of one of the hotels. "Check that out."

"Nice, right?" he says grinning at me. "But it looks even better at night."

He rubs his eyes then yawns loudly. We're just inching along the strip, since there's so much traffic.

"I bet you've seen it a thousand times," I mutter, my eyes still fixed on the dance of water.

"I don't know about a thousand, but I've been here a few times, yeah," he says, moving closer to me and wrapping his arm around my shoulders. All the tension between us is gone. We're just two lovers here to have a good time. And I mean for us to have a very good time.

"Let's just see if they have a room here," he says, pointing at the hotel the fountain is attached to.

"Why not indeed?" I say. "Seems as good a place as any."

I wink at him, and then his lips are on mine, the desire rising inside me mixing with the excitement all around us into a blinding, breathtaking combination.

Loud honking pulls us apart. I've forgotten to watch the line of cars in front of us, and left a huge gap. The driver of the car behind us is yelling something I can't hear, but which can't be very nice. I accelerate, pull up to the hotel.

The receptionist smiles widely, offers us a newlyweds suite, and I know I'm blushing as Tommy says yes. I've been to a ton of fancy hotels in my life, but I never enjoyed it this much, never enjoyed it at all. Whatever happens after today, I want tonight to be perfect.

Our suite is all done up in light pastel shades of white and pale pink, blue and green. It's romantic, but not tacky, and I feel like I just walked into a dream. My dream. One I forgot I ever even had.

The view is of the fountain, and I just stand there gazing at the delicate interplay of water for awhile, thinking about how it would feel to stand under those jets, feel the water land against my skin. Tommy comes over, wraps his arm around my shoulders and pulls me close.

"We'll find your sister, you'll see," he says, and I want to believe him. But I'm also annoyed he brought it up again, which is immediately followed by a surge of guilt, and all those conflicting emotions are now wrapped up in a soft haze of desire that his hard body pressed against mine is stoking higher and higher.

"How can you be so sure?" I ask.

"I always get lucky in Vegas."

The sharp remark I was gonna make is just wiped clean from my mind as I look up at him.

Those worlds I want to visit are there, bathed in moonlight, beckoning to me from his eyes. So I don't say anything, just believe, because I now know miracles are possible.

"How about we try out the bed?" he asks, grinning at me.

I grin too and nod, take his hand, lead him to the bed and lie down. The mattress is soft like clouds, standing in perfect contrast to the hardness and the weight of his body pressing me into it. His kisses are sending waves of pleasure through my entire being, and feel like the calmest evening breeze, taste like the clearest waters.

We just kiss, for a long time, lost in this oneness we share, this perfect dream that weaves itself around us whenever we're alone. He takes off my shirt, and I help him out of his. And then we kiss some more. Our jeans follow, and then we kiss some more, our bodies pressed so close there is no space left between us.

There is no urgency to do anything more than just kiss, not on my part and not on his. His hands and his lips are exploring my skin, and mine are mapping his. We have time, so much time. Around us the whole world is still, waiting for us. And I love just enjoying the soft, pleasant heat radiating all through my body from the smoldering, glowing embers of our desire.

"How about we get some dinner now?" he asks once the sky outside turns a dusty pink. "Because if we don't stop soon, we won't be leaving the hotel room tonight."

"You're right," I say, resting my head against his chest. "And maybe we can hit a casino too."

I shoot up right after I suggest it, staring at the large shopping bag that contains all I packed.

"What?" he asks grinning at me.

"I don't have anything to wear." I packed some of the new dresses, but none are fancy enough for what I want to do tonight. "And I bet you didn't either."

His hand slithers down my side, comes to rest on my ass. "I pictured this more as a clothes optional sorta getaway."

"I bet you did," I say, giving him a peck on the lips then climbing off the bed. "But we're going shopping."

He groans, but doesn't put up much of a fight.

"There's a couple of floors dedicated to shopping right here in the hotel," he says, checking the information guidebook while I'm combing out my tangled hair.

"Everything's bound to be super overpriced here,"

I say, not even sure why I care. But despite always having more money than I could spend at my disposal, I was always a cheapskate. Sam's words, not mine.

"Let's not overthink this, and just do that." Tommy says and sets down the guidebook, then unzips his duffel bag, his back turned. He pulls out a wad of money, all hundreds, and I can clearly see there's a lot more of it in there. In fact that's all that's in there.

But I won't ruin the mood again by asking him to explain. He's absolutely right, I mustn't overthink this.

The first store we pass has a gorgeous, flowing turquoise dress in the window. It looks like something movie stars in the fifties wore only a lot more daring, with its low v-shaped neckline, and an impossibly high split along the left side.

"You should try that on," Tommy says, chuckling as I look at him in shock.

"My boobs would fall right out," I protest, but I do like his suggestion.

"Yeah, that too, but it would also go great with

your eyes." He's got the biggest grin on his face as he says it.

"No one would notice my eyes if I wore that," I say, my eyes sliding back to the dress, some of my old fears of getting lewd looks starting to creep in at the edges of my mind.

"I would notice," Tommy says softly, chasing the fear away, leaving behind only a soft waterfall of love.

"Alright, let's do it," I say, charging into the store like I'm about to attack. Which in a way I am. Attacking my fears, meeting them head on, not letting them control me anymore.

I look good in the dress, even if I do think so myself, and it is very sexy. But the second Tommy's eyes take me in as I walk out of the changing room, I know I'm buying it. And a hundred more like it, just so he'll always look at me like that.

I find a pair of silver stiletto sandals to go with it, then start scanning the store for a suit for Tommy.

"Suits are for funerals," he grumbles, following me around, but showing no enthusiasm for actually trying on any of the ones I show him

"And for weddings," I counter, and I actually feel the air shift as he looks at me sharply. He knows I meant our wedding, and it probably scared him. I don't know much about men, but I heard they're very scared of commitment. So I won't mention marriage again. I was only joking anyway...for now.

"Try this one," I say, shoving a light grey silk suit into his arms, my voice shaky.

He does as he's told without even grumbling about it this time.

"You look very handsome," I say, walking up to him as he emerges from the dressing room, and smoothing down his lapels. "You should wear a suit more often,

He wraps his arm around my lower back, pulls me close, his hard cock jabbing me in the belly. "Any-thing for you, Tara."

He chuckles as he says it, but I know he means it. There's no doubt in my mind that he means it.

CHAPTER TWENTY-FIVE

TOMMY

At least she didn't say no, said she'd come with me when I left. And she meant it. I know she did. But she wants to know her sister is alright before she does, I get that.

She's taking a shower now, and I can just barely make out the outline of her perfect curves through the steam covered shower door. Everything inside me is screaming to go join her. But I have something to do first. Something I should've done before now. Right after she told me Shade might be holding her sister prisoner.

So I somehow manage to peel my eyes from her, and step out into the hallway to make the call. It rings and rings, until I'm sure he won't even pick up.

"Where the hell are you, Tommy?" Shade says into the phone. "We have some talking to do."

"Yeah, we do," I say.

"I'm glad you're seeing sense again," he interrupts, completely misinterpreting my meaning, though as it turns out, I am finally seeing sense. Just not the kind he's thinking of.

"I want to know where you're holding Tara's sister," I say. "It's better that you just tell me."

"Who the fuck is Tara, and who is Tara's sister?" he snaps.

"You know who I'm talking about. Her sister is a pretty brunette with blue eyes that looks a lot like my mom. She was seen in your company at Christmas at the Nest, and she's been missing longer than that. I think you know where she is, and I want you to tell me."

"Still not ringing any bells," he says. "You know how many whores I got working for me?"

"No," I say though I'd like to find out. Up until last night when Crystal told me had an escort service in Vegas, I didn't think he had any whores working for him yet. But I need to keep this conversation on track. "Think harder, or you won't have any."

The silence that follows makes me think he hung up.

"Is that some kind of threat, Tommy?" he asks slowly.

"Yes," I say, since there's no point denying it. I'm dead anyway, if I can't be with Tara. Nothing means more to me than keeping the promises I made to her. I feel rotten to the core just thinking about betraying the MC, but even that pales in comparison to a life without Tara in it. Not just pales, disappears.

"I know things, Shade, lots of things, things that'll put you in jail for life. And there are plenty of people who'd love to hear me tell them the full story. So I'll ask you again, where is Tara's sister?"

"You wouldn't betray me, or the MC, you wouldn't dare."

But he doesn't sound very certain of that at all.

"Don't make me do it," I say, surprised at how much I actually mean it.

"You should've been put down too," he yells. "Years ago. Along with your whore mother."

"Tell me what I want to know and let me walk away in peace. This is a one time offer."

"Fuck you!"

"Alright, suit yourself," I say. "But Shade, if anything happens to anyone I care about, I'll kill you. And I'll do it slowly."

He knows I mean all of what I said, I can hear it

in the gasp he's trying to hide, the silence that follows.

"If it means so much to you, I'll give you this girl you want to find," he says, a lot more complacently, though there's still an edge in his voice. "But I'll need a few days. Come back here, and we'll talk."

His initial anger at me has subsided, he's just trying to find a way to save the MC now. If I go back, I'll be walking into a bullet. But he doesn't have to know that I know.

"Fine, I'll be back in a couple of days," I say. "I expect you to have Tara's sister ready for me."

"Yes, yes," he says, sighing in exasperation. "You and your women."

He's given me enough. There's a chance he is holding her somewhere and selling her, since he didn't deny it outright. He can't save the MC now, or himself. I already made my final decision while I watched Tara twirl around in front of the mirror admiring her new dress. She'll get her sister back, and I'll give her—give us—the life we both deserve.

Tara is breathtakingly gorgeous in her new dress. I don't even notice any other woman in this whole restaurant, but I see the guys checking Tara out very clearly. And I'm both pissed off that they're looking and proud that she's mine, that she chose me. Though on the whole, I have trouble thinking about anything other than taking her back to our room upstairs, and ripping that dress off her.

But she deserves more than that, she deserves romance, flowers, gifts, candle-lit dinners, afternoons spent with me just kissing her perfect body. Which is why I won't be getting her drunk and asking her to marry me in some cheap all-night wedding chapel in Vegas. She deserves a diamond ring, a wedding on an exotic beach, or in a beautiful medieval cathedral in the heart of Europe. She deserves to be treated like a princess, which is exactly what she already looks like. There won't be many people attending our wedding, but just the two of us will be enough.

"What?" she says, sliding a lock of her honey colored hair back behind her ear and blushing a soft pink. She did something with her hair, pulled it all into a side bun and hiding that stupid undercut. No, that's not right. She could be bald, and I still couldn't keep my eyes off her. I love even her undercut.

"What?" I echo.

"You've just been staring at me since we sat down at this table," she says softly. "Why?"

She's wrong. I've just been staring at her since she got out of the shower and put on the dress, did her hair and makeup. But it has gotten worse since we sat down at this candle-lit table in the dining room.

"Because you're the most beautiful woman I've ever seen," I say, and it sounds so cheesy, but it encapsulates what I feel pretty well. Doesn't do it justice, but it comes close. "No, what I mean is that you're the most gorgeous, classy, smart and kind person I've ever met."

That doesn't sound much better, so she's right to be frowning at me. I can do better. I can find the right words to describe why I can't stop looking at her, and thinking about her, and why I don't ever want to stop doing either of those things. Or tell her how she makes me yearn to be a better man, the kind she deserves.

"Oh my God," she breathes more than says, her eyes suddenly growing very wide. She's looking right past me.

"What is it?" I ask, confused by her reaction.

"That's...that's Samantha."

She's out of her seat, rushing away from the table before I even turn fully. She's heading right for a brown-haired girl hanging on the arm of some puny businessman with glasses as they wait to be seated by the hostess. The girl doesn't notice Tara until she's right next to her, and then her face goes through so many emotions it's hard to tell what she's actually feeling. There's surprise, pain, happiness, fear, and that's just the ones I see before Tara wraps her arms around her, squeezing her tight. The businessman is still holding onto Samantha's arm, and there's only confusion on his face, nothing else.

I walk over, though I have no idea what I'll do. I told Tara luck always followed me to Vegas, but that was just a dumb line, yet somehow I was right.

"Tara, I can't believe this. Is it really you?" Samantha says, tears flowing from her eyes now. Tara nods enthusiastically, her whole body shaking, but at least she's not crying.

"I think our table is ready," the businessman says to Sam, eying me warily as I approach. When Sam sees me, she takes a step back, bumping into the hostess.

"Why don't you go sit at that table by yourself," I tell the businessman, and he lets go of Sam's arm like he's just gonna obey. But then his face settles on defiance. The idiot probably did a few lines of Coke before Sam was delivered to him, and it's making him brave now. But I'm not reluctant to start any kind of scene here.

"We have to go, Sam, right now," Tara is saying, pulling on her arm, but Sam won't budge. She's still looking at me warily, her eyes darting over the tattoos on my hands, and the ones on my neck, which the suit doesn't quite hide.

"It's OK, Sam, everything is gonna be OK now. Tommy's with me," Tara says, glancing back at me as though looking for support, or maybe for confirmation, like she's still not sure I'd actually do anything for her. I would. I would do absolutely anything for her. Even let her go, if that's what it takes. I'm not planning to, but I would.

"Yeah, let's go," I say, nodding at Tara and hoping she understands I really mean it.

Sam visibly relaxes as Tara wraps her arm around her and starts to lead her out of the dining room.

"Hey, I paid for the whole night," the business says, his voice shrill.

I glare at him. "We should let the girls talk. Go wait at your table. Or are we gonna have a problem?"

Most of the patrons are staring at the scene we're causing, but I don't think any of them are here tonight just to make sure Sam does her job. Though they might be. Any one of these well-dressed diners could actually be working for Shade. Though he probably has another way of keeping track of her. It doesn't really matter, since I'm sure the FBI station can't be far from here. And we probably have some time, since, as far as I can see, no one's getting up to follow Sam and Tara.

The man shakes his head and walks away, and I join Tara and her sister by the door. We could be stopped at any time as we try to get out of this hotel, but I don't let any of that into my voice as I tell them to follow me.

It's time to roll the dice and see how much my insurance will actually buy. Shade might have given me Samantha, though that was doubtful, but he certainly won't just let me take her.

TARA

Tommy's nervous, I can tell by the firm set of his jaw, and the way his eyes are so dark I see absolutely nothing in them. He's also not saying much. But it will be fine, all will be OK now that we found Sam.

"You don't know how much I missed you," I say,

hugging her again in the elevator as we're riding up to our room.

She's stiff in my arms, but she's leaning against me like my body's the only thing holding her upright.

"I missed you too," she says, her voice hollow. "I thought I'd never see you again."

It's a statement of pure fact, not a throwaway line, and the way she says it chills me to the bone. I don't know this silent, hollow-voiced Sam. Before, she was always talking, always smiling, always cracking jokes. Sarcastic ones mostly, but still. And now she's just leaning against me, stiff and shaking a little.

"Grab what you need and then we're going," Tommy says as he unlocks the hotel room door. He slings the duffel bag over his shoulder and grabs the smaller bag he packed his clothes in.

"We should change, don't you think?" I ask.

"No time, we can change in the car," he says picking up the shopping bag with my clothes too. "Is this all your stuff?"

I nod, even though all my makeup and other toiletries are still in the bathroom. And then he's preceding us back out of the room, renewed urgency in his step.

"Can we really trust him?" Sam whispers into

my ear.

He's already at the elevators, but I know he heard her, and is pretending he didn't.

"Yes," I whisper back. "I'm positive."

She eyes him warily, and he's still ignoring her. I know he's doing it to make her feel more at ease, and I love him so much for it my heart's about to burst.

We don't stop at reception, just ride all the way down to the garage where our car is parked. He paid for the room in cash when we arrived, so no one stops us.

"Sam, how do you feel?" I ask, once we're finally on the road. She's gripping my hand so tight that hers is shaking, while staring out the window blankly, and her odd behavior is starting to scare me. I've never seen my sister act like this, not since we were very young, not since our father first started touching her too. And that realization is bringing all the darkness back faster than I can fight it.

She made her peace with all that, much better than I did, lived a full life after we were finally freed from it, and to see her get sucked back down into the depths of that depression by this horrible thing she must have been through, hurts me like someone just slashed my chest open.

Tommy keeps glancing at us in turn, then

reaches into his pocket and hands me his phone.

"You said the FBI is looking for her?" he asks.

I have trouble thinking straight.

"Tara?" He says my name with such care, such concern, such compassion, that it rips through my fear like a ray of sunshine.

"Yes, they are," I answer.

"Find their address in Vegas, that's the safest place for you now."

I take the phone but don't turn it on. "They can't know she's gone yet, we can go home—"

"They know," he says. "If nothing else, that guy called them and asked for a refund."

Sam turns to us sharply, gripping my hand even tighter, her whole body shaking again.

"Just find the address," Tommy says. "I'll take care of it."

And the confidence is there in his voice, but it's not prevalent. And now I'm scared of losing them both, and I could never handle losing just one of them.

"Come on, Tara, you're strong, you got this," Tommy says, smiling at me, his face awash with the bright neon lights all around us. He kisses me after he says it, a soft whisper of warmth passing through my whole body, giving me the strength I need.

I find the address, and he takes us there.

"Go tell them who you are, insist you need protection," he says once we're standing by the entrance of the tall, dark FBI building that looks more menacing than any I've ever seen.

"You're not coming with us?" I ask, my voice breaking.

Sam's still clutching my hand, but that doesn't stop him from pulling me into a tight embrace, kissing me so urgently, so deeply, so hungrily that it feels like a goodbye forever kiss.

"Tara, I need to go and take care of this now, but I'll come get you as soon as I can," he says, but for the first time since I met him, I'm hearing an empty promise.

"Just stay with me now, come in with us." He's trying to move away from me and leave, but I'm clutching his waist so tightly he has no chance to.

"I can't, I need to take care of this," he says, firmly but not angrily. "Don't let them let you out of their sight. Call your father, he can use his connections to give you the protection you need."

I gasp at his suggestion, and Sam starts shaking harder. But Tommy's eyes never waver as he looks directly into mine.

"You can protect me," I say. "You're the only one

who can do that."

His eyes lose the edge as he cups my cheeks and kisses me again, slower this time, more lasting, and I can feel all the love I have for him, that he has for me in that kiss. It fills me to the brink, any more and I'd burst apart.

"I have to do this now, or you'll never be safe," he says. "Just trust me. Don't make this so hard."

But letting him go *is* hard. It's the hardest thing I ever had to do. And I can't do it. I can't just let him walk away. I can't face never seeing him again.

"Please, Tara," he whispers. "It will be OK, and I'll be back soon, I promise."

He's yet to make me a promise he didn't keep. So I nod, and let go of his waist. But it feels like a huge chunk of flesh was just ripped right from my chest, as I watch him drive away, and I don't know how I'm even still alive, because I should be bleeding to death.

"Oh my God, Tara, you're crying," Sam gasps, sounding almost like her old self for the first time since I found her.

And she's right, hot tears are streaming down my cheeks, more following. I haven't cried in over twelve years, but now I can't stop. And I might never stop, not until Tommy comes back for me.

CHAPTER TWENTY-SIX

TOMMY

At least she didn't cry. If she'd cried, I would have stayed, walked right in that building with her and told the FBI everything I know. But now that she has her sister back, and they're both safe with the Feds, other options are open. Ones that won't make me a rotten backstabber, won't make me betray the brothers. Because with the shit I know, they're all going down.

I can't let Shade run the MC. Not the way he wants to, which is exactly the same way my father ran it. But I can give him the chance to step down instead of destroying it all. Someone else can take over, someone who would follow the plan Blade had for the MC. I know there are still those loyal to him in the MC, and loyal to me. Guys who didn't want Shade to take over. The President position has been hereditary until now, passing from father to son to brother, but that's just the way it always was, not even a written rule. I'm leaving no matter what. I crave that quiet life with Tara, just the two of us traveling the world, with nothing to worry about except making each other happy. I've done enough worrying and hurting for five lifetimes, and so has she.

"Tell me that was some other blonde chick and black haired thug that took one of my whores," Shade says as he picks up the phone, his voice shaking from the strain of trying to control it.

"It wasn't someone else." Back when he was VP, and I just one of the enforcers, I used to love goading Shade just to get a rise out of him. Because when he gets mad, his eyes bulge, the veins on his neck pop out, and his face turns three different shades of red. I'm pretty sure this is all happening right now.

"How'd you even find her?"

"Pure luck," I tell him.

"You stepped too far out of line now, Tommy. I might have given her to you, but you can't just take what's mine. You're either with me now, or you're against me. Make your choice."

"I want you to step down as President, let

someone else take over. That's my choice, take it or leave it. Or I go to the cops and tear it all down." My heart's racing in my throat as I make this demand, grows faster as he laughs a guttural laugh any villain would be proud of. "I won't be a part of any establishment that sells human beings."

"Whores are not human beings. And you don't make demands of me," he says. "You apologize to me."

"No, Shade, you don't understand. Either you go, or everything goes."

He stops his growling, and the silence that follows is tense, charged.

"Let's stop pretending you'll carry out your threats, Tommy. We both know you won't betray anyone. Hurry back and you might still make it in time," he says, and I can hear the smile that must be on his face.

"In time for what?"

"Just hurry back and we'll talk in the morning," he says. "Drive safe now."

He hangs up, doesn't pick up when I call back. But I keep trying. I call Crystal too, and the club, but no one's picking up. I finally get Brett on the line after trying at least thirty times.

"Where the hell are you, Brett?"

"In Tijuana, man, with the hottest little redhead

you've ever seen. Her name's Candy, and it fits her perfectly," he says, his voice thick with bravado and having a good time. "What do you need?"

"Never mind, you just stay in Mexico. Don't come back."

I could use him tonight, but I'm glad he's out of harm's way. At least one of my friends will be saved from whatever happens after tonight.

"What are you talking about?" Brett says, his tone completely serious now, and more than a little worried.

"I'm sorry, but there's no other way. Don't come back until I tell you to, is that clear?"

"Yes, but—"

"No buts, I'll explain when I can."

I have four hours of the drive left. Three, if I step on it. Less if I had a faster car. But I don't need to complicate this situation any further by stealing a car, so Tara's rented pickup will have to do.

Even if I got there faster, I doubt I'd be in time to prevent whatever revenge Shade is planning.

The sky over the east part of town is illuminated a bright orangey red, but it's only a couple of minutes before four AM, hours still left until sunrise. Crystal's is on the east side of town, and the orange light gets brighter the closer I get.

The road's blocked by patrol cars and ambulances, fire trucks visible in the distance. I park and run towards what's left of the building, ignoring the cops' shouts as I slip under the yellow crime scene tape.

All that's left of the strip club is a blackened, smoldering hull. Behind it flames are rising from Crystal's house, the firefighters still battling that fire.

"Tommy!" Crystal calls from somewhere to my left, and I let out the breath I've been holding.

She's swaddled in a blanket, standing next to an ambulance with the rear door open. I run over.

"What happened?" Through the open ambulance door I see Bear laying unconscious on a stretcher, an oxygen tube attached to his nose, and a bandage covering his forehead.

"It was those damn Mexicans, the Vagabundos," Crystal says, her teeth chattering because she's shaking so hard. "They came and trashed the place then burned it all down. We put up a fight, but there was nothing we could do. There were too many of them. Ten's been shot, and my Bear—"

Tears stream down her face, and she can't finish

the sentence. She turns to look at Bear's unmoving form on the stretcher, shaking even harder.

"Will he be alright?"

She shrugs. "I hope so. He got hit on the head and has smoke poisoning. He's so old, Tommy. But you should've seen him today. He fought for me, for us, like he was a young man again."

I caused this. No way the Vagos just attacked on their own. Crystal's has always been untouchable. There's nothing to gain by targeting it. The only reason would be to get back at me. Shade is behind this.

"And the others?" I ask, checking around to see where the girls are. If any of them were hurt—

"They're already at the hospital," Crystal says. "Nothing serious, just scrapes and bruises, and smoke inhalation. They were after the club, not the girls, thank God."

"We're leaving now too," the paramedic working on Bear informs us. "Are you coming?"

I offer her my arm to help her climb into the back. "I'll take care of this, Crystal, I promise."

Her home is gone, her club is gone, and her husband might die soon. There's precious little left for me to take care of. I should've said I'll avenge this.

She smiles at me anyway, nodding her head. "I know you will."

I'm already locking eyes with Sheriff Lance Williams. It's time to finish this. Shade shouldn't have gone after Crystal and her girls. I warned him. I tried to get him to back off. My conscience will never be clear over what I'm about to do, but I am doing the right thing. Because I can't stand by and just watch innocent people get hurt anymore.

"Something I can help you with, Tommy?" the Sheriff asks as I walk up to him.

"Yeah," I say. "You can take me down to the station. I have something to tell you."

He eyes me warily. The last time we spoke, I threatened to expose his secret unless he turned a blind eye where the MC's dealings were concerned. Right now, I'm about to make his career.

"It'll be worth your while," I assure him.

"Alright," he finally caves. "Follow me."

"So you're telling me you're willing to rat out the entire MC?" the Sheriff says after I tell him what I can offer. "You? The founder's grandson and the

President's brother? Forgive me if I have trouble believing you."

I don't like his tone, but he's absolutely right. I am a rat. "Lance, we've been over this already. Either you make a deal with me, or you get the FBI or the ATF down here to talk to me. Or even the fucking Border Patrol. One of them is gonna give me what I want in exchange for the information I'm offering. And they'll be getting it cheap."

"Witness protection?" he asks.

"For me plus one," I say nodding. "A new name and a new identity."

"And a house with a white picket fence, I suppose," the Sheriff says, a mocking half smile plastered across his face. "I didn't take you for the settling down type. Or for a traitor."

It stings, him calling me that. But there's no denying it either.

"You know what people will do for love, Lance. After all, you're one of those who'd do anything for love."

He knows what I mean, can't hide his anger now. As liberal a state as California is, on the whole, a gay sheriff is still not something that's tolerated. Especially not up here in the hills. A married sheriff with a long time gay boyfriend on the side probably wouldn't be tolerated anywhere. All it took to get him to look the other way where the MC was concerned was threaten to expose that secret of his. We didn't even have to bribe him.

"Be smart about this, Lance. The info I can give you will make your career. You won't have to worry about anything after that. I want a new name and a new identity. For me and my girlfriend. And I won't testify at any trial. But I'll buy my own house."

I can see him considering it, the anger no longer the main expression in his bloodshot brown eyes.

"I'd rather we handled all this here and now, but if you won't take what I'm offering, I'll go elsewhere. I can give you enough to destroy Viper's Bite MC and make a huge dent in the Vagabundos' operation in the area."

This is the last time I'm repeating myself tonight. He either takes the deal, or I'm taking it to the Feds.

"I'll get the DA on the phone, see what we can do."

The sun's already up now. I should've called Tara long ago. "You do that, and I'll wait in the hall."

He lets me exit his office without putting up any fight, though he's still eyeing me warily.

I could still change my mind. Walk out of the station and forget all about this. Not be a traitor.

But I can't look the other way anymore. I tried for years, and it nearly killed me. I might never get rid of the guilt of betraying the brotherhood. But it won't be so bad once I hear Tara's voice.

"Tommy?" she breathes into the phone, sounding like I woke her up. "Is it really you?"

I laugh at her question, because just the sound of her voice makes me feel rested, ready to take anything on. No sacrifice is too great, if it means I never have to leave her side again.

"Why wouldn't it be?" I ask, still chuckling.

"I was afraid you'd get hurt, that I'd never see you again."

"Nonsense, Tara, don't worry about me. I can take care of myself," I say. "How are you? What's happening there?"

"They questioned Sam, and then they took her to the hospital. We've been here for hours," she says. "When are you coming back?"

"Soon, Tara, but I can't come just yet," I say, wishing I was next to her right now, holding her hand, letting her lean against me. "Make sure you both have protection around the clock. Call your father, have him arrange it."

She sighs. "I'd rather not see him."

I feel like I just swallowed a block of ice. "I know,

baby, I know. But sometimes we have to do stuff we'd rather not. This is one of those times. So please, call him. Get him to hire you bodyguards or something. I'll be there soon, and then you'll never have to see him again if you don't want to."

"Are we in very serious danger, Tommy?" she asks, and I don't know if she means just Sam and her, or the three of us. Probably the latter. That's how she is. Selfless and caring, thoughtful and kind.

"No, Tara, it's gonna be OK. I just want to be extra careful. Say you'll call your father, do it for me."

"OK," she murmurs. I hate myself for asking this of her, because I know how hard it will be for her to ask this favor of her father. I couldn't have asked it of mine. Though if it meant keeping Tara safe, I would probably have done it.

"I'll be there soon," I say. "But now I have to go."

The Sheriff is waving me back into his office. It's fucking show time.

CHAPTER TWENTY-SEVEN

TARA

Tommy keeps calling, keeps promising he'll be back soon, but he's not telling me what's keeping him, and it's been days. I called Dad like he instructed me too, and Sam's still angry with me over that. He had them move us to LA and got Sam checked into an expensive clinic so she can begin healing. I'm staying with her, sharing the double bed in her fancy suite. They haven't asked me to leave yet, but I assume eventually they will.

   She's not eating much, and not talking a lot either. They want her to testify against the men that took her, but she's refusing to. I've been trying to convince her to do it, since Tommy said it'd be a good idea, and because I think so too. But she spends her days sitting by the window and won't be swayed.

"Want to go to a yoga class this afternoon?" I ask, checking the schedule of group events. "I think that actor goes too, you know the one you liked, what's his name?"

This place is full of celebrities of all ages. If Sam was her old self she'd be having a blast. The doctor says she's just been through a lot, that she needs time to heal, and I get that, but I don't know this new person she's become, and it's frightening.

"Yeah, that's exactly what I need, Tara," she snaps. "A new man in my life."

"I'm sorry, I wasn't thinking," I say, laying the schedule down and walking over to the armchair by the window in which she's been sitting since breakfast. "I just thought a diversion would do you good."

She looks at me in mock surprise, her bloodshot eyes very wide. "A diversion? Who are you and what have you done with my sister?"

I could ask her the same thing.

"What do you mean?" I sit on the arm of her chair.

"It sounds like something I used to tell you," she says. "But I guess now that you finally got laid, you know best."

The venom in her voice cuts me to the core.

"I mean, I'm happy for you that you found someone to fuck you, God knows it took you long enough, but now it's just Tommy this, Tommy that, Tommy says call dad and you do, Tommy says put Sam in an asylum, and here I am. What's next?"

She's always been harsh and sarcastic, but never this insulting. I'm getting mad at her, and I don't want to. She's been through so much.

"He never said that," I tell her as calmly as I can. "But I get it, you're angry. Yet if it wasn't for him, you'd still be..."

But I can't finish the sentence.

"A sex slave?" she says. "Still having trouble with the S word, I see. It's probably for the best, because that biker boyfriend of yours isn't coming back. And maybe it's time you started accepting that."

"He says he'll be here soon," I murmur.

"Don't get your hopes up, Tara. I know guys. They make all sorts of promises and rarely deliver. You'll never see him again, mark my words. First his calls will get fewer and fewer and then they'll stop." From the corner of my eye I see Sam is still glaring at me. But I don't look at her, because she'll be able to see the uncertainty in my eyes that her words are causing. "Besides, you probably gave him quite a challenge before he got you in bed, am I right? But even playing hard to get only works until they, well, get you."

"I trust him. He hasn't let me down yet." I move away from her and go to the bed. My phone's charging on the nightstand, and it hasn't rang once today. It's almost lunchtime. Tommy usually calls in the morning and the evening. But he hasn't called since just after breakfast yesterday. I tried calling him half an hour ago, but his phone is off. What if she's right? What if something happened to him? No, nothing happened to him. He told me he was perfectly safe, and I believe him. I have to believe him, or I'll go mad. Besides, I could feel it if something happened to him, I know I would.

No, whatever he's doing to take care of everything so he can come back to me is just keeping him busy.

I should just try calling again. And I do, but his phone is still off.

"I'm sorry, Tara," Sam says, suddenly standing right next to me, and I didn't hear her come over. She draws me into a tight hug, her whole body shaking.

"I'm being such a bitch to you, and I don't mean to be. I'm so happy that you found someone to love, and who loves you back," she mutters into my shoulder. "For what it's worth, I think he does love you, judging from the way you said your goodbyes. But now he's not calling you anymore, and I just don't want you to get hurt."

I hug her back. "I know. But you know I'm tough. You just worry about getting better."

What I want to say is that Tommy hasn't lied to me yet, that he'll be back if he says he'll be back, but I'm afraid saying that will just cause her to flare up again.

She releases me and sits down on the edge of the bed, pulling me down beside her. She's smiling, and if it weren't for the strained fear in her eyes that hardly ever goes away completely now, I'd think my Sam was back. Her eyes used to sparkle. She didn't used to have a care in the world. Now she looks at me with the same strain in her eyes that was always in mine.

"I do know you," she says, squeezing both of my hands in hers. "You used to wrap yourself in layers of icy detachment and cold righteous anger, but your center was always whole and undamaged, always shining brightly. You just pretended to be dead inside so you could protect that. But me, I was always dead on the inside, and I tried to hide it by having so much fun I could hardly keep up with myself. Now it's caught up with me."

"That's just not true."

She squeezes my hands tighter. "Let me finish."

But I don't want to hear any more of this. Because what she's saying is so dark, and her voice is so cold that I just want to cry.

"You've finally let your inner light shine through again, Tara, and you're beautiful, you're gorgeous, like I always knew you were. And I'm so thankful to you that you went to such lengths to find me and bring me back home. But I'm afraid it was a wasted effort. And I don't mean to push you away, but maybe I should. Because I'll just drag you down with me. I'm beyond saving this time. I am dead inside, and I don't have the strength or the will to pretend otherwise anymore. I'm so sorry."

She starts sobbing, fat tears rolling down her cheeks. I wrap my arms around her and draw her closer, tears streaming down my face too.

"Sam, you'll be fine. Even after Tommy comes back, I'll stay here with you, make sure you get through this."

She hiccups, rips herself from my arms, and glares at me with tear filled eyes.

"Don't you dare sacrifice anything more for me.

You go with him, if he wants you to. Far away from me, because I'll just drag you back down, and I don't want to do that. I really don't want to do that, Tara. I can deal with this on my own. I promise I can."

"OK, OK," I say hugging her tight and letting her sob into my shoulder.

This is the most she's said at one time since we rescued her. I hope it means she's getting better, that she's finally breaking out of the haze of despair caused by having been held captive for so long, and forced into prostitution. But I will stay and make sure she gets the healing she needs. Tommy will understand. He'll wait for me if I ask him to.

TOMMY

Three fucking days the whole thing took. I gave them everything I promised yesterday morning, right after they gave me my immunity, a new identity, and a letter of promise to do the same for Tara. They monitored my calls before then, but they took my phone away completely after that, and locked me in one of the cushier holding cells, where I've just been staring at the walls going slowly insane for the last 36 hours.

Apart from bringing me food, no one's looked in on me once. Maybe they just mean to hold me here indefinitely; while they figure out how to recant the immunity they gave me.

Sure they offered good reasons for holding me. They want to make the arrests without me having the chance to alert anyone to the danger beforehand. It makes sense, I'd do the same thing. But that hasn't helped the voices in my head. Which are mostly just calling me a scumbag backstabbing traitor the whole time, and I can't even call Tara to get away from them for just a little while.

I haven't told her what I've done yet. Mostly because I couldn't, since the cops are already too suspicious of me, but I've also been too ashamed to.

Though I'm starting to think I made my decision to destroy the MC the night my mom died. It just took me fifteen years to carry it out. After Blade took over, decided to go legit, it got better. But then he died too. And Shade is even worse than my father was. At least my dad played with me, took me to ball games, and let me ride with him on his bike before my feet even reached the ground. He also stopped running whores for me, so I'd forgive him for mom. I'll never forgive him, but at least he made an effort.

But Shade would take the MC to such vile pits,

no one would remain unscathed. It's quite possible I'm just rationalizing my betrayal. But I'm sure of it nonetheless. On some level, betraying them all was absolutely the right thing to do. But on the surface, I couldn't do anything worse. I was orphaned at twelve, the MC was my family since. So I actually betrayed my whole family, but I would have taken it over eventually. I would be making all the calls one day. By destroying it all now, I just fast forwarded to that day.

Maybe I could've just challenged Shade. Taken over the MC, then handed it to someone else once Shade was out of the way. But that would've taken months. And I want peace for Tara and me, not a lifetime of looking over our shoulders.

The lock rattles and then Sheriff Lance is staring at me. "You can go now. Your brother and the rest of the execs are in custody, as are most of the local MC members. You have maybe half a day before what you did becomes common knowledge, you know how fast news travels in a small town. I suggest you haul ass out of town, or your witness protection won't be worth shit."

I jump off the bed. "You already told them it was me, didn't you?"

It's his payback, I get that, I even admire him for having the balls to do it.

"No, but they'll know soon enough," he says, but I know he's lying. "You sure you don't want that escort out of town."

"I'll make my own way from here," I say, making sure to bump into him as I exit the cell.

It's unfortunate that people already know about my betrayal, because it gives me less time to do what I still need to do before I return to Tara.

"I need my phone now."

He hands it to me, but the battery's dead. What else did I expect? Of course the bastards didn't charge it for me.

"I'll see you around, Lance." I hope to Christ I'm wrong, and I'm pretty sure he's thinking the same thing.

I take a cab to Crystal's, luckily find Tara's pickup still parked where I left it with my money still inside. It's not even most of what I have, but starting a new life can get expensive. I have three more bags just like this one buried out in the hills, and it'll probably take me the rest of the day to dig them up. But first I need to say my goodbyes.

My first stop is Sara's beachside club in the hills. She's sitting alone at the bar, the place deserted. Her head turns as I enter, but the hopeful expression on her eyes is quickly quenched by shock.

"Tommy, what are you doing here?" she says. "They've been arresting MC members all morning. They even came here looking for Brett. You need to get out of town."

The fact that she doesn't know it's all my doing is a relief. But she'll know soon enough, and I should be the one to tell her.

"I am getting out of town. But I'm not in any immediate danger," I say instead, and carry the bag of money into the back room.

She follows me, staring at it with narrowed eyes. "What is that, Tommy?"

"That's the money Ian left in my safekeeping when he went to jail," I tell her. There's more in that bag than what he left with me, but leaving Sara a little extra is the least I can do. Who knows when Ian will be getting out of jail now that I've betrayed the MC. There was no way to keep his involvement in the club's dealings a secret, he was too enmeshed in it. And warning him wouldn't have done any good either, since he's already locked up. Knowing him, it would just make him do something stupid, like try to escape and come after me. "It's yours now."

"I don't want his dirty money," she shrieks, her ears starting to twitch.

I don't have time to argue with her. I just came to say goodbye. "He wanted you to have it, if things went south, so take it up with him, if you don't want it. I haven't told him your secret. That's up to you as well, but I suggest you do it."

She's blinking at me, her mouth open like she's about to argue some more, but I just give her a quick hug.

"I'm leaving, and I won't be back for a long time," I say. "Everyone getting arrested is my doing. And I am sorry, but I had no other choice. Shade is crazy, and I couldn't stand by and watch what he was doing. I had to protect the woman I love."

Her eyes keep growing wider and wider as she processes what I just told her.

"You?" she finally breathes and it truly encapsulates all she's trying to say. I used to be the MCs fiercest warrior, and I swore I'd never fall in love.

"I knew you'd understand," I say, giving her another quick hug and a peck on the cheek. "But now I really have to go."

"Will I ever see you again?" she asks once I'm already at the door, her voice kinda teary.

"Maybe," I say without turning, because she'd see the lie in my face.

Bear is lying in one of the glass-walled ICU rooms, hooked up to at least five machines. Crystal is sitting next to him, wrapped in a cardigan, and clutching his hand in both of hers. I don't want to interrupt. I don't want to know there's no hope for him to ever wake up. Though the selfish part of me is glad he's sleeping. Bear is the last person who'd understand what I did. Crystal might, but I'm not counting on it.

She sees me, gasping in shock before releasing his hand and coming out into the hall.

"Where have you been, Tommy? Shade's been arrested, the cops even came looking for Bear, and no one's telling me anything." She's out of breath by the time she finally pauses.

"How is he?" I ask, glancing at Bear's motionless form again.

"Not great," she says shivering slightly. "But they think he has a chance."

Ava and Lola are standing next to the vending

machine on the other side of the long hallway. They both see me at the same time, start walking towards us.

"I'm leaving, Crystal, I just came to give you this." I fish a set of keys from my pocket. "They're for Blade's house. I want you to have it. He'd also want you to have it after what happened. And you'll find some money under the floorboards in the attic. Use it as you see fit, but make sure Simone gets all the medical care she needs. She's probably gonna need plastic surgery as well."

She wraps the cardigan around herself tighter. "I can't take that. It's too much."

"Nonsense," I say, jangling the keys in front of her. "The house is yours. Just take it."

Ava and Lola have almost reached us, but I turn my back on them to discourage an interruption. "Look, I'm going away for a very long time. I want to know you're provided for."

Her good eye grows wide. "You're going to jail?"

"No," I say. "I'm just leaving, disappearing."

Her hand flies to her mouth. "It was you."

"I did what I had to," I say, still holding out the key stupidly.

Her eyes are mere slits, and I'm expecting her to start berating me, calling me a traitor at any moment. But she takes the keys, and gives me a hug.

"I know that can't have been easy, Tommy. But for what it's worth, I think it might have been for the best. Your grandfather had a good vision for the MC, but it got all twisted in the end. I doubt even Blade could've fixed it. Thank you for the house, and for everything else," she says. "Go see Simone before you leave. You saved her life, and she wants to thank you."

She gives me another hug, and kisses both my cheeks, then returns to Bear's bedside. I watch them through the window, trying not to think of anything. But at least she has a house now and the money to start over.

"Are you really leaving, Tommy?" Lola asks. Her usually giggly voice is very somber. "Where's Tara?"

"She's waiting for me in LA, I should go to her now." I don't want to see Simone, I just want to get out of town as fast as I can.

"Simone's sleeping right now, but she wakes up from time to time," Ava says. "She wants to thank you, like Crystal said. That guy who used to come to the club every night to watch her dance visits her too. He's alright. He got Lola, Gwen and me out of the club when those Mexicans came. He was in the military once upon a time, apparently. I think he's really in love with Simone. Maybe he'll marry her when she gets better. Wouldn't that be nice? What's gonna happen to us now, Tommy?"

I've never heard Ava speak so much in one go. And she's practically crying now, so it's especially unnerving. "Crystal will take care of you, don't worry. Let's go see if Simone's awake."

I really don't want to see her ruined face again, but maybe I should. I need all the reminders of why I did what I did fresh and clear in my mind, so I can call them up when my thoughts turn dark.

Simone's awake, and she tries to speak, but can't really, because her jaw and lips are still too swollen.

"Crystal will take care of your face," I say dumbly. She nods, and I hope I never forget the thankfulness in the one eye she can actually open. Her fingers are flexing against the sheets like she wants me to take hold of her hand and I do, squeezing once before releasing her.

"I have to leave now," I say, and none of them try to stop me. I hope I treated them OK. I really do.

No one saw me leave town, or followed me to the

hills when I went there to get the money. The plans I made held. I imagined riding out of town on my bike when I originally planned my escape. It'd be kinda poetic to pick up Tara with my bike, and then we'd ride off into the unknown on it, but I had to leave it behind. I spent years working on it, but I don't deserve it anyway. Not after what I did.

My phone charged fully while I was digging up the money. It's almost four PM, and I should've called Tara before now, but I needed to make sure I was actually getting out of town alive today, so I wouldn't make her a promise I can't keep. There's nothing but highway in front of me now. My luck held. It's a five hour drive to LA, but I can make it in four.

I'm holding my breath as I dial her number, growing more and more afraid she won't pick up each time it rings. I leave a message when the voicemail comes on then call back right after.

There's no reason to panic, she'll call back. She's probably just not near her phone right now. The feds are watching them. There's no way Shade could've gotten to her. Him and the rest of the MC were too busy getting arrested, if nothing else. She's safe. And she will call back. She has to. Me and Tara, we're

TNT, things get explosive when we're together, and nothing can stop us.

I still try to reach her a bunch of times more, with no luck. In the end, her phone just starts going straight to voicemail. But that just means the battery went dead. It doesn't mean anything else. I won't think of the worst. The worst is behind me. It's time to start thinking only of the best.

My phone finally rings when I'm about half an hour out of LA, but it's not Tara, it's Jerry.

"What was that?" he asks, since he probably heard the end of my curse as I picked up.

"Nothing, what did you want?" I need to keep the line clear for Tara's call.

"I...umm...finally found some stuff," he says slowly, like it's hurting him to say it. "You know, the producer and his...you know."

"Yes, I know," I snap. "Will it be helpful?"

"I haven't been able to find much, he keeps it secured pretty tight, but I found some older stuff, like ten years old, or more...it's only a couple of videos, and they're fucking horrible," he says, exhaling loudly. "Should I send them through? But I don't know if you want to see it."

"Yeah, send it to me." He's right, I probably don't

want to see it. Just the way he's talking about it makes my stomach twist in rage.

"Alright, done," Jerry says after a slight pause. "Please do something about this guy."

"Oh, I will," I promise him, then make my good-byes. I'll probably never see Jerry again.

He doesn't ask any unnecessary questions.

I'm stuck in gridlock traffic on the LA highway, and I could easily watch the videos he sent me. But I keep tossing the phone back on the seat each time I decide to, and not doing it.

I'm such a pussy. Seriously, Tara lived through it, and I can't even watch it on video?

I pick up the phone again and hit download on Jerry's mail.

My worst fear comes true as I see Tara's face in the video. She's young, maybe fourteen, possibly younger, and she looks so scared, so lost, so angry and sad over what's being done to her. She fights the man —her father—as best she can. It's not nearly enough; she has no chance to escape it. And the resigned look that rests on her face after she realizes that is more horrible than all the fear and sadness before. It fucking breaks my heart the way nothing ever has.

I only watched a couple minutes of the video, and I almost puked. She survived years of that torture. Her father's gonna pay for that. Maybe not right now, because he needs to be able to keep Samantha safe, but eventually I will make him pay for what he's done to Tara. And I will spend the rest of my life making sure that look of anguish never crosses her face again.

CHAPTER TWENTY-EIGHT

TARA

Dad came to visit at noon, insisted he take us out to lunch. The visit took all afternoon, he just kept jabbering on about nothing at all, and he's still here now. Sam didn't touch any of her food, or said more than yes and no all afternoon. So I was stuck talking to him, memories I've been so good at keeping away these last few weeks pushing in, taking over. By the middle of our meal, I started to feel like I was sitting beside myself, an invisible Tara occupying an empty chair at the table, just watching what was happening, but not taking part in any of it, not letting anything get to her. I know her well, she used to be with me all the time growing up. But I never wanted to see her again. Because she scares me so much, makes me feel like I'm going insane. And to top it off, I forgot to bring my phone to lunch.

But Tommy hasn't called in two days. Sam could've been right about him. But how could I have been so wrong? How could he let me down like this after all the promises he made and kept so well?

Of course, he never planned to stick around, the voice of my memories keeps telling me now. You're too damaged. Why would he want to deal with you? He knows he can get ten girls just like you, better than you, to sleep with him any time he wants. I'm trying not to listen, but it's getting harder and harder. But listening to that voice is still easier than thinking something might have happened to him. I can't think about that. Not ever.

It's almost dinnertime and we're back in Sam's room, but Dad's still here, trying to make plans for us to do something over the weekend. Suggesting we go on the boat.

I hate that boat. I have no good memories from aboard that boat. I used to wish it would sink with me and everyone else on it.

I hate my dad too. So much so, that I can't even listen to him speak anymore.

Sam is sitting in her armchair by the window, holding onto her knees and rocking gently. My phone's charging by the bed, but the screen is still blank.

"Why won't you just leave, Dad?" I yell at him, much too loudly. I'm sure they heard me out in the hall. "Can't you see what you're doing to Sam?"

And to me, but I don't say that. I've always been the strong one, the tough one.

His face changes in a split second, the lazy half smile morphing into an angry grimace. I know how quickly his face can change like that, I've seen it a thousand times before. But it still causes such primal fear to rise in my chest, I forget to inhale.

"You won't talk to me like that," he says softly, menacingly.

"Or what?" I manage to choke out. He shouldn't scare me anymore, I'm free of him. But he does.

My phone rings and I rush to it before he can stop me.

"Tara, where are you?" Tommy asks, and I let out a happy little whimper that sounds too much like a sob.

"What's wrong?" he asks, but by now I'm already smiling. Of course he called, he promised he would.

"Where are *you*?" I ask.

"At the reception of this weird spa you're staying at. They won't tell me where you are."

I laugh, all the fear I felt just moments ago so far away now I don't even remember it. "I'll be right down."

"Now you wait," Dad says, tries to grab my arm. But he can't catch me, and he certainly can't stop me.

The world just freezes as I see Tommy, everything but him floating off into a hazy distance at the very edge of my sight. Nothing's moving except his head as I call his name from the foot of the stairs. His eyes are shimmering with the light of a billion stars as he opens his arms to catch me. I practically fly into his arms, and then his lips are on mine, the kiss chasing away the last dregs of my memories, silencing that dark voice forever, invisible Tara waving goodbye before she disappears for the last time.

Applause erupts, making the world spin again. A few of the residents are gathered around us, all of them clapping, some whistling.

Tommy frowns at them, and I'm sure I'm blushing a bright crimson, though I can't fight the smile spreading across my face.

"Ready to go?" he whispers into my ear, kissing me softly one more time and preventing me from answering.

I look back at the stairs leading up to Sam's room.

Her and Dad are standing behind the people gathered around us. I catch her eye and she smiles. The
way she used to smile back when there was nothing
to worry about.

I move away from Tommy so I can go to her, but
she shakes her head.

"Don't you dare, Tara," she calls out. "Just go."

And she's still smiling.

"I'll just go say goodbye to her and my father,
OK?" I say to Tommy.

He tenses in my arms, the anger in his face
almost scary enough to make me take a step back.
"Your father's here? Where?"

I glance back, see my father retreat up the stairs.
"In the room, I guess."

Tommy lets go of me, but keeps a firm grip on my
hand. "Come on, you can introduce me to him."

"Tommy, no, it's fine. I'll just get my things, and
we'll leave," I say, because that's murder in his eyes,
and I only just got him back, I can't lose him now. I
try to bodily stop him from going up the stairs, but
he's just sorta dragging me along now.

"I need to have a word with him first," he says. "I
won't hurt him. Yet."

I don't know how to keep arguing, and I don't

really want to. So I take him up to Sam's room, kinda hoping Dad won't be there, kinda hoping he is.

Dad's standing by the window, but turns as we enter, a very defiant look on his face.

"Who's this, Tara?" he asks.

"You'll shut up and listen now," Tommy says, slamming the door behind us.

Dad sneers at him, makes for the door, which Tommy is blocking with his body. "No one talks to me like that."

Dad shoves me aside as he tries to reach the door, making me stumble. And judging by the pure rage now boiling in Tommy's eyes, he just made the worst mistake of his life.

Tommy's arm shoots out, and he grabs Dad by the throat, slams him against the door. The rational part of my mind is telling me I should stop him. But this is exactly what I wanted to happen to my dad so many times. For someone to come to my rescue, get him off me, make him hurt the way he hurt me.

"Me and Tara are leaving now," Tommy hisses in my Dad's face, still clutching him tightly by the throat. "After we leave you will hire a team of body-guards who will watch over your daughter Samantha around the clock. She doesn't have to see you if she doesn't want to, but you will make sure nothing happens to her. Nothing at all."

Dad's face is turning purple, and he's clawing at Tommy's hand. But it's as though Tommy doesn't even feel it.

"I'll be calling you from time to time," he says. "And I want to hear nothing but good news. Or else I'll be back, and this sick shit will be all over the evening news."

He pulls his phone from his pocket, looks for something on it, then shows the screen to my dad. A few seconds later, I hear myself scream in the video he's playing for him. I don't have to look to know what's on the screen, but somehow even faced with the video version of my worst memories, the darkness stays at bay.

"I'll let you go now," Tommy says, such power in his voice, my whole body is taut, standing at attention. "And all I want to hear from you is a, Yes, Sir."

Dad almost crumples to the ground as Tommy releases him, but manages to stay upright.

"Yes, Sir," he croaks out.

"Good." Tommy says and turns to me. "Ready?"

I nod, hugging Sam tightly, and promising I'll call her all the time, before following Tommy out the door.

"Where to?" I ask, once we're sitting in the car. Seeing him manhandle my dad, save me from him the way I always wished someone would, made burning flames of primal desire surge through me, and they're still not abating, still burn in my belly like a pool of molten lava. I want to be completely alone with him right now, for days, for weeks, for years. I want to be with him in all ways a man and a woman can be together.

He's looking at me, the midnight in his eyes pure velvet, enveloping me like the softest cloak. "Wherever you want, Tara. But it'll have to be far."

"Then far it is." I smile at him, then kiss him softly.

But he's tense again, so I pull away. "What?"

"I want you to know exactly what you're getting yourself into by coming with me," he says, silencing me by laying the tips of his fingers over my lips when I try to speak. "I betrayed the entire MC, turned them all in so you and your sister won't have anything to worry about. So me and you won't have anything to worry about. But I have to disappear now, because they'll all be looking for me. Looking to kill me."

A pain so raw stabs through me as he says it that a tear trickles from my eye. But he's still silencing me with his finger.

"I can promise you I'll stay with you and make sure nothing and no one ever hurts you again, that I'll love you the way you should always have been loved," he continues, my tears flowing freely now, but I'm not sad, not at all. This is all I ever wanted to hear from him. "I can offer you peace and adventure, a fresh start, even a new name. But you can't return home. Not for a very long time, maybe never, if you come with me."

He's running his thumb across my lips as he tells me all this, and I take his hand once he's done speaking, kiss it, then peel it away from my mouth.

"That all sounds terrific, and I'll just take your name," I say, but hastily add, "I mean eventually, down the line sometime, when we're both ready." I'm rambling, not wanting to scare him off with my premature suggestion of marriage. It was just a joke, but not really.

He smiles widely, the vastness in his nighttime eyes expanding, showing me all those glorious worlds I never believed existed, but which are now finally mine to reach, to explore, to get lost in.

"So that's a yes?" he asks.

I nod, but that's not nearly affirmation enough. "You saved me, Tommy. I was sure I was dead, but you brought me back to life. I want to spend my forever making it up to you, loving you, having adventures with you, getting lost with you—"

He interrupts me with a passionate kiss, stoking the heat of my desire for him higher and higher.

"So, yes, forever yes. Please take me with you," I conclude once we pull apart to breathe.

"Alright, then let's start this adventure already," he says grinning at me.

"Yes, let's do!" I say, matching his excited tone.

I scoot closer to him and he starts the car, rests his arm around my shoulders as we drive off.

"We'll make it, right?" I ask, pressing even closer to him.

He glances at me, then wraps his arm tighter around my body.

"Of course we will. We're TNT," he says, in a grandiose sort of voice.

"What's that supposed to mean?" I ask.

"You know, Tara and Tommy," he says. "TNT."

I chuckle. "Good for you Tommy, you can spell our names, but I still don't get it."

"Oh, come on." He sighs, looking at me. "TNT,

like dynamite. When we're together, explosive things happen and nothing can stop us."

"That's so cute," I say slipping my arm behind his back and hugging him tight. "But you do know we're T and T, while TNT is an abbreviation."

"Well, Miss Smarty Pants, phonetically it sounds about right." He kisses the top of my head as he says it, so I know he's not really annoyed with me.

"I love it," I breathe, kiss his cheek and hug him tighter. "And you're right, nothing can stop us."

No stars are visible in the night sky over the city, but they're all there in his eyes, shimmering down on all I ever wished for.

EPILOGUE

ONE YEAR LATER

The sun is rising with no clouds in sight. It's gonna be another perfect summer day. Dawn and Tara are forever tied together in my mind. Probably because she gets up to watch it so often, like she's doing right now, sitting at the very edge of the cliffs and staring off at the horizon. Her long honey-colored hair is falling in thick waves over her back, moving slightly in the breeze.

I can't believe it, but Tara is still the only woman I want. That doesn't mean I don't notice others, especially the ones that frolic around topless on all those

European beaches we visited. But Tara is still the
only one I want to come home to, go home with, kiss,
make love to, and fuck. That last is important. Tara
still has moments when she can't quite surrender to
me, but they're fewer and further between now. So
much so, they surprise both of us when they happen.

A year ago, if someone said I would be settled
down, I'd have laughed and laughed, and probably
call them an idiot or worse. But I can't deny it now.
And it's not funny. It's just perfect. It's ridiculously
perfect. I've never been this happy. I never even
wanted to be. And I certainly didn't know what I was
missing.

We've travelled all over Europe. London, Paris,
Rome, Venice, Greece, Romania, even Monte Negro
and Croatia. But it's Italy we keep returning to.
We're in Sicily now. And it's time.

Tara turns and smiles as she notices me watching
her from the doorway of our bus-home. No picket
fence, but it's got everything else we need.

I smile back and walk over to her. I'm so nervous
my legs are stiff. But I don't think I need to be. And
I'd have to be unable to move and think to not want
Tara beside me. Hell, I'd have to be dead.

The paperwork took forever to assemble, and I
think she was getting a little suspicious of all my

absences while we were in Rome. But she didn't say anything. That's not Tara's way. She almost never complains, and doesn't ask for very much at all. She's grateful for everything, and I still want to give her anything she wants. Sometimes, I'd rather she did just ask, because then I'd know for sure what she needs. But guessing isn't that hard either.

She leans against my leg once I stop next to her. The touch of her fingers as she runs them along my calf sends a jolt of electricity through me, burning away my nervousness. She looks up at me and smiles. "It's going to be another sunny day."

"Yeah, it looks that way." It's the best I can do, my nervousness now back and constricting my throat like an iron fist is clutching it. I know exactly what she means though. We've had nothing but icy cold rain and gale-force winds, since we arrived back to Italy a couple of weeks ago. It got so bad they paused the ferry transfers to Sicily for awhile. But these last two days, the weather's held.

Maybe I should have picked a more romantic way of doing this, but sunrise is her favorite time of the day and this is one of her favorite spots in the world. She told me so before we returned to Italy to spend the rest of the summer here.

I stroke her soft, luscious hair then reach down to

take her hand and guide her to her feet. It's time. And me kneeling won't exactly work if she's sitting down.

She gives me a puzzled look, which only grows more surprised as I go down on one knee on the rocky ground, open the little box I've been clutching in my hand, and offer her the ring. "I love you, Tara. More than I've ever loved anyone. I want you to be my wife. Will you marry me?"

I practiced the words. But there was no need. They'd just flow from my mouth anyway. Her hand is covering her lips, but she's nodding fast as she drops down to her knees too. She grabs the ring with one hand, pulls me into a hug with the other.

"Yes, Tommy, I'll marry you," she finally says, her lips less than half an inch from mine, her eyes glistening.

I kiss her deeply, passionately, lovingly, until everything but the soft touch of her lips, the warmth of her presence disappears, becomes inconsequential. Because it is. She's all that matters.

Her eyes are brimming with tears when we finally break apart and she lets me put the ring on her finger. And I'd prefer it if she weren't crying, but then again, she's not doing it in sadness but joy, and tears are just one of those things I was able to give back to her. And I count that as a win, however messed up it sounds.

I wish I could give her my real name though, not this new one the witness protection program assigned me, and that desire is assaulting my mind pretty hard right now, taking chunks out of what should be a happy moment.

We're sitting side by side on the cliffs now, and she's leaning against me, her arms wrapped tightly around my waist, mine around her shoulders.

"Can we get married here?" she asks admiring the way her ring sparkles in the sun's rays.

"Yes, we can," I say grinning at her. "I have all the paperwork ready. We can do it today, if you want."

"You have all the paperwork? How did you know I'd say yes?" she asks wryly, smirking at me, her eyes the exact color of the ocean stretching out below us.

"I wanted to be ready," I tell her. "And I was pretty sure you'd say yes."

She nods slowly, knowingly, her eyes changing color again until they're exactly like the summer sky just after sunrise.

"I thought that little church on the hill would be

perfect," she says and points off to the right. I know exactly which one she means. She goes there to pray sometimes. And the fact that she'd been imagining our wedding there just makes this moment that much more perfect, even lets me forget about my inability to give her my real last name. I betrayed the MC. I made my choices. I can't say I regret them, not exactly, but maybe it could've all gone a different way.

"Yeah, I thought you'd say that," I tell and pull her closer to me. She's my rock and my reasons. "We can get married anywhere you want."

She presses even closer to me until there's literally no space left between us. I could just sit here, holding her all day. All year. My whole life. And maybe I don't deserve to be this happy, but Tara does. And that's the only thing that really matters.

THE END

Ready for the next installment in the Viper's Bite

MC series? Check out **OUTLAW'S SALVATION** (Viper's Bite MC, Book 2), which tells Brett and Samantha's story. AVAILABLE NOW in Paperback and eBook!

VIPER'S BITE MC SERIES - A steamy and
suspenseful biker romance series (Completed)

OUTLAW'S HOPE, BOOK 1

OUTLAW'S SALVATION, BOOK 2

OUTLAW'S REDEMPTION, BOOK 3

DEVIL'S NIGHTAMRE MC SERIES

CROSS - Available Now

TANK - Available Now

ROOK - Coming Soon

ADAM (OF THE ARCHERS, BOOK 1) — A full-
length, standalone BBW Military Romance

HIS FOREVER - An Alpha Billionaire Romance Serial
(Completed)

RICHES TO RAGS - A Stepbrother Romance
(Completed)

NOT LOOKING FOR LOVE - An NA Contemporary
Romance Series (Completed)

Made in the USA
Middletown, DE
28 July 2018